THE WRATH OF LORDS

KYLE ALEXANDER ROMINES

ALSO BY KYLE ALEXANDER ROMINES

Warden of Fál

The Wrath of Lords

The Blood of Kings

The City of Thieves

The Will of Queens

Tales of Fál

The Fortress of Suffering

The Price of Hate

The Path of Vengeance

The Way of Rage

The Heart of Magic

The Keeper of the Crows

The Chrononaut

A Sound in the Dark

Bride

Atonement

Drone

Seeking to Devour

To sign up to receive author updates—and receive a FREE
electronic copy of Kyle's science fiction novella, The
Chrononaut—go to http://eepurl.com/bsvhYP.

And when Nora of Connacht, last of the line of Áed, took up her uncle's crown and drove the Lord of Shadows from Fál, the five kings and queens gathered at Tara, where the High Kings of old once reigned. When Queen Nora touched the Lia Fáil—the Stone of Destiny—the stone let out a roar heard across the land, and the kings and queens cast their crowns at her feet. That was how Nora became High Queen of Fál.

But there were many evils left in the land. To ensure the dark times never returned, Nora named five wardens to keep the fragile peace between the realms: Golden Darragh—first and greatest among them —Callahan the Brehon, Niall the Wise, and Connor the Younger— all heroes of renown. But when she named the fifth, a great uproar greeted the name of Esben Berengar, the Bloody Red Bear. Berengar was not beloved as the others, for it was thought he was a monster, a killer against whose wrath none could stand. But wise Queen Nora knew not everything is as it seems, and when heroes fail, sometimes it takes a monster…

—Morwen of Cashel, *The Annals of Inis Faithlinn*

Five Kingdoms.

Five Kings and Queens.

One High Queen Sits Above All.

Her Wardens Keep the Peace.

CHAPTER ONE

HE KILLED the first man with his bare hands.

It was just before dark, and the forest in which Berengar had concealed himself was already alive with the sounds of stirring creatures. Freshly fallen rain left the earth soft and damp, masking his footsteps. He waited until his first victim, the lone sentry standing guard outside the fort, ventured to the forest's edge to relieve himself.

No sooner had the sentry reached the bushes than he appeared to hear something rustling in the brush. When he raised his torch to investigate the sound's source, the sentry's gaze settled on a pair of eyes belonging to an exceptionally large wolfhound. "What the devil are you supposed to be?"

Before he could speak again, Berengar grabbed him from behind and clamped a hand over his mouth to prevent him from crying out and alerting his companions. The sentry tried putting up a fight, so Berengar simply broke the man's neck and dragged the body deeper into the forest. By the time the others realized he was missing it would be too late. He wouldn't have let the sentry live in any event, though he might have preferred to interrogate him first. The members of the company he hunted showed no such mercy to their victims, and likewise they would receive none from him.

Intrigued by the prospect of a fresh meal, a crow hopped from its perch and landed a short distance away. When Berengar finished with his task, the crow and its kin would eat well. A faintly perceptible whistle called the wolfhound to his side. She was Faolán, his sole companion, and her savagery almost matched his own. With the sentry dealt with, there was no one to notice their approach. The others were inside, no doubt seeking warmth and shelter behind ancient stone walls. The pair emerged from the brush under cover of darkness. Only a sliver of moonlight escaped the clouds, which threatened yet more rain.

Berengar was after Skinner Kane, the leader of a vicious company of thugs and killers known as the Black Hand, wanted for atrocities in each of Fál's five kingdoms. The brehons proved unequal to the task of putting an end to the company's savagery, so it fell to Berengar to deal with them. It was bloody and dirty work—the kind of job Berengar preferred. He was happy to let the High Queen's other wardens settle disputes between quarreling nobles and attend to diplomatic matters. He preferred keeping the peace his way, usually at the end of his axe.

He'd tracked the killers to an abandoned goblin fort near the border between Meath and Leinster and waited for night to come. Berengar had pursued the company for the better part of the spring. He nearly had Kane twice, but the man was a slippery bastard, and both times managed to elude his grasp. It had taken him weeks to find their trail again, and Berengar was determined there would not be a third escape.

He slipped through the entrance like a wraith, unseen. Apart from the trickling sound produced by renewed rainfall, the fort lay utterly still. A chill hung in the air. The warden's eye quickly adjusted to the lack of light, and he found himself in a bare stone hall where a partially collapsed wall prevented him from advancing into the next room. Two sets of stairs loomed on opposite ends of the chamber. The nearest staircase ran upward, and the other led down, into darkness.

Berengar was about to start the climb when he heard a pair of voices coming from below. He motioned for Faolán to follow before creeping along the path down to the dungeon. As he made his descent, the voices grew louder. A hint of torchlight was visible at the foot of the stairs.

"How much longer do we have to wait in this hellhole before we get paid?" one voice asked another.

"We'll get paid when we get paid," the other replied in a condescending tone. "What's your rush?"

"I hate this place. It's cold and reeks of goblin. That scholar better come through for us after what we went through to get our hands on that rune he wanted."

"He'd better," the second voice said. "Otherwise, he'll have to deal with Kane."

Berengar listened carefully. He'd heard rumors that a valuable thunder rune purchased by King Mór of Munster for his court magician had been stolen, but this was the first he'd heard that the Black Hand was responsible. He had a deep dislike and mistrust of all things magical, which would only serve to further complicate his task. Still, he had come to kill Kane, not recover some missing artifact. If Mór wanted the rune, he could claim it himself.

"That rune's probably worth a hefty sum," the first voice added. "I still don't understand why we don't just kill the scholar and sell it ourselves, especially if we're not getting paid for the hostages."

Berengar frowned at the mention of hostages, and he suspected he knew what awaited him in the dungeon.

"You know how he gets around magic. I think it's the only thing he's afraid of—just don't tell him I said that."

He quietly eased his blade from its sheath. Although the battleaxe strapped to his back was his weapon of choice, the staircase's narrow confines made his short sword better suited to the task at hand. The torchlight grew brighter as he approached the guards, each of whom noticed him a half-second too late. Faolán leapt from the stairs and pounced on the nearest guard, mauling him with her teeth and claws. Before the remaining guard could cry out to alert those above, Berengar grabbed him and bashed his head against the wall several times in rapid succession. Faolán silenced her victim's whimpers by tearing out his throat as Berengar used his blade to finish off his foe.

When he reached the bottom of the stairs, it became clear why the killers did not expect to receive payment for those they had taken hostage. The warden lowered his sword and put it away. It was almost like stepping into hell. Unlike the chill that hung about the fortress, a searing heat greeted him in the chamber below, where a pile of logs lay beside a roaring fire filled with brands. Bright firelight licked the dungeon's bloodstained walls, revealing the bodies strewn throughout the chamber on the floor, in cells, and in shackles. Without exception, they appeared dead. Some seemed to have been burned; others starved. Most had scorch marks on their clothes. All bore marks of torture.

A cough came from the center of the room, and Berengar's gaze fell on yet another hostage—a young woman barely out of adolescence, shackled to a table.

Berengar was accustomed to his appearance causing alarm. The mere sight of him was often enough to send children running in the other direction, and not without cause. He wore a hooded bearskin cloak over his leather armor. He had nearly the size of a bear to match. In addition to the battleaxe and short sword, he carried a bow slung across his back and a silver dagger hidden in his boot. He hesitated before approaching, careful to keep the ruined half of his face turned away from her so as not to scare her.

He needn't have bothered. The young woman was too close to death to notice much of anything. When she saw him, she simply watched him through narrow, swollen eyes. Her face was bruised, and cuts and gashes marred her sweat and soot-stained skin. Like the corpses, she had also been marked with one of the brands.

"It's all right. I won't hurt you." Though he tried his best to make his words sound soothing, his voice was coarse and harsh. If there was ever a time when he sounded different, it was long ago, and he no longer remembered how to comfort.

She opened her mouth in an attempt to speak but produced only a dry rasp. Berengar cradled her in his arms and pried the lid from his drinking horn. She was too far gone for the water to help, but perhaps it would ease her passing. Water spilled over the young woman's face as she eagerly gulped down the horn's contents. She stopped and for a moment looked at him with a hint of gratitude before the life left her eyes.

The warden's arms began to shake with an all too familiar fury as he gently lowered the girl's body to the table. When he turned away, his face was a stone mask, barely betraying his gathering rage. No trace of softness or vulnerability marred his expression—the hostages were dead, and his vengeance would serve them far better than mourning their demise. In a way, their deaths almost came as a relief, as they spared him from having to make the decision of whether to rescue the hostages or finish the job.

Berengar climbed over the twin corpses left in his wake on his way from the dungeon. It would not be long before the rest of the Black Hand joined them in death. Their passage would be swift, but he didn't intend to make it easy. He reached again for his sword. The cruelties Kane and his men had inflicted upon the hostages would be visited upon them a hundredfold. Berengar returned to the entrance hall and slowly ascended the staircase leading deeper inside the fortress. He kept to the shadows, just out of sight. The torches were few and far between, as the killers wanted to avoid attracting unwanted attention. Unfortunately for them, he had found them all the same.

When he first began his pursuit, the Black Hand numbered seventeen strong. Berengar whittled that number down to thirteen in Ballivor before Kane eluded his grasp, and counting the sentry he killed earlier, he had now taken the lives of three more. The sounds of the storm muffled his progress. Despite the warden's size, he moved with considerable stealth. A few guards patrolled the hallways of the upper levels, but most were gathered in the great hall where the goblins that built the fortress once held their feasts. He took the guards apart one by one. Behind him, Faolán's eyes gleamed, watchful and hungry.

Finally, he reached the top of the tower, which loomed above the great hall. A large portion of the ceiling had collapsed long ago, rendering the night sky visible and allowing rain to run freely around the periphery of the chamber. Kane, another of his men, and a robed individual sat around a broad stone table beneath the tower balcony while the others warmed themselves beside the fireplace.

"It's too blasted quiet in here," one remarked as Berengar crept closer to the balcony, where an archer stood with his back to him. "Where have the others gone?"

For a moment, no one spoke, and there was no sound in the chamber apart from the dull echo of raindrops against cold stone. Then Kane's voice filled the room. "Why so jumpy, Alastair? There haven't been any goblins in these woods for a long time."

Berengar could practically hear the mocking sneer on the killer's face. As he neared the balcony, he saw Kane leaning back in his chair, his boots on the table. Across his lap lay his sword, freshly polished, and a tankard was fixed in his right hand.

"It's not goblins I'm worried about," Alastair replied, nervously glancing at the shadows. "The Red Bear is on our trail."

"Esben Berengar is a fable," interjected the robed man at the table with a dismissive shake of his head. "A myth spread by those loyal to the High Queen to strike fear into the hearts of her enemies."

With that, the robed individual returned to tinkering with a shimmering white stone under candlelight. Berengar assumed this was the scholar the guards in the dungeon spoke of, which made the object in his hands the stolen thunder rune. A small pile of books and scrolls were stacked beside him.

"He's no myth," Alastair answered. "I saw him with my own eyes at Ballivor, where he took out four of our lads. Big as a giant he was, and he wore the skin of a bear as a cloak, just like the stories say."

The scholar laughed derisively. "And I suppose you think he killed said bear with his bare hands when he was a child? Or that he's a demon sent by the Fomorians? You and the others would be better served finding me more subjects for my experiments and spending less time worrying about some tall tale." As he spoke, the rune began to glow and vibrate in his hands. A burst of thunder shook the tower, and Berengar realized where the scorch marks on the clothes of the victims in the dungeon had come from.

"He's real enough," Kane told the scholar. "Let him come. The warden is just one man. We can chain him below. Maybe he'll last longer than the others. They were starting to bore me."

Berengar's blood boiled with fury at the memory of the bodies strewn across the dungeon. The archer posted at the balcony stiffened, as if suddenly aware something was behind him, but before he could react, Berengar drove the sword through his back and hurled him over the ledge. The archer's corpse landed in a heap on the table below, the blade protruding from his back. Those at the fireplace turned to see the source of the commotion as Kane and the scholar leapt back from the table, stunned. Lightning flashed outside the tower, illuminating Berengar, who loomed over those below.

The corner of Berengar's mouth turned upward in response to their fear.

"It's him," Kane stammered, the characteristic arrogance in his voice replaced by a hint of fear.

Berengar reached for his axe and started down the stairs as the outlaws scrambled to arm themselves. "I've come for you, Kane," he called, his grip tightening around the handle. "But I'll gladly cut through your men to get to you."

There were seven in all, including Kane and the scholar, who waited in the center of the chamber, flanked by archers on either side. As three swordsmen rushed forward to meet him, an arrow from a panicked archer missed him by a wide margin and vanished, lost to the darkness. Berengar whistled to Faolán, who quickly outpaced him, running the archer down before he could fire another shot. The warden countered a blow from the first swordsman to reach him, with such force his attacker was thrown on his back. He crushed the man's windpipe under the weight of his boot while at the same time bringing his axe around to meet the wrist of the next to approach. Blood spurted in the night, and Berengar seized the man by the hair and used him as a shield as another arrow came streaking toward him. The swordsman caught the arrow in the chest, and then another, as Berengar fought his way closer to the stone table. He pushed the swordsman's lifeless body away and split an archer's face in half with a stroke of his axe. A sharp cry came from the last of the swordsmen as Faolán dragged him across the floor with a bloodstained maw.

Berengar turned at last to face Kane, who stood with his sword at the ready. The two warriors regarded each other for a prolonged interval, each sizing up the other's strengths and weaknesses until Kane glanced at the stairway, as if expecting the rest of his men to come to his aid.

"No one's coming," Berengar told him, his voice low. "They're all dead. It's just you and me now."

Kane lunged at him suddenly, hoping to catch him off guard.

Berengar battered the killer's sword away with ease and knocked him back, sending him crashing into the stone table. "I thought this would be more of a challenge. Is that the best you've got?"

Kane's eyes flashed with hate, and he swung his sword at Berengar several times in rapid succession with deadly precision. The warden stood his ground. Turning his foe's momentum to his advantage, he reached out and caught Kane's wrist in his free hand, wrenching the sword away. Before Kane could react, he drove his knee into the man's groin and broke his nose with the flat of his axe. Though he might have easily shattered his attacker's wrist, he instead released his hold and nodded to the fallen sword.

"Pick it up."

Kane regarded him with a curious expression until it seemed to dawn on him that Berengar was toying with him —as he himself had toyed with so many of his victims over the years—and all the color drained from his face at once. "Wait! Perhaps we can strike a deal. Tell me what you want."

Berengar bared his teeth in contempt at the show of cowardice, not that he expected any better. The other wardens might have allowed Kane to surrender, but Berengar wasn't like the others. "I want your head." Like the monster hunters of old, it was the surest way to show the deed had been done. "Now pick up that sword."

Kane reluctantly reached down and retrieved the sword, but before Berengar or Faolán could strike, a bolt of lightning shot through the open ceiling, causing the chamber to tremble. Berengar stared past Kane to the spot where the scholar held the thunder rune clutched in his hand.

"Stay back!" The rune pulsed with white and yellow light, which seemed to flash brighter in response to the timbre of his voice. When Berengar took a step in his direction, the scholar raised the rune, said something in a strange tongue, and called down lightning from the sky. "Keep away!"

A bolt streaked from the rune, but Faolán tackled Berengar out of the way before it could hit him. Instead, the lightning knocked over the wall behind him, and stones fell from above as more of the ceiling collapsed around them. Berengar looked for Kane, but the killer had seized his opportunity to flee the chamber and had disappeared down the staircase. Before he could give chase, the scholar again pointed the rune in his direction and spoke the same incantation, causing the rune to glow. The warden dived underneath the stone table and turned it over to use as a shield. Mercifully, the table absorbed most of the impact, even as the blast shook the tower, causing part of the floor to cave in on itself.

If this keeps up, that idiot is going to bring the whole tower down on our heads, he thought.

On the other side of the room, Faolán deftly avoided several blasts from the thunder rune, drawing the scholar's attention away from him. Berengar stuck his head out from behind the table and watched the scholar, who continued to back away. He appeared to have little influence over sparks from the rune, which nearly caught his robes on fire as flames began to spread. Smoke rose from the rune, and Berengar saw that the flesh of the scholar's arm was burned and charred. The man was dealing with forces beyond his capabilities to control, which came as little surprise. There was a reason magical relics were best left to magicians and the like. In the wrong hands, such a powerful artifact could be dangerous.

Berengar jumped from cover just before another bolt incinerated the table. The scholar doubled over in pain, nearly dropping the thunder rune. "Don't come any clos-er," he said to Berengar, wincing. That was when he noticed Faolán crouched on his other side, ready to strike.

"Give up," Berengar told him. "You might get me before I reach you, but you can't hit both of us at the same time." He made a show of lowering his axe. "I came for

Kane. I'm not here for you. Give up the rune, and I'll let you walk away. You have my word."

The scholar surveyed the spreading fire, the structural damage to the tower, and the ruin of his own hand. He finally let go of the rune, which clattered to the floor, and breathed a sigh of relief.

Berengar closed the distance between them in an instant and gutted the man with his axe. He pictured the young woman he found in the dungeon in his mind as the scholar collapsed in a heap on the floor, writhing while clutching at his entrails. The warden turned his back on the dying man, picked up the rune, and added it to his satchel, careful not to let it make contact with his skin. Then he hurried from the tower. He would have to worry about disposing of the rune later. The job wasn't finished yet, and there remained yet one more life to claim.

Kane was nowhere in sight when he reached the entrance. Not far away, the earth was disturbed where hoofprints had been left behind in the mud. The rains had stopped, at least for the moment, allowing the moon's light to peek out from behind the clouds, and he noticed the prints were part of a set of tracks leading away from the tower.

He can't have gone far. Berengar headed for the spot where he'd concealed himself in the woods earlier that day. His horse waited nearby, tied to a tree. "Come," he muttered to Faolán, and together they started on the outlaw's trail as flames engulfed the forsaken fortress behind them.

B erengar pursued Kane south, into Leinster. Kane fled as if the devil himself were at his back. Berengar followed over hills, across rivers, and through forests. He did not relent. Each day he grew closer. No doubt Kane hoped Faolán would lose his scent in one of Leinster's many bogs or marshes, but he would never get far enough for that to happen, not with Berengar hot on his trail. This time there would be no escape.

On the third day he caught up to his prey. Kane had hidden himself in a thicket. It was a cold morning, and dew clung to the grass. The outlaw glanced about nervously and reached for his sword at the slightest sound, as if he knew death was coming. After a moment, he relaxed. Berengar waited until he cupped his hands, reached into the stream, and lowered his face to drink from the water before taking out his bow. He nocked an arrow and took aim as casually as if he were after a deer.

The shot struck true. It wasn't a fatal wound, which was by design. Berengar wanted him to suffer. Kane crawled across the grass and managed to get to his horse, but the end was only a matter of time now, and they both knew it. Berengar lowered the bow and returned to his mount, this time with his quarry in sight.

He chased Kane to the outskirts of a nearby town. Faolán ran down the killer's horse, which threw its rider from the saddle. Interrupted from their daily tasks, a number of townspeople watched Kane hit the ground before their attention shifted to Berengar, who dismounted and approached on foot, axe in hand. Kane stumbled back, lost his balance, and landed in the mud, losing his sword. He scrambled to his feet and ran toward the church, leaving the blade behind. When the priest appeared outside the church, drawn by the commotion, Kane threw himself at the man's feet and kissed the hem of his robes.

"Please, show mercy, Father."

The priest took note of Berengar and nodded, allowing

Kane to slip past him and bolt the door closed. When Berengar came to a halt just outside the church, the priest took a nervous step back at the sight of him. "Stop where you are. You will go no farther."

"This man is a murderer," Berengar declared, loud enough for the crowd of townspeople that had assembled to hear him. "He slaughters men, women, and children for sport. He deserves to die."

"Vengeance belongs to the Lord of Hosts alone," the priest replied sternly. "This man has sought sanctuary in the house of the Lord. He is unarmed. You cannot harm him."

Berengar snarled, feeling a wave of anger rise up inside him. "I am Esben Berengar, Warden of Fál and servant of the High Queen."

At this pronouncement, the crowd murmured loudly among themselves. Some looked on him with fear, others with hate.

"The law of the Lord of Hosts is above that of any earthly ruler," the priest said solemnly. "There are some laws even a warden cannot break, and the right of sanctuary is one of them."

Berengar looked at the priest and again at the crowd. The priest was right. More than any other kingdom, Leinster valued piety above all. To violate the right of sanctuary was an unspeakable act. None of the other wardens would even consider such a thing.

Berengar didn't hesitate. He strode forward, and when the priest moved to block his path, he knocked him into the mud. He broke down the church doors with his axe over the priest's protests.

"Stay here," he told Faolán, who guarded the entrance while Berengar ventured inside the sanctuary. A trail of blood stretched across the chamber, leading to where Kane clung to the altar.

"Please," his victim screamed as he approached, but Berengar seized him by the hair, jerked his head back, and held him in place as he struggled.

Then he took Kane's head and left his body at the altar.

CHAPTER TWO

His task complete, Berengar looked upon his handiwork with a small measure of satisfaction. The debt had been paid. Perhaps it would be enough to bring some comfort to the Black Hand's victims, be they living or dead. Berengar felt no such relief. Even with Kane's lifeless body at his feet, the warden's thirst for vengeance was only partially sated. The rage that drove him never really went away. Fortunately, there was always another task waiting for him to take care of, if not in one kingdom, then in another. He kept to the road more than any of the High Queen's other wardens—returning to Tara mostly when summoned—and that was the way he preferred it.

A bark from Faolán shattered the temporary lull inside the sanctuary as he stuffed the head into a sack. Berengar turned toward the entrance, where some kind of commotion had started. Carrying his axe in one bloodstained hand and the sack in the other, he left the church the way he came. The throng had only grown in his short absence and now appeared openly hostile.

When he emerged, cries of "murderer" and "monster"

rang out from members of the crowd. Armed with stones and torches, they blocked the warden's path to his horse.

The priest Berengar had pushed aside gasped at the sight of the blood-covered sack and stared at Berengar with an all too familiar mixture of fear and loathing. "This is sacrilege! You have committed murder at the sacred altar of St. Brigid's Church. There can be no forgiveness for such a crime against the Lord."

Berengar cursed his luck. Next to Padraig himself, Brigid was one of the most sainted and revered figures in Fál. That meant Berengar had tracked Kane to the town of Kildare, which literally meant "church of the oak." *Of all the places for Kane to seek refuge, he had to choose one of the holiest sites in Leinster.* Something like this would follow him. At the least, this was yet more fodder for the bards to spin ballads of his misdeeds. At worst…

"Blasphemer!" one of the angrier townspeople shouted, spittle flying from his mouth. "Blood for blood! The Lord demands justice."

"Kill him!" another replied. "Hang his body from the oak!"

It wasn't all that unusual for his actions to stir up the locals, though most of the time they had the good sense not to threaten him outright. He could usually count on his appearance to frighten away potential enemies. The warden towered over all the townspeople in sight, but it wasn't just his size or the weapons he carried that intimidated. Three deep, jagged scars raked down his face from his forehead to his lip. A leather patch covered his missing right eye, the result of his encounter with the bear whose fur he now wore as a cloak. Even his hair, bright red like an open flame, drew unwanted attention his way.

Berengar bared his teeth in displeasure, causing a few to back away. "Get out of my path." Faolán bounded to his side, snarling at the closest potential attacker. None of the townspeople made a move toward him, but neither did they clear a path to his horse. The tense standoff continued until at last the warden raised his axe and pointed it at the crowd. "Last warning. I'll go through the lot of you if I have to."

Someone threw a stone at him, which fell short and landed at his feet.

This is about to get ugly.

"People of Kildare, make way!" a voice proclaimed before the frenzied mob could attack.

The crowd parted to allow a number of guards to pass through their ranks. The townspeople obeyed without question, and with good reason. The guards were well armed and impressively armored. All wore blue woolen cloaks. There were almost fifteen men in total—a surprising display, even for a town the size of Kildare. Berengar eased off his grip on the axe's handle at the guards' advance, though he remained careful to keep the weapon close at hand.

"Stand down," the guards' captain ordered one of the more irate townspeople—who nodded meekly and stepped out of the way—before taking note of Berengar. "What is the meaning of this?"

The priest hurried to the captain's side and jabbed his finger in Berengar's direction. "This man violated the right of sanctuary and committed murder on St. Brigid's altar—in cold blood, no less! In the name of all that is holy, he must be made to pay for his sins."

The captain's eyes narrowed in Berengar's direction. "Take him."

The guards quickly moved to surround the warden, encouraged by the crowd.

"I wouldn't do that if I were you," Berengar said when

the captain reached for the sword at his side. "I am Esben Berengar, Warden of Fál. I answer to the High Queen alone."

The guards halted at this declaration, and their captain's eyes lingered on Berengar's scars before wandering to the brooch clasped to his cloak, which bore the sigil of the silver fox.

"The man was Skinner Kane, leader of the Black Hand," Berengar continued. "He was a butcher and a criminal, deserving of death many times over."

The captain exchanged a brief look with one of his lieutenants at the mention of the Black Hand.

"These are Laird Margolin's lands," said a guard who wore a particularly nasty expression. "We won't answer to some whore of a queen, or one of her dogs that's slipped its leash."

Berengar moved without hesitation. Before any of the guards could react, he seized the man's hand and snapped his wrist like a twig. "Insult the High Queen in my presence again, and I'll kill you."

The guard muttered a string of profanities, which quickly ceased when Berengar increased the pressure applied to his broken wrist.

"Enough," the captain of the guards said. "Let him go." At his command, archers across the town square took aim, their bows trained on Berengar.

The warden growled but reluctantly released his grip on the guard, who toppled over at his feet, whimpering in pain.

The guards' captain nodded, and the archers lowered their bows. "Servant of Tara or not, you have committed a grievous offense, Warden Berengar. Relinquish your arms and surrender yourself to our custody. Laird Margolin will decide your fate."

Berengar weighed his options. He might have fought his way past the crowd to his horse, but there was little chance of cutting down Laird Margolin's guards in broad daylight. He had hardly slept in the last three days. On the other hand, nobles could always be counted on to cut deals if there was something in it for them, and as a servant of Leinster's boy-king, the local lord would likely be more favorably disposed toward him than the mob of peasants calling out for his blood.

"Very well. I'll go with you to the castle, but if you try to take my weapons, we'll have trouble."

The captain grimaced at this response, clearly unaccustomed to having his authority challenged, but nevertheless agreed, prompting sighs of relief from his subordinates. "As you wish. This way. You'll accompany us to Castle Blackthorn."

Berengar reluctantly handed the sack containing Kane's severed head to one of the guards and followed the captain from the town square, the people of Kildare glaring behind him.

What have you gotten yourself into now?

T hey reached their destination just after midday. Despite the hour, the land was again shrouded in darkness under a veil of black clouds. The guards' wagon splashed through a puddle and rolled to a stop, followed by those on horseback. The outline of a towering structure was visible through a thin layer of fog. As Berengar and the others made their way through the dense hedge of thorns and briars surrounding the castle, the stronghold's features grew more distinct.

Castle Blackthorn had an austere, imposing appearance, even from a distance. While by no means the largest castle Berengar had beheld, Blackthorn was nonetheless impressive for such a rural setting. Though the surrounding lands were flat, neighboring swamps and marshes lent the remote castle added protection. Any attacking force would have a difficult time even finding the castle, let alone launching an assault. Dark blue banners bearing the sigil of a leafless, bleeding tree hung from the walls, thrashed about by frigid winds that held no promise of the summer to come.

Berengar scanned the castle's walls, noticing a number of sentries, archers, and spearmen at their posts.

"Open the gate," the captain bellowed to those on the other side.

After a brief pause, the gate slowly opened, granting them entrance. A faint whisper of thunder echoed in the heavens, like a slumbering giant soon to wake, as Berengar passed under the watchful eyes of the sentries above. A trio of corpses hung from gallows inside the courtyard, which had attracted no small number of crows. In more populous areas of Fál, it wasn't uncommon to find a castle as part of a larger city or community. This was not the case at Black- thorn, where the castle was far removed from the towns and villages under its lord's control. It seemed likely that any traveling merchants, farmers, or emissaries would have to stay the night in the castle before returning to the road.

To Berengar's surprise, there wasn't a church or chapel in sight—which was unusual for Leinster, where the worship of the elder gods was strictly prohibited. Although devotion to the elder gods—beings divided between the benevolent Tuatha dé Danann and the monstrous Fomo- rians—had slowly diminished since Padraig brought the word of the Lord of Hosts to Fál, the old ways remained strong in many places, especially in the north.

The gate closed behind them, and the captain whispered something into a messenger's ear before nodding in Berengar's direction. The messenger stared at the warden in alarm until Berengar returned his gaze, causing him to promptly hurry in the opposite direction. A mud-covered stableboy who barely reached Berengar's waist appeared to take his horse, but not before Berengar made sure the satchel with the thunder rune was safely secured in his possession. That was one object he didn't want falling into the wrong hands.

"This way," the captain said as the boy vanished into the stables with Berengar's horse.

He accompanied the guards through the courtyard and farther into the castle. They encountered mostly servants along the way, though the warden noticed a few lesser nobles in attendance—possibly guests of Laird Margolin. Most were quiet or kept to themselves, but some carried themselves with an added air of wariness and suspicion, hinting at an atmosphere of fear hanging over Blackthorn. Though his duties frequently drew him into the affairs of lords and lesser nobles, Berengar disdained regional politics. He knew relatively little about Margolin, but what he had witnessed so far wasn't particularly promising.

I should have killed Kane at the border when I had the chance. When Nora of Connacht ascended to the High Throne, she appointed the wardens to uphold peace between the realms. In theory, Berengar's authority as a warden extended to each of Fál's five kingdoms, though as current circumstances proved, reality often operated by a more troublesome set of rules. For various reasons, he tried his best to keep out of Leinster. The death of the kingdom's previous king with his sole heir in infancy had left the kingdom under the rule of a Prince Regent more interested in pleasurable pursuits than governance. A weak boy-king and a powerful central church allowed the lords of Leinster to exert an outsized influence over the land.

Walking through the castle's joyless halls felt like entering a tomb, which seemed in keeping with the grim mood. Shadows lorded over cold, sparsely decorated chambers and corridors. A faint melody emanated from deeper within the castle. The sound grew stronger as Berengar's armed escort led him to the entrance of the great hall, a quietly lit chamber where a number of the castle's guests were gathered.

"Wait here," the guards' captain muttered sternly.

Berengar folded his arms across his chest and did his best to remain unnoticed by the hall's occupants—no small feat for a man his size. The music came from a bard playing a harp with obvious skill; all who listened were mesmerized by her voice.

Berengar recognized the song as "The Queen's War", which told the story of how Nora of Connacht brought an end to the Shadow Wars and united the five kingdoms of Fál. He had spent enough time in taverns and inns to know many of the more popular ballads by heart, which, to his chagrin, often included the songs sung about *him*. Most were exaggerations—tales spun into myth with each retelling—but some hit closer to the mark than he cared to admit.

His gaze wandered to the opposite end of the room and fell on a throne hewn from twisted blackthorn branches, upon which sat the castle's lord. Margolin's black locks were interspersed with gray, and Berengar estimated the man was somewhere in his forties. He wore a dark blue cloak over a gold and scarlet tunic, but it was the crown on his head that merited Berengar's attention.

Fál consisted of five kingdoms, with Ulster to the north, Munster to the south, and Connacht, Meath, and

Leinster in between. The kings and queens of each kingdom wore crowns of silver. Only Nora, the High Queen, wore a crown of gold. Margolin's crown, crafted from iron, meant he was a *Rí Tuaithe*—one of several underkings, or greater lords. If Margolin was in fact one of the *Rí Tuaithe*, it seemed strange to find his seat of power in such an isolated part of Leinster's countryside.

As Berengar looked on, a man prostrated himself before the throne, beseeching his lord to forgive a debt of some kind. With the wave of a hand, Margolin had the man dragged from the room before returning to the contents of his goblet. "Who's next?" he demanded of a scholarly-looking courtier reading from a scroll.

"Fergus O'Rirdan, the representative from Curragh."

Fergus, a ruddy-faced, balding peasant, waited with his family for Margolin to acknowledge him.

"It seems the good people of Curragh have again failed to meet their obligations," said a man perched behind the throne. His voice was soft and inviting, and he spoke with a smile, but there was something vaguely menacing about his eyes. Though clad in black robes, no cross hung from his neck, which made it unlikely he was a priest in the service of the Lord of Hosts.

"That's Thaddeus," muttered a man beside Berengar, taking note of his interest. "Laird Margolin's chief adviser, and the only man he seems to listen to. Curious fellow, if you ask me. No one knows where he's from."

Berengar said nothing but continued to observe. Thaddeus was an unusually pale man, with unruly black hair and a thin, spindly build.

Margolin lowered his goblet and gestured for Fergus to come before the throne. "Approach." The lord's voice was as harsh as his adviser's was smooth, and as he spoke,

Berengar noticed an impressive scar across his neck, suggesting at least one previous attempt on his life.

Fergus swallowed nervously and did as he was asked, hat in hand. He knelt before the throne and lowered his gaze until Margolin bade him to rise. Even then he had trouble meeting his lord's eyes. "My lord, I can explain..."

"Silence." Margolin regarded his subject with considerable disdain. He held himself with the bearing of a man accustomed to the trappings of power and authority. "You were not summoned here to give excuses or to plead for mercy."

"Your village, and others like it, flourish under the protection Laird Margolin provides," Thaddeus reminded Fergus, who glanced at the lord's adviser with obvious discomfort. "The costs of cleansing these lands of goblins have proven considerable. It is only natural that your obligations should increase in turn to afford the cost of soldiers and treasure. Would you now deny your lord that which is rightfully his?"

"We have brought what we could afford," Fergus protested. "We will make good on our debts when the harvest improves. I give you my word."

Margolin greeted this pronouncement with a cold sneer. "Of that, I have no doubt. I sent for you to deliver a message to the rest of your village. You must now pay three times what you owe, and you must do it by the new moon. If not...the consequences will be severe." His eyes swept from Fergus to a young woman behind him. "Is this your daughter?"

Fergus looked from Margolin to his daughter, who seemed caught off guard by the court's attention. "Aye." The trepidation in his voice was clear.

"She will remain here until your obligations are met. Should you fail to properly motivate the people of

Curragh, I am sure she will make a fine wife for one of my soldiers."

"But my lord—"

Fergus reached for his daughter, but she was pulled away by a group of guards.

"If you are not out of my sight by the time I finish my wine, I will have you thrown into a cell," Margolin said.

Fergus gave his daughter one final look and fled from the room with the rest of his family as his daughter's anguished cries filled the chamber.

Berengar knew cruelty when he saw it. Watching Margolin, he was certain this was not a man to be trifled with. He would have to proceed with caution, something that didn't exactly come naturally to him.

The music resumed, and the clamor of the hall began anew.

"It appears the patrol from Kildare has returned," Thaddeus said, observing the guards who had traveled with Berengar to Castle Blackthorn. "What news is there from Kildare?"

The guards' captain stepped forward and nodded to his companions, who ushered Berengar toward Margolin. "This man assaulted a priest and murdered a man granted sanctuary in St. Brigid's Church. He claims he is one of the High Queen's wardens."

The captain reached into the sack and produced the severed head of Skinner Kane to the collective gasp from those gathered in the hall. The bard's playing stopped abruptly, and silence spread through the chamber as every eye in the room fell on Berengar.

Better get this over with.

Murmurs came from the crowd when he approached the throne with Faolán, flanked by guards on either side.

"So it is true," Thaddeus muttered. "Esben Berengar—

the Bear Warden. There were rumors he was traveling through the area."

It was an unfortunate consequence of his distinctive appearance and well-deserved infamy that he was easily recognized.

Margolin regarded him with a steely gaze. "What brings a Warden of Fál to my domain? Speak."

Berengar met his eyes without flinching. "I entered your lands on warden's business, after tracking the Black Hand to an abandoned goblin fort at the border with Meath. I dealt with the outlaws, but their leader fled into Leinster. When I tracked the coward to Kildare, he thought he could escape me by seeking protection from the church. He was wrong."

"This is an outrage!" a lesser noble bellowed. "Murder, in a sacred place?"

"The people of Kildare demand justice," the guards' captain said, gesturing to the priest. "The town's priest insisted on accompanying us here to plead with you personally."

The priest, who rode in the wagon on the journey from Kildare, gave a curt bow before addressing Margolin. "My lord, this man must be punished for his crime. Such barbarity cannot be tolerated in Leinster, no matter who he serves. The church will not stand for it."

Margolin stroked his beard, deep in thought. "Enough. I wish to speak with the warden alone. Everyone out."

The order was a demonstration of power. If Margolin wanted to discuss something with him in the absence of prying ears, he might have done so in private with ease. The lord's subjects obeyed without hesitation, although the priest glared balefully at Berengar on his way from the room. Berengar briefly locked eyes with the bard, who frowned before leaving with her harp. Apart from the guards, only Thaddeus remained behind, a signal of his influence over Margolin.

The lord set his goblet aside and descended from the throne, stopping just short of Berengar. "Were you one of my subjects, I would have you killed and be done with it. What, then, am I to do with you, Warden of Fál?"

Berengar stared down at him, arms still folded across his chest in a show of defiance. *Rí Tuaithe* or not, he didn't like being threatened. "I don't answer to you. That man deserved to die. I'd do it again if I had the chance."

Margolin's brow furrowed with visible anger. "You would do well to show respect, Warden Berengar. You may be a favorite of the High Queen, but here you are in my abode. If I wished your death, be assured your body would vanish into a swamp and never be found. I am certain there would be many who would be glad of your demise."

"Perhaps there is a way a man like him can be of use to you, my lord," Thaddeus suggested. "I understand there was a hefty bounty on Skinner Kane. Surely his head would fetch a handsome price."

In the end, it always came down to greed. There was always a deal to be made. "Take it. I have no use for the reward."

"Of course, there is the matter of the church," Margolin said before he could leave. "It will not be long before word of your actions at St. Brigid's begins to spread. Dún Aulin is not far from here. I understand you've had issues with church leadership in the past?"

Berengar stopped dead in his tracks and turned back to face him. *Issues* was an understatement. Of all Fál's kingdoms, Leinster was the least tolerant of nonhumans and magic. After the upheaval of the Shadow Wars, when the dark sorcerer Azeroth nearly conquered Fál, public sentiment quickly turned against anyone with even the slightest connection to magic, resulting in a number of riots and purges. The most violent of these riots took place in Dún Aulin, Leinster's capital. Berengar was sent in to restore order, which he did with bloody efficiency, something the leadership of the powerful Church of Leinster had never forgiven him for. He could only imagine how they would take the news of his deeds at Kildare. Given the church's influence over Leinster, it was not something he wanted to consider.

"If she is as pious as the stories say, I assume the High Queen would also take issue with your actions in her name," Margolin continued.

Berengar gritted his teeth. A follower of the Lord of Hosts, Nora had a great deal of respect for the church, and the queen's opinion was the only one that mattered to him. "I'm listening."

"Of course, it would be a simple task for me to suppress the news. My guards can be very persuasive. One command from me and word of what you have done will never leave Kildare. Do we understand each other?"

Berengar studied the man across from him. Margolin had him in a bind, and they both knew it. "We do. And what is it you want from me in return?"

Margolin returned to his throne. "Are you familiar with the Bog of Móin Alúin, which rests on my lands?"

"I've heard of it."

"An ogre that dwells in the bog has been causing trouble for the locals. Then, three nights ago, the monster abducted my niece, Lady Imogen. I want you to rescue her, if she is still alive, and slay the beast."

Berengar accepted without hesitation. "We have a deal."

"Good. I expect you will want to rest before setting off on your quest. You are welcome to do so, but I warn you not to tarry too long. If my niece is out there, it is unlikely she will long survive on her own. In the meantime, you are my guest. Eat and drink your fill. I will have a bedchamber prepared for you. When you are ready, Thaddeus will fill you in on the details."

"Very well."

The moment he was dismissed from Margolin's presence, Berengar left to find his way to the kitchens. His dogged pursuit of Kane had left him tired and hungry. Soon he would hunt, but first he needed sleep.

In truth, the task before him was rather straightforward. Though Lady Imogen was most likely dead, Berengar intended to find her, whatever her fate. Ogres, while nasty creatures, were nothing he hadn't handled before. For once, luck seemed on his side.

What could go wrong?

CHAPTER THREE

BERENGAR WOKE EARLY to prepare for the hunt. Sunrise remained a ways off, but there was work to do before then. He had just finished arming himself when an eerie wail came from somewhere outside the castle. The low, mournful cry reminded him of someone in torment. He glanced around the confines of his modest room and listened, half-expecting to hear the noise again.

Must've been the wind, he thought, but something about the sound left him uneasy.

Faolán, whose animal senses were more attuned to the supernatural, growled, and her fur bristled in response to an unseen threat. Berengar motioned for her to follow and eased open the door. Castle Blackthorn lay still in the dead of night. Even the servants showed no signs of stirring. Only the guards on patrol were awake. Berengar made his way through quiet, dark halls and deserted corridors. A pair of guards regarded him with suspicion at the castle's entrance, but he ignored them and proceeded to the court-yard, which lay bathed in the moon's pale light. From there, it was only a short climb to one of the round towers, from which he could see the grounds beyond the wall.

Berengar scanned the area, seeking anything that might shed light on what had transpired the night Lady Imogen was taken. According to Margolin, his niece had been abducted outside the castle, but if that was true, what was she doing on the other side of the wall in the first place? Though an ogre might approach a human settlement if hungry enough, even it wouldn't have been thick enough to do so in a place so well defended. It didn't add up.

Suddenly, another wail rang out above the wind. Berengar peered past the dim torchlight toward the swaying trees that lay beyond the maze of shrubs and thorns around the castle. For a moment, he thought he glimpsed several figures watching from the shadows, but before he could get a better look, he heard someone approach behind him.

"What has you on the prowl at this hour, Warden Berengar?"

It was Thaddeus, Laird Margolin's chief adviser. His tone was friendly, but Berengar saw mistrust in his eyes.

"Daylight is too valuable to waste. I want to reach the ogre's hunting ground before dusk, and I plan to learn as much as I can before departing." He preferred to avoid going in blind when he could avoid it. In his line of work, proper preparation often meant the difference between life and death. Besides, things weren't always as they appeared on the surface.

"In that case, I am pleased to offer whatever knowledge you require. You'll find the bog between the Shannon and Liffey rivers. The village of Alúine, to the east, is the closest human settlement. Although the goblin population has dwindled thanks to Laird Margolin's efforts at extermination, those who are left have caused no shortage of trouble for his lordship's subjects. The ogre has killed more than a few villagers already, but if you plan to venture into the bog, you should also be aware of the hag."

Berengar followed him back inside the castle, and they walked together in the direction of the great hall. "What hag?"

"A witch said to dwell deep within the bog. There are rumors of other unusual happenings in the area—of strange disappearances, ghostly apparitions, and the like—but most of the accounts are unverified and may amount to nothing more than local gossip. All the same, these are dangerous lands, Warden Berengar. You would do well to remember it."

"I'm a dangerous man."

"You do not understand. This part of the realm is not as tame as other areas of Leinster. The old ways still have a hold here. Padraig may have vanquished the Fomorians, but many powerful creatures linger."

Whether the elder gods were truly gods, as the fairies believed, or demons, as the church believed, most acknowledged they existed, or at least had at one time. It was thought by some they had spawned entire races of monsters. Thanks to Azeroth's attempted conquest of Fál and the purges of magicians following the Shadow Wars, there were fewer magic-capable beings to deal with monsters, leaving the task to mercenaries or men like Berengar.

"What else do you require?" Thaddeus asked.

"I want to speak with anyone who knows Lady Imogen or her habits, as well as witnesses to the ogre sightings."

The request seemed to surprise Margolin's adviser. "I'll see what I can do. I've also arranged for three soldiers to show you the way and accompany you on your quest. All are skilled hunters."

"I prefer to work alone."

Thaddeus shook his head as if to indicate the matter was not up for discussion. "It is the express will of Laird Margolin."

Berengar grunted in half-hearted assent. "Fine. Just see to it they don't get in my way."

"I also suggest you consult with the castle alchemist. He might be able to brew a decoction or poison that would be of use against an ogre."

At this, Berengar raised an eyebrow. Despite the fact that most alchemists and herbalists had not a drop of magical blood, there were few of either left in Leinster thanks to the purges. He wasn't particularly fond of ingesting strange potions or elixirs, but an alchemist might prove useful nonetheless. "I will. Anything else?"

Thaddeus took a step closer and lowered his voice. "About your time hunting Skinner Kane…rumor has it the Black Hand acquired a very rare item intended for King Mór of Munster—a thunder rune, I believe? You wouldn't happen to know what became of it, by chance?"

Berengar didn't trust Margolin, but he trusted his adviser even less. Whatever his interest in the thunder rune, it couldn't be good. He looked Thaddeus dead in the eyes and shook his head. "It's no concern of mine what happened to some relic."

He left the great hall and returned to the task of readying himself for what lay ahead. The alchemist, as it turned out, was not particularly adept—and also quite possibly mad as the result of inhaling too many dangerous fumes over the years. Nevertheless, Berengar left with bait to attract the ogre, along with a purported vial of poison of questionable efficacy.

When the sun rose, he set about questioning the castle's inhabitants about Lady Imogen's disappearance. Most of the servants were reluctant to speak with him, and others still refused outright to do so, as if they feared to even discuss the subject. He gleaned very little about Imogen apart from her age and appearance. The poor girl seemed well liked but had few friends, and Laird Margolin kept her under strict supervision—though apparently not strict enough, as she'd managed to slip outside the castle the night she went missing. According to the servants, there was a storm that night, so it wasn't out of the realm of possibility the sentries missed the ogre, but it still raised the question of what Lady Imogen was doing beyond the wall in the first place.

The few witnesses who claimed to have seen the ogre were equally unhelpful. One described seeing a creature that could have easily been a werewolf, and another was nearly blind. Berengar, who didn't enjoy the company of others to begin with, found the process deeply frustrating and couldn't help feeling there was something more the people weren't telling him. Once his preparations for the journey were complete, he was on the way to the stables to meet the soldiers Laird Margolin sent to accompany him until he came across the bard practicing in the courtyard.

When she saw him, her fingers stopped moving, and the harp's strings fell silent.

"I'd like a word," Berengar said. "I'm—"

The bard spoke with a distinctly Caledonian accent. "I know who you are, Bear Warden. My name is Saroise. What do you want with me?" She was clearly not pleased to see him, which came as little surprise. If she believed even half of what the songs recorded about his deeds, she had good cause to be wary of him.

"I've heard of you." Saroise of Caledonia wasn't just

any bard. She was well-known across the kingdoms of Fál, her talents sought after by kings, princes, and lords alike. "What are you doing in a place like this?"

"When my wagon broke down in the marsh, Laird Margolin offered me food and shelter in return for three moons' stay at court." Her tone evidenced her obvious displeasure. "What is it to you? I've broken no laws, Warden of Fál, and I'll have you know I'm somewhat fond of my head."

"I don't have time to trade barbs." Saroise was an outsider at Blackthorn, which meant that she was his best chance to gather more information. "During your stay, did you spend time in the company of Lady Imogen?"

To her credit, she met his gaze without blinking. "Aye."

"What kind of person is she?"

"She's strong, although she'd have to be to live in a place like this. Blackthorn isn't known for its hospitality. The people miss her. Unlike her uncle, Imogen is liked and respected by Laird Margolin's subjects."

"Was it common for her to go outside the castle in the evening?"

Saroise shook her head.

"Did you notice any unusual behavior from her the day of her disappearance?"

The bard pursed her lips, mulling the question over. "I believe she had an argument with her uncle. The man is a tyrant, and I doubt there's much love between them. I take it he has asked you to find her?"

Berengar nodded. "Aye. And kill the thing that took her."

Saroise stared at him curiously. "Tell me—what will you do if you find her alive?"

"Bring her home, of course."

"Don't."

She left him standing there without another word.

Another village, another monster—if the stories were to be believed, anyway. Panicked villagers running for their lives didn't make the most reliable witnesses. Truth be told, Berengar didn't care if it was an ogre, troll, or even a skin changer. He just wanted something to sink his axe into.

His stallion left a trail in its wake as they traversed a field littered with puddles. Faolán followed at a distance, her fur coated with mud. It was supposed to be spring, but it felt more like fall. The untrimmed hedge of hawthorn trees was not yet in full bloom, the trees' sweet scent masked by an earthy musk. The sun had all but disappeared. A light mist hung about the air. Already he could see his breath—not that the weather bothered him. Berengar had been born in the Kingdom of Ulster, far to the north, and seasoned by many winters there. That, and the heavy cloak he wore, rendered him nearly immune to the cold's effects.

He was already in a foul mood, mostly because he tried to avoid traveling this far south if he could help it. While the High Queen's wardens shared equal authority in all five kingdoms, each assumed most of the responsibility for a specific territory. For his part, Berengar preferred to operate out of Meath, so he was not pleased to do the bidding of some rural lord from Leinster who seemed more concerned with unpaid taxes than missing villagers.

Still, hunting monsters was better than enduring the endless web of treachery and deceit found in great halls and royal courts. He didn't care a whit about Margolin, and the man's niece was very likely dead, but at least he might prevent more locals from falling victim to the ogre's monstrous appetite.

Let Darragh and the others rescue maidens and attend peace summits, he thought. Or whatever it was the Captain of the Wardens did in sunlit Munster while men like Berengar did the dirty work. He'd already prepared the bait he would use to lure the beast. Unlike goblins, ogres possessed an underdeveloped sense of taste. As such, they were attracted to foods with especially strong aromas and flavors most humans found repugnant. The rotting, fly-infested meats Berengar had obtained from the castle's alchemist would do the trick nicely. In the grand scheme of things, stalking and killing an ogre was a simple enough business. Berengar was a skilled tracker. Before he was a warden, he was a soldier, and before that, a hunter. Before that...well, he tried not to think about it.

His companions were loud enough to wake a slumbering troll—no easy feat, the warden knew, though the blasted things did have a nasty habit of waking at the most inopportune moments. None of the three soldiers sent by Laird Margolin to accompany him on the hunt had said more than a handful of words to him for the duration of the journey, which was perfectly fine by Berengar. The men jumped whenever he so much as glanced in their direction.

He brought his horse to a halt and held up a hand to silence the others. "Quiet." Something didn't feel right. The trail had ended some time ago, and they were close enough to the bog already.

"What is it?" one of his companions said, staring into the encroaching darkness. "I don't hear anything."

That meant nothing, though Berengar didn't bother saying it aloud. Despite their size, ogres could move quietly enough if they had cause, aided by the soft earth of the marshes and bogs in which they dwelled.

The wind changed directions, and a putrid aroma tickled the warden's nostrils. "It's close," he whispered just loud enough for the others to hear. Goblins and trolls weren't particularly pleasant-smelling either, but ogres possessed a distinctive, overpowering stench.

As he motioned for his companions to dismount, Berengar caught a flurry of movement out of the corner of his good eye, and Faolán barked a warning. The others reached for their swords, but they were too late. The ogre burst from the hawthorn hedge with a ferocious growl. With one swing of its club, the ogre knocked over one horseman in mid-dismount, and the horse collapsed on its rider, crushing him. After successfully making it to the ground, one rider tried in vain to flee only to sink into the mud, and the ogre caved in his head by bashing him with its club.

Berengar's horse reared at the sight of the ogre, and he allowed himself to fall away, landing on his feet.

"Steady," he said to the remaining soldier, who instead charged the beast in a blind panic, waving his sword about like a madman. Berengar heard bones crunch and snap as the ogre seized his companion in its massive hand. The beast sank a set of oversized if slightly dulled teeth into the soldier's neck and ripped out a chunk of flesh, sending blood spurting freely from the wound.

The ogre rounded on Berengar, its yellow eyes gleaming under the light of the full moon. Despite its size, at just under seven feet tall, the monstrous creature was only slightly the larger of the two. Its bulky, muscular frame was covered in fungi and vines. Its hairless skin was a muted orange, a few shades duller than Berengar's fiery red hair.

"You're an ugly brute." The warden fastened his grip around the handle of his battleaxe. Faolán growled at his side, baring her fangs. "And that's coming from me."

When the ogre charged him, Berengar stood his ground, his gaze fixed on its exposed flabby belly. One well-placed slash from his axe would spill the creature's entrails. After that, it would be a simple matter to take the creature's head. Unfortunately, the ogre lowered its shoulder at the last second, and Berengar's axe was dragged the length of its forearm. The impact rattled his grip enough that the following swing from the ogre's club knocked the weapon from his hands. Before the ogre could bring the club down on him, Faolán sank her teeth into its ankle, and Berengar lunged forward and grabbed its wrists, wrenching the club free.

With a surge of strength, the ogre lifted him off the ground and slammed him into a rock. Faolán leapt onto its back, distracting the creature long enough for Berengar to retrieve the dagger hidden in his boot and stab it through the hand. The ogre fell back with a pained cry. Though his axe remained out of reach, Berengar drew the short sword sheathed at his side and held it in front of him, ready to continue their bout.

The ogre gazed down at the viscous, brown blood leaking from the wound, and its eyes widened in surprise.

"Come on, you orange bastard. What are you waiting for?"

It stared at him a moment longer before bounding away, the earth shaking under its weight.

It's headed for the bog. He considered reaching for the bow at his back, but the thing was moving fast. Once the ogre reached Móin Alúin, it would have the advantage. He swore and returned his sword to its sheath.

Fortunately, his horse had the good sense not to bolt

with the others, even if it had thrown him. "Looks like this one's going to make us give chase," he muttered to Faolán. "Hunt it down."

Faolán took off in search of the ogre. If their quarry did make it to the bog, the hound could guide Berengar safely to its lair.

When the warden stooped to retrieve his axe, one of the soldiers moaned and reached for him from the ground. It was the soldier who had attempted to flee.

"Help me," the man croaked. "Please."

The soldier lay beside one of the ogre's footprints, his face covered by mud and blood. He was still alive, but barely. His body was broken. It was clear the man would not last the hour, much less the night. Berengar stepped around his body and started toward the horse.

"Don't leave me here alone," the soldier begged. "I'm so cold. Please, have mercy…"

Any of the other wardens would have stayed behind to ease the man's passing. Darragh would probably have even managed to find a healer, bury the fallen, and slay the ogre in one fell swoop. Remaining there was the compassionate thing to do, but the soldier was done for, and nothing Berengar did could change that. If he wavered from his task, even for a moment, the ogre would escape, and more innocent lives would suffer. Still, he let go of the reins and approached the wounded man. A fallen sword lay visible nearby. Berengar picked it up and placed it in the man's trembling grasp.

"This is the best I can do for you." His meaning was plain. The soldier would either use the blade or wait to succumb to his injuries, hopefully before the wolves found him. "I'll tell your family you died with honor."

Berengar swung himself onto the saddle and galloped across the plain in pursuit of the murderous ogre. He rode with the full moon to guide his path and did not look back. Ahead, a murky haze gathered around Móin Alúin, obscuring the stars above. He heard Faolán's call through the mist. So the ogre had reached the bog. That meant he needed to proceed with an extra measure of caution, though perhaps the ogre's lair would contain evidence as to the fate of Margolin's niece.

A monstrous howl caused him to jerk back on the reins. *That didn't come from Faolán.* No hound could make a sound like that. The ogre didn't make it either; the howl came from the direction opposite to Móin Alúin.

Before he could explore further, a human-shaped form emerged from the bog and fled on foot, headed east. For a moment, he thought it might be Imogen, but the figure was too small to belong to Margolin's niece. The clouds peeled away from the moon, and Berengar realized the fleeing figure was a child.

Where did he come from? Berengar wondered. What was a boy doing alone at night? More importantly, what was he running from?

The boy tripped over something in his path and glanced over his shoulder at Móin Alúin, where a rider emerged from the mist in pursuit. The rider was dressed entirely in black, as if cloaked by the night itself. Clutched in its right hand it carried what appeared to be a lantern, which illuminated its path in an otherworldly light. It sat astride a mount with glowing red eyes and hooves matted with crimson blood. A cruel greatsword was sheathed at the rider's side, and in its left hand, it wielded a peculiar-looking whip.

The boy quickly scrambled to his feet, but the black rider closed the distance between them with inhuman speed.

Berengar took out his bow, the ogre momentarily

forgotten. The first arrow missed and sailed into the fog behind the rider. He nocked a second arrow, taking his time even as the rider reached for the child with a gloved hand. The next shot found its mark and struck the rider's mount, which collapsed to the earth in a heap.

Berengar spurred his horse forward and extended his hand toward the child, who regarded him with a terrified expression. "Take my hand, boy. This is no place for you."

A coarse, rasping noise sounded nearby, and the child slowly turned in the felled rider's direction. When Berengar followed the boy's gaze, he found himself looking at a creature unlike any he had ever encountered.

The rider had no head—at least not one that was currently attached to its body. The "lantern" it carried was in fact the decaying remains of its head, which shimmered with an unnatural light, and its whip was fashioned from human spines twisted together.

"What are you?" Berengar demanded.

The rider responded only by pointing a finger in the direction of the boy. Though it did not speak, he understood the creature's meaning perfectly. It wanted the child.

"Get out of here, boy." Berengar took hold of his axe and rounded on the rider. "If you want him, you'll have to go through me."

The rider held out the head it carried, and its eyes fixed themselves on the warden's mount, causing the horse to go wild. Having been unhorsed once already that evening, Berengar held onto the thrashing animal with all his might and charged the rider, who held fast at his approach. They met in a violent collision, and the impact carried them through the fog and into the marshy bog.

The rider brandished its whip with lightning speed, and the bony lash tore through Berengar's leather armor and into the flesh of his back. As the horse landed on its back, Berengar spilled from the saddle, losing his grip on his axe in the process. He lunged for the weapon, but the rider wrapped the whip around his hand, causing dozens of bony spurs to tear into his skin. Rather than resisting the pull of the whip, Berengar drew his short sword and hurled himself at the black rider. The struggle took them deeper into the mist, until finally Berengar forced the blade into the creature's chest.

The rider took a few steps back, and for a moment Berengar thought the fight was done. Then the rider pulled the blade from its chest and cracked the whip, which wrapped around Berengar's ankle like a vise. He found himself on the ground and barely rolled away in time to avoid the sword, but before he could fully recover his footing, the creature lashed him again with the whip. He stumbled forward and grabbed hold of a tree to steady himself, and the whip drew blood from his exposed side.

Unarmed, Berengar attacked in a blind fury, using his rage to propel him. He struck the rider again and again, bloodying his fists to no avail. His brashness was rewarded with a shallow slash across the chest from his own sword, quickly followed by a blow from the creature's steel gauntlet that sent him spinning away. Panting for breath, Berengar stared at his enemy. He tasted blood, and his vision was starting to swim. He could hardly stand.

"You're tough. I'll give you that. But I won't go down so easily."

Before the rider could again crack the whip, Berengar lowered his head and tackled it. As the pair tumbled downhill, the creature lost its grip on him. When he grabbed a branch to slow his momentum, it snapped, and he fell off an embankment and landed in the swamp. Berengar staggered to his feet. The rider was gone, at least temporarily. At the moment, he was in no condition to continue the fight. He needed to find his way out of the swamp before the rider found him again. Bruised and bloodied, he dragged himself through the mud until finally he collapsed from sheer exhaustion.

Something was singing to him. Berengar stirred. The sound was wrong and unsettling. Instead of a soft, gentle tune, the song was harsh and dissonant, like something out of a nightmare.

The warden's eye fluttered open. *Where am I?*

He was lying flat on his back, covered in shallow swamp water. The sky was pitch black. Flies and gnats danced in the thin sliver of moonlight that pierced the trees while reeds and tall grasses looked down at him from above.

The air felt heavy and thick. His thoughts were disoriented and confused. He tried to sit up but only succeeded in grasping at the mud under his right hand. When he opened his mouth to speak, his tongue felt heavy in his mouth and no words came out. It was as if he was under a spell.

Something coarse and unpleasant stroked his face as the song continued, and that was when he saw the witch.

She knelt over him, holding his face in her crooked, spiderlike fingers. The witch's skin was bloated and wrinkled, and a pair of bulbous eyes protruded from their sockets. Her hands were webbed and claw-like. It was clear years spent practicing black magic within the swamp had changed her considerably. She no longer appeared remotely human, if she ever was in the first place. Berengar's skin crawled with revulsion at her touch, but his body failed to respond to his mental commands.

"Quiet." Her breath smelled of rot and decay. "Hush now."

It was the hag Thaddeus had warned him about. Berengar marshaled all his will in an effort to break free from her hold on him. He managed to liberate one of his hands and wrapped it around her slimy arms, trying to pull her away, but it was as if all the strength had been drained from him.

The hag took his injured hand and raked a long fingernail across the blood, which she lifted to her tongue. A series of shivers racked her body, and she stared down at him with a malicious grin.

"Your soul is stained with blood. You will serve me well."

"Go to...hell," Berengar managed to say.

The hag took a long, rusted nail and drove it through his hand. Her spell prevented him from screaming, but the pain was not dulled.

"You are ruled by rage and hate. Your heart is stone, and stone you will become, unless you bring me the sacrifice." She held up three fingers. "You have three days. Then you will die, Berengar One-Eye." She stopped and sniffed the air. "You carry something of power. What is it?"

She reached toward him, drawn by the thunder rune, but before she could take it, a bark rang out, breaking the hag's spell. Berengar glanced across the swamp and saw Faolán approaching.

The hag flashed a set of pointed teeth in anger and withdrew her touch. "Remember—bring me the sacrifice, or the curse will claim your life."

Then she was gone.

Berengar forced himself to his feet, waded from the bank, and leaned against the nearest tree for support. Though free of the witch's trance, his body still reeled from the aftereffects of his battle with the headless rider. All attempts to pull the nail from his palm failed.

When Faolán reached his side, he stroked her behind the ears, and she licked his face. "I owe you one. Now let's get out of here."

He limped away, hoping he could find his way out of the bog before he lost consciousness.

CHAPTER FOUR

HE WOKE to the sound of the witch's laughter. Berengar bolted upright and instinctively reached for his axe before he remembered losing it the night before. The hag was gone, and he was no longer in the bog. After sitting up to look around, he quickly discovered he had been moved indoors. Shafts of sunlight spilled between the wooden beams that made up the walls of a chilly, shabby-looking room. His cloak and armor lay in a neat pile beside his cot. In their place he wore a white tunic and a pair of brown trousers that didn't quite fit. Much to his surprise, someone had bandaged the wounds he'd sustained in his fight with the headless rider.

How did I get here? Everything that followed his encounter with the Hag of Móin Alúin remained a blur.

The sound of burning logs, which he initially mistook for the hag's cackle, drew his gaze to the chimney, where a woman with her back to him tended to the fire. Faolán, much too large to fit on the cot, gave a low whine when Berengar stirred, prompting the woman to turn around.

"Good. You're awake."

She was in her mid-thirties, or at least that was how she appeared. Those in rural areas often looked older than their years—a result of a difficult life. A few premature strands of white ran through her brown hair. Her eyes were somber, but her face was otherwise unmarred by time. She wore a scarf and a hooded sheepskin cloak over a gray linen dress for warmth.

The woman poured a steaming liquid from a kettle into a cup, only to be warned away by Faolán when she attempted to approach.

"You have a loyal companion. She has hardly let me get close to you."

"Don't take it personally. She doesn't like most people." In that respect, she was similar to her master. He snapped his fingers, bringing the wolfhound to heel. "Easy, Faolán."

The woman seemed vaguely amused by the name. "Little wolf? An odd name for a hound of her size."

"I didn't name her."

"I'm Rose," she said by way of introduction when he declined to elaborate. "I was gathering herbs near Móin Alúin when I found you. You were probably too out of it to remember getting you on my wagon. I brought you back with me to patch you up."

"Where are we?"

"On my farm, a safe distance from the bog and a decent ride from Alúine."

Berengar scanned the room for a sign of other inhabitants and found none. Still, the tunic and trousers he wore were a man's clothes and had to come from somewhere. "You live here alone?"

"Aye, since my father's death."

"Considering what's out there, why not go to the village?"

Rose's brow momentarily knotted in anger. "This is my

49

home. I'm more than capable of managing on my own. Besides, I have little use for village life."

In that respect, he could relate. "Are you a healer?"

She shook her head. "No, but I'm as close to one as you're likely to find around these parts. What happened to you?"

He hesitated, unsure of how much to share. Berengar made it a point to trust no one. Still, she'd rescued him from the bog, so she deserved at least something in the way of an explanation. "My horse fled once we entered the bog, and I lost my way."

"You took quite a beating." She bit her lip, and her voice wavered just a little. "Did something attack you?"

"I came across a boy pursued by a headless rider. We fought. Do you know anything about it?"

At the mention of the rider, Rose oddly seemed to relax, as if she had been expecting him to say something different. "I'm afraid not, although I don't venture into Alúine often enough to hear the latest gossip."

"I need to get to the village. I can pay." Almost as soon as the words left his mouth, he remembered that he had lost his money with his horse. Berengar muttered a string of profanities under his breath.

"There are some things I should see to in the village. I can take you by wagon, but first let me check your wounds." Rose reached into her cloak and withdrew the warden's dagger. "No offense, but you have a dangerous look about you and I don't want any trouble. Behave yourself and you'll get this back when we reach Alúine."

"I mean you no harm."

She studied him curiously. "You're not dressed like one of Laird Margolin's men. Who are you? Some kind of mercenary?"

"Something like that."

Rose knelt at his side and inspected the bandages. "You seem to be healing well. Luckily, none of your injuries were serious, but…"

"What?" he asked, noting her discomfort.

Her eyes lingered on the bandages wrapped around his left hand. "This is a cursed wound. The nail won't come out. I've tried. The hag's handiwork, it appears."

He stared up at her. "You've had dealings with her?"

"Perhaps," Rose said evasively. "You'd be better off speaking to Friar Godfrey." She offered him the cup. "Drink this. It will make you feel better."

Berengar took the cup and lifted it to his lips. His body still ached from the brutal beating he'd endured. The nail no longer caused him pain, but he could feel black magic slowly spreading through his veins. The hag told him he had three days before the curse finished him—three days to bring her the sacrifice she spoke of, whatever that meant. It was bad enough the ogre had slipped from his grasp, and even worse that he'd gotten his backside handed to him by a rider with no head. Now he had to find a way to break a curse before it claimed his life. *I really hate magic.*

His stiffness and fatigue had improved considerably by the time he finished the draught. Apart from a few scrapes and bruises, he was mostly no worse for wear. Rose shared some porridge with him, after which he stuffed what remained of his belongings into a sack and emerged into the cool air.

Like the cottage, the farm appeared in a state of disrepair. On the way to the barn, he passed a stretch of fence with several conspicuous gaps in it. Whatever her insistence to the contrary, it was quite clear that Rose had a rough time since her father's death. Weeds sprouted freely across the property, and judging from the barren field, Berengar had a hard time believing the harvest would prove plentiful. It was quiet, too—and with good reason. Many peasants were too poor to afford cattle, but neither did he see any sheep, goats, chickens, or pigs.

"Predators came for the chickens at the start of spring," Rose said when she saw him staring at an empty coop. She opened a stall door and ran a hand along the crest of her horse. "I had to sell the others to make ends meet. Tillie is the last one left." She led the horse outside, and Berengar helped her hitch the mare to the wagon, which also looked to have seen better days.

It seemed strange she would choose to live so close to Móin Alúin on her own, especially with predators in the area. Then again, perhaps memories of her father made it difficult to abandon her home. It was the way of things that some people were determined to cling to the past while others tried their best to run from it. There was a reason Berengar preferred life on the road. Although he had his own quarters in the warden's tower at Tara, he hadn't called any place home since before the Shadow Wars.

He whistled to Faolán as the wagon started down the path. Instead of jumping onto the wagon, she trailed behind, a sign she still hadn't warmed to Rose. The ride was peaceful, with no hint of the horrors that stalked Leinster's countryside by night. They rolled through open, dark green fields where the earth was still damp from the recent rains, and they had to stop three times when the wagon's wheels got stuck in the mud. The air warmed as morning passed, if only a little. The sky was mostly clear, though the sun remained a pale, muted color. Rose said next to nothing during the journey, which suited Berengar just fine, as he wasn't fond of making small talk. He'd been on the job long enough to know when someone was keeping secrets, but her affairs weren't any of his business. He had far more pressing matters to concern himself with once they reached the village.

It was still early when they arrived, which was a good thing, considering the curse the hag had placed on him meant his supply of time was limited. Ahead lay a modest, unguarded gate, which Berengar thought unlikely to prove much use in the event of an actual attack. Alúine was considerably smaller than Kildare. Even the church—the only building in the area made from stone and not wood—was plain in comparison to St. Brigid's. The villagers lived in thatched huts of varying sizes gathered around a central well. Berengar doubted the population numbered more than forty people, if that. A great hill looked over the village to the west, in the direction of Móin Alúin, and a forest loomed to the south.

He turned his attention to the villagers, most of whom were occupied with the business of their daily lives. Despite its size, Alúine was home to an assortment of tradesmen, and Berengar spotted a baker's stand, a blacksmith's forge, a butcher's shop, and a carpenter hard at work on what appeared to be a coffin. Given the probable difficulty of farming the surrounding lands, it seemed likely the village depended on trade with neighboring towns and settlements. Though it was not quite as ominous as Margolin's castle, there was a palpable sense of discontent about Alúine, perhaps the result of hard times or the recent trouble with the ogre. None of the villagers seemed particularly cheerful—including the children, who appeared far too busy helping their parents with their labors to play.

Without his distinctive cloak and weapons, Berengar went unrecognized by the locals. Some nonetheless looked on him with the same level of suspicion reserved for any outsider, but for the most part, the people of Alúine seemed largely too preoccupied to care.

Rose pulled back on the reins and brought the wagon to a stop. "Here we are." She took out the dagger and held it out to him. "As promised." She hesitated before handing it to him. "There are good people here. Don't make me regret this."

Berengar tucked the dagger into his boot. "Don't worry. It's for protection only." It was a lie, but one that might set her mind at ease. He retrieved the sack of his belongings and climbed off the wagon in time to greet Faolán.

"Farewell. I wish you good fortune."

"Wait," he said gruffly, and she turned back to face him. "Thanks." It wasn't often strangers treated him with kindness, and in lieu of payment, the least he could do was show a little gratitude.

"Rose?" said a voice nearby. The voice belonged to a huntsman in the process of selling a stag's carcass to the butcher. At the sight of Rose, the huntsman quickly pocketed the coins and hurried in their direction. He appeared close to Rose's age, and based on his concern it was obvious they shared a history. "What are you doing here? Are you all right?"

"I'm fine, Evander. I just came to gather supplies, that's all."

"I've been worried about you. It's been weeks since you last visited the village." He stopped and noticed Berengar for the first time. "Who's this?"

"A traveler. I found him on the outskirts of Móin Alúin."

"The bog?" Evander gripped Rose by the shoulders. "You know you shouldn't be living out there by yourself, not with what's out there."

Rose brushed away his hands with a pained expression.

"I can't stay here, Evander. I'm sorry." With that, she turned and walked away.

"Rose, wait." Evander cast one last look at Berengar and went after her.

The warden peeled back the bandage wrapped around his left hand and grimaced. The skin around the nail was gray and discolored. The affected area extended almost the full width of his palm. What started as a simple task had grown considerably more difficult. Before he could proceed, he needed to recover his weapons from the bog, which would require hiring a guide. That would cost money he no longer possessed, which meant finding work that would put his talents to good use. He had three days to find a way to break the hag's curse. Then there was still the business of the ogre and Laird Margolin's missing niece, not to mention the mysterious rider. First, he had to find a place to stay during his time in Alúine.

Given his reputation in Leinster, it would be better to keep his identity to himself, at least for the time being. The last thing he wanted was another bloodthirsty mob on his hands. Besides, the locals would be much less likely to answer his questions if they knew who he was, and he wanted to be able to move about the region without attracting too much attention.

Berengar started down the path that led to the inn, a humble, one-story building. The sign posted outside read *The Green Flagon*. Innkeepers were generally the friendly sort, especially when their palms were oiled with coin. They were also, almost without exception, better informed on local gossip and goings-on than anyone else in a given area, which made the inn the best spot to start his search for answers and find paying work.

When he drew nearer, he overheard an argument close to the stables. Angry shouts came from a scowling middle-aged man accompanied by a young woman who appeared to be his daughter.

"I told you before, stay away from her, you beast!"

The *beast* in question was a towering behemoth of a man who had offered the young woman a flower. In all Berengar's years, he had only seen a handful of human individuals taller than himself, but the stableman was easily among their number. The man had a left-sided limp, and his arm and hand on the left side was shrunken and contorted, as if neither had properly developed.

"Father, it's all right," the man's daughter said. Her words were kind, but her eyes were red, and there was something sad about her. "Silas is harmless."

"Quiet, Leona." The veins in the man's forehead throbbed as he looked at Silas. "I've seen the way he looks at you."

As a rule, Berengar made it a point to avoid getting drawn into local disputes. *This doesn't concern you.* He had enough to do already, a thought accompanied by a brief stab of pain in his left hand.

Leona's father plucked the flower from Silas' hand and stomped on it. Though Silas might have easily snapped the young woman's father in half, instead his face reddened with embarrassment, and he cowered in shame.

Berengar ground his teeth in anger. Tendency to avoid getting involved or not, he didn't like bullies. "Is there a problem?"

The man's anger didn't abate. "This is none of your concern, stranger. Get out of my way."

"You just made it my concern. I don't take kindly to being threatened."

The man's expression faltered, and he took a step back when Faolán growled at him.

"What's going on here?" demanded the shorter of two

guards, both of whom were dressed in Laird Margolin's colors.

"He's at it again," Leona's father told them. "I tell you, I won't stand for this. He should be locked up."

The innkeeper materialized at the entrance to the inn and stepped in front of Silas, who relaxed in his presence. "Apologies all around. I promise you, Hirum, Silas doesn't mean anything by it."

Leona's father jabbed a finger in the innkeeper's face. "That's not the point, Iain! I don't care how you do it, but you'd better keep that half-witted brute away from my daughter."

"Of course." Iain turned to the guards and flashed a smile. "I'll tell Silas to stay away from Leona. Now why don't we all share a round of drinks on me and forget about this unpleasant business?"

"Sounds good to me," said the taller of the guards, who reeked of alcohol already.

Leona's father shook his head and stormed off. "Come, Leona. We're leaving." He went on his way, but not without a parting glare at Silas.

"Ignore him, my friend," the innkeeper said, giving Silas a friendly slap on the back. "Hirum's just a little possessive, that's all."

The pair returned to the inn. When Berengar attempted to follow, the shorter of the guards blocked his path.

"And who's this, then?" the guard asked his companion with a sneer. "I haven't seen your like around here before. What's your purpose here, stranger?"

Even without his weapons, Berengar wasn't intimidated. He could easily wipe the sneer from the guard's face if he chose, and he doubted the man's companion was sober enough to put up much of a fight. While both were in Margolin's service, he didn't want to risk revealing himself when he wasn't sure whom he could trust. "I come from Ulster. I was on my way south to…seek penance for my sins, when I lost my way in the bog."

The shorter guard took another step closer to inspect him. "Looks like you've been in a scrape recently. You aren't going to cause us trouble, are you?"

We'll see, Berengar thought. "I'm just looking to earn some coin to purchase supplies and a new horse."

"Very well then. Be on your way, but I've got my eye on you."

Berengar fought the urge to laugh. He'd known men like this his whole life—thin-skinned and bitter with a taste for power. One flash of the brooch with the High Queen's sigil and the guard would be shaking in his boots.

"Let's go," the guard said to his companion.

"What about that drink?" the taller guard replied, looking with longing at the inn.

"Later. We have work to do."

Berengar watched them go before making his way inside the inn.

The innkeeper, busy polishing tables, greeted him with a welcoming gesture. "Come in. I was hoping you'd find your way inside." He nodded to Silas, who stood nearby with a broom. "Silas here was just telling me what you did for him."

"It was nothing," Berengar said to Silas, who avoided eye contact and retreated to the corner of the room to sweep the floor.

"Don't mind him," the innkeeper said. "He's shy around strangers." He held out his hand, which Berengar shook. "I'm Iain. I own this humble establishment. Silas helps me with chores and odd jobs."

"Has he always been like that?"

"He came into the world with the cord wrapped around his neck. Word is, his mother did something to provoke the hag's wrath. He's never been quite normal, but he's a good lad." Iain set the tablecloth aside and motioned him to the bar. "Anyway, thanks for the help. I promised his mother I'd look after him when she passed. If it weren't so early in the day, I'd offer you a drink to show my appreciation. How about a meal instead?"

"Fine by me. I'll take the drink too, as long as you're offering." Based on the way things were going, he was going to need it.

Iain raised an eyebrow but did as requested. "I hope the guards didn't give you too much trouble. Phineas is always looking for an excuse to swing that sword of his."

"I assume he's the shorter of the two."

"That's the one. He's the real devil of the two. Man seems to think he's Margolin himself. The other one's named Tuck. He's actually a decent fellow when he's not drunk."

"Are they the only two guards in Alúine?"

Iain set a tankard before Berengar. "Aye. We've pleaded with Margolin for more to ward off the ogre, but our requests have fallen on deaf ears. He's too preoccupied collecting taxes for his campaign to exterminate the goblins."

Berengar took a large swig from the tankard and choked the substance down. Ale in Leinster was more watered down than in any of the remaining kingdoms of Fál. The accompanying cottage pie tasted much better, though perhaps that was due to his ravenous appetite.

Snores came from the inn's sole other patron, who was slumped over at the end of the bar. "That's just Duncan. Better he's passed out here than home mistreating his wife and boy."

59

Berengar declined to make a response and took another bite of pie instead.

"We don't get many newcomers here," Iain continued. "Usually just traveling merchants or soldiers. Where are you from?"

Berengar swallowed a chunk of beef before answering. "North. What can you tell me about this place?"

Iain laughed. "Alúine? Centuries ago there was a great battle on the hill, between the High King of Fál and the King of Leinster. Not much has happened since then, apart from the occasional haunting or monster infestation. I suppose the last few years have been harder than most. Drought and disease have ravaged the whole region." He propped his elbows on the counter and leaned closer. "So tell me, what brings you here?"

The warden shared the same story he'd given the guards—that he'd been traveling south and wandered into Móin Alúin. "I was hoping you could point me in the direction of some work. I'm looking for a place to stay and I'm short on coin at the moment." He was rarely in need of funds, one of the advantages of being in the High Queen's service. Though he cared little for wealth or material possessions, gold had its uses, and not sleeping outside in a ditch was one.

When Iain opened his mouth to speak, the church bell chimed before he could say the words, and his smile faltered.

"Goblins!" cried a voice beyond the inn's walls.

Berengar sat up, instantly alert. Suddenly, the door crashed open, and a creature darted inside. It was short for a goblin—just over four feet—and adorned from head to toe in rudimentary armor, which goblins usually wore only when at war. A large wolf pelt covered the goblin's back like a cloak, and a pair of angry eyes stared back at him through the mask it wore. It held a shield in one hand and a curved dagger clenched in the other. The goblin scurried across the room in a flash, pinned Iain against the counter, and tried to pry the wedding band from his hand.

Berengar threw himself at the goblin, and they both crashed to the floor. The goblin regained its footing in an instant and leapt on him in the next.

Blasted things are fast. He grabbed the goblin's wrist to hold off the dagger. Faolán sank her teeth into the creature's leg, prompting a hiss, and Berengar heaved it off him.

"You made a serious mistake." Familiar anger rose within him. He might have to wait to settle his scores with the ogre and the headless rider, but finally he had something he could kill.

When the goblin rushed him again, he grabbed it with both arms and swung it across the room. It hit the wall and dropped its shield, and its exposed eyes darted from Berengar to Faolán. Before either could move to intercept it, the creature fled from the inn as the bell continued to toll.

As Silas ran to the bar to help Iain to his feet, Berengar and Faolán hurried from the inn in pursuit of their attacker.

Outside, chaos gripped Alúine. Panicked villagers fled or hid while the band of goblins roamed the streets, pillaging as they went. A few locals joined forces with the guards to fend off the raid. Berengar approached and picked up a fallen shield, using it to batter an attacking goblin to the ground. Faolán pounced on a second attacker, who scurried up the side of a thatched hut to get away. The pair joined forces with Alúine's defenders at the well, and the tide of the battle turned. A horn blew, and the goblins crawled over the fence and retreated into the forest, but not before Berengar locked eyes with the goblin holding the horn.

Recalling his scuffle with the goblin in the Green Flagon, he reached for his belt.

The thunder rune was missing. The goblin had taken it.

CHAPTER FIVE

BERENGAR STARED into the forest with barely suppressed rage. If he'd only had his axe, he might have cleaved each of the goblins in two. As if he didn't have enough to do before, now he needed to recover the stolen thunder rune. Goblins were greedy, dangerous creatures, and there was no telling what might become of such a valuable object in their possession.

One by one the people of Alúine emerged from their hideaways to inspect the damage and loss of property in the aftermath of the attack. Nearby, a few villagers used water from the well to extinguish a fire licking one of the thatched huts as the two guards looked on.

Phineas put away his sword in disgust. "Another raiding party."

Tuck took a swig from a flask at his side to the visible annoyance of his companion. "I wonder what they stole this time."

"Probably the same as last time—some animals, medicines, and as much coin as the filth could get their slimy little hands on." Phineas shook his head and spit in the dirt. "We're going to have to do something about them. If this makes the villagers late paying their taxes again, Laird Margolin will have our heads."

Berengar dropped the goblin shield and found the guards looking in his direction.

"I should have known this one would be handy in a fight, judging by the size of him," Phineas said. "Have you ever considered the life of a soldier?"

"Once," Berengar muttered. "This isn't the first attack? How often do these raids happen?"

Phineas gestured for him to come along as the guards resumed their patrol. "They stick to ambushes mostly—attacking travelers who pass through the forest. Occasionally one or two will sneak into the village after dark and steal as much as they can carry. They've never raided the village in broad daylight."

"They must be getting desperate," said Tuck, who seemed to be the quieter of the two. His eyes were glossy and red, and he spoke with a slight slur.

"Why?" Berengar asked.

"There aren't many left. Laird Margolin decided to stamp them out. Had us burn whatever settlements we found." There was something haunted about his demeanor.

To Berengar's surprise, the damage inflicted by the goblins appeared minimal, perhaps because the raid was so brief. A few villagers looked a little rattled, but none were seriously harmed. "Odd. I fought goblins to the north, and it's rare to suffer an attack like this without any casualties."

Phineas shrugged dismissively. "They're afraid of provoking Laird Margolin, I'm sure. Better to remain a nuisance than be seen as a threat. We know the last of their number live somewhere in the forest, but we haven't found them yet." He regarded Berengar with a shrewd expression. "In fact, we have something planned for tonight. If we clear the final goblin hideaway, the reward would be great. We'd make it worth your while."

"Count me in." Helping the guards was the perfect way to recover the thunder rune and earn some coins in the process. Still, something didn't quite sit right about the attack. Goblins were usually more concerned with stealing gold and valuables than food and medicine, and doing so without causing harm was unusual behavior. Whatever it was, he would have to worry about it later.

Berengar left the guards to their task and set out to explore the village in search of additional work. He didn't get far before he ran into a familiar face—Iain, the innkeeper from the Green Flagon. At Berengar's approach, Iain—busy helping the baker clear away debris from his stand—stopped what he was doing and made his way to the warden's side.

"There you are. I owe you one, and I don't say that lightly. That ring is all I have left of my wife since the plague took her. I couldn't stand to lose it to a goblin." Iain delved into his pocket and handed Berengar a key. "You mentioned you were short on coin. The room is yours for as long as you're here."

"Thanks." Berengar took the key and nodded in gratitude. That was one less thing to worry about.

"Think nothing of it. I'm not sure I could have afforded repairs if that goblin had ransacked the place. I'll have Silas take your things to your room. In the meantime, there's something I want to show you." He led Berengar up the road toward the church. "If it's work you're seeking, I'd suggest starting there. Most people here leave messages for Friar Godfrey on the church doors when they need help."

Finally, some good news. He could already think of more than a few ways to put his earnings to good use. "Is there a tanner in the village who can mend leather armor? I'll be needing a new mount as well."

The innkeeper looked at him quizzically at the mention of armor. "Avery should be up to the task." He pointed out one of the huts. "As far as the horse is concerned, these are lean times, so there should be someone who will part with one for a fair price. I'll ask around and tell you what I've learned when you return to the inn for supper."

"There is one more thing," Berengar said. "I need a guide who can lead me through Móin Alúin."

Iain's brow furrowed. "Why the devil do you want to go there? You'd have to be mad to go back with that ogre on the loose."

Berengar kept his tone firm. "I left something I need behind, and I plan to get it back, one way or another."

Iain sighed reluctantly and stroked his beard, contemplating the request. "Well, if your mind is truly made up… There is a man who might be willing to help with such a dangerous endeavor—Evander, the village huntsman. I can send word to him if you like."

Berengar recognized the name. *He's the man who greeted Rose when we arrived.* "No thanks. I know what he looks like."

"In that case, I will see you tonight upon your return." With that, the innkeeper went on his way.

Berengar started on the path to the church, a tall building that seemed to keep watch over the rest of Alúine from relative seclusion. Moss and vines grew freely over the dark stone surface. The church bell had fallen still within the round tower belfry, and the area was quiet and deserted.

Berengar hesitated on the steps, remembering the last time he'd entered a church. In his mind's eye he saw himself cutting down Skinner Kane, and his left hand throbbed again with a sudden, stabbing pain. He winced and focused on the doors, where a number of notices were nailed. Most were written in the same hand, which wasn't surprising, considering the level of illiteracy among the common folk, especially in more rural areas. Berengar was well into adulthood before he learned to read and write, and he wasn't particularly fond of either. His hands were made for wielding axes and swords, not quills and parchment.

He examined each of the messages in turn. There were rewards posted for killing the ogre or providing information to the guards about the goblins' whereabouts. Another was a request for help finding a predator responsible for killing villagers' livestock. One more interesting notice warned of a group of dangerous outlaws encamped in the forest—men condemned to death by Laird Margolin himself.

"This could be promising," he muttered to Faolán as a final notice caught his attention. It was short on details but promised paying work.

Help wanted. Could be dangerous. See Friar Godfrey for details.

There wasn't much in the way of a reward; forty copper coins might be enough to get his armor repaired, but they probably wouldn't buy him a decent horse. Still, it was a start. He took the notice and pushed open the door. It was dark inside the church. A few candles rested at the altar, all unlit. The rest of the sanctuary was cold and bare, save for some pews. It was probably the best the villagers could manage in such lean times.

Faolán's ears perked up, and when Berengar listened closely he heard the sound of digging beyond the stone walls. He walked outside to the cemetery, where a man was digging a fresh grave. A short distance away lay the same coffin the carpenter had been working on upon Berengar's arrival in Alúine.

The gravedigger was a stout man in long brown robes. His hair and beard were gray, and a crucifix hung from his neck.

"You're Godfrey? Where's the undertaker?"

"Dead," the friar replied, his work complete. "Taken by the plague, and the priest before him. I'm all that's left, I'm afraid." He nodded at the coffin. "Help me with that, will you?"

It was then Berengar noticed a wooden prosthesis in place of Godfrey's right hand. He considered telling the friar to get on with it, as his time was short and he wanted to proceed with the business of the notice. Instead, he stifled a sigh and trudged over to the coffin, which he moved without assistance. As he worked, he shared an abbreviated version of the events that had led him to Alúine. The job of filling in the dirt went much faster with a two-handed man wielding the shovel, and despite the work, the pain in his hand seemed lessened by the time he finished.

Godfrey retrieved a satchel from the ground, fished out his drinking horn, and offered Berengar a drink. "I take it you're here about work, then."

"Aye." Berengar used his forearm to wipe the water from his lips before returning the horn to Godfrey.

"Donald O'Dohetry and his family haven't been seen in the village in a few days. His sister is worried and asked me to look into their disappearance. She's the one offering the reward for information. The family lives on a farm near the woods three miles south of here. With the goblins lurking in the forest—not to mention the ogre—few dare venture far beyond the village. Even the guards aren't up to the task without Margolin's boot up their backsides."

"Sounds simple enough. When can we get started?"

"Now, if you're willing." Godfrey bent down and picked up a walking stick leaning against a gravestone.

"Lead the way. Where's your wagon?"

Godfrey laughed heartily. "I'm a friar, not a priest. We have no need of horses. I wander Leinster and go where the people need help."

Together, they set off on the road south on foot with a cool wind blowing at their back. Godfrey whistled a lively tune for most of the journey. Despite the circumstances, he walked with mirth in his eyes and the hint of a smile on his face, as if he knew some secret about life he found amusing. Berengar, who saw little good in the world, found the friar's cheer off-putting.

"I'll warn you, I don't know what awaits us at the farm," Godfrey said after a while. "I arrived in Alúine at winter's end. Spring brings rebirth and renewal, but here it has brought only death and disease. There is a pestilence upon the land. Mark my words, the missing villagers and monster attacks are not by chance. I sense a darker influence at work in Laird Margolin's territory."

Though the words were unsettling, Berengar agreed. There were already fewer magicians, herbalists, and alchemists in Leinster than anywhere else in Fál. With the advancement of human society, the fairies had all but disappeared, and the church's monster hunters had driven the populations of other magical creatures to the brink of extinction. That so many missing persons and monster sightings were concentrated around a specific area was likely no accident.

"Could it be the hag?" Perhaps Godfrey could shed light on the witch that had cursed him. "What do you know about her?"

"Her name has been lost to time," Godfrey said. "None

know her true age. The people believe she's lived in the bog for at least a century, if not longer. She has a hold over Alúine. Desperate villagers seek her out for her magic, but she makes deals that always turn out ugly for those involved. Even those wise enough to avoid the bog still fall under her sway, as it's believed she visits villagers in their sleep and influences their actions and behaviors through their dreams."

Faolán let out a growl as the farm's outline slowly materialized under the gray sky. While modest, the property boasted a barn and a well of its own. Hoofprints marred the soil, suggesting that someone else had traveled to the farm relatively recently. There was no sign of the occupants.

Something's not right. The breeze died, and the sound of buzzing flies filled the air. The air was thick with the overpowering smell of decay. It was a scent Berengar knew well —one that meant death. Goats and pigs lay dead in their pens and enclosures. A precious few clung to life, but only just. *They're starving.* His gaze fell on the door, which stood open. "It's been forced. Keep on your guard."

Faolán barked to them from the spot where a corpse lay propped against the well. Godfrey waved away the swarming flies and knelt down to inspect the body. "It's Donald, poor devil."

"Look at this," Berengar said. The farmer's shirt was stained with dried blood. "He's been stabbed." The dead man held the handle of a broken hoe clutched in his hand. "Whatever it was that attacked them, he tried to fight them off, and they left him for dead. Looks like he managed to drag himself to the well before he died of blood loss." He glanced at Godfrey. "I've heard there are brigands living in the area. Do you think they had a hand in this?"

"It's doubtful. The brigands are enemies of Laird

Margolin and those loyal to him. It's not like them to butcher commoners. It would turn the people against them." Godfrey bit his lip, obviously troubled by something. "Donald's sister mentioned that when he and his family were last in the village, his wife told her something about an apparition that gave her quite a fright."

"What sort of apparition?"

"She didn't say."

Faolán sniffed the air and led them to the barn, where a woman's body rested on her side.

"It's Maude," Godfrey said. "Donald's wife. These bodies haven't been here long."

Berengar was well acquainted with the process of death and decay. It seemed curious a friar shared his familiarity with the subject. He studied the corpse. "It looks like she was trying to reach the stables when she died." There were lash marks on her back. "These wounds are strange." He reached into one of the wounds and dislodged a bony fragment embedded in her back. "I've seen injuries like this before."

"Where?"

"At Móin Alúin, I stopped a rider in black from riding down a child. The rider used a whip fashioned from human bones." Berengar held up his bandaged hand. "And…he had no head."

Godfrey's expression darkened considerably. "It can't be. I heard stories about him as a lad, but I always assumed he was a myth."

"The thing I fought was no myth. Tell me what you know."

"He's known as the Dullahan," Godfrey explained. "He roams the earth collecting souls. According to the stories, he can only speak one word: the name of his intended victim, which brings death when uttered."

"What does he want? Can he be stopped?"

"I don't know, but if the Dullahan is involved, the situation is more dire than I thought. The legends say he comes from the underworld to travel the land until he finds his next victim. He should have moved on to somewhere else after killing Donald and his family, but you saw him at Móin Alúin."

"Could something be controlling him? The hag, perhaps?"

"Only very powerful magic could control a being like the Dullahan. Even the hag may not be capable of it." As if struck by a sudden realization, Godfrey stiffened and slowly looked around.

"What is it?" Berengar asked, sensing his discomfort.

"There are only two corpses here. Donald and his wife had a daughter."

Berengar followed his gaze to the woods. "Do you think she might still be alive?"

A low moan came from the forest, and the friar shook his head. "No. I don't think that at all."

As Berengar looked on, a shadow detached itself from the trees and took on a humanoid shape. Its skin seemed to ebb and flow, almost translucent in the pale light. The shade staggered forward, all but ignoring Berengar and Godfrey as it wandered the farmstead. Loose strands of raven-colored hair covered much of its face like a shroud, and two empty holes occupied the place where its eyes should have been.

"It's her," Godfrey said. "Or what's left of her. I think she's returned as a sluagh."

Berengar thought again of the things that lurked in the darkness beyond the castle walls. "I saw something like it at Blackthorn."

"What were you doing at Margolin's castle?"

"It's a long story. What are we going to do about this one?"

The friar took a moment to consider the matter. "The church believes the sluagh are the spirits of sinners doomed to wander the earth without peace. Those who hold with the old ways believe they are lost souls unable to pass on to the next life. In either event, she will haunt this place until her spirit finds peace. That means we must lay her to rest."

"And how do we go about doing that?"

Faolán paced back and forth in front of them, watching warily as the sluagh moaned and rasped like a creature caught in a trap, bound to follow a variation of the same path.

"I'm a friar, not a spiritist. I have no power of my own —only faith. Though I suppose I could attempt an exorcism."

"Isn't that dangerous?"

Godfrey shrugged. "Tradition says they're harmless during the daylight hours." He delved into his satchel and removed a bottle of holy water. "If you don't mind standing watch, I know the words."

Berengar nodded in assent. "I'm ready."

Godfrey pried the lid off the bottle with his teeth before closing his eyes and invoking the words of the ritual under his breath. At first, the sluagh kept to its course as if nothing had happened, but when Godfrey sprinkled holy water on it, the spirit spun around in anger. Its eyes glowed with fiery red light and a mouthful of razor-shaped black teeth took shape. The creature reached out a shadowy hand, and Berengar intercepted it before it could reach the friar only to find himself in its grasp.

"I thought you said they were harmless," he said, struggling against the restless spirit.

Godfrey continued chanting as if he hadn't heard him. Berengar reached into his boot and plunged the silver dagger into the creature's side. The dagger passed through the spirit with no resistance, and tendrils of shadow quickly filled the hole it created. He swore and brought an arm up to shield himself from its open jaws.

The sluagh drove him back in the mud in an effort to get at Godfrey, who to his credit refused to budge an inch. It reached out with long, slender fingers that stopped just short of the friar's cross, as if paralyzed, and Godfrey took hold of his walking stick and cracked the creature over the head with surprising speed. When the sluagh stumbled back, Berengar seized it from behind and hurled it against the well. It roared with anger and crouched to leap at him, and he braced himself. Just before the collision, the sluagh dissolved, replaced by a blackbird that took to the sky and vanished into the trees.

Berengar wiped a bead of sweat from his forehead and took in a deep breath. "You handled yourself well."

Godfrey chuckled and held up his wooden hand with a grin. "I wasn't always a friar."

"I don't know many priests who can use a walking stick like that."

"I learned early in life there is evil in the world. I wasn't going to spend my life in some monastery poring over scrolls when I could do my part to fight it."

Maybe he's not so bad after all. For a holy man, anyway. "So is that it? Did it work?"

"Aye. I believe it did. All the same, I should purify the area to prevent any chance of her return." Godfrey gestured to the bodies of the farmer and his wife. "We need to bury them."

Berengar pried the hoe from Donald's grip and set about the task while the friar sanctified the farmstead.

"You said the sluagh were souls of the dead. Do you think this one was somehow related to the Dullahan?"

"It can't be a coincidence. If the Dullahan was here, he probably killed the girl's parents and abducted her to claim her soul. Her shade must have returned here afterward out of some fleeting sense of familiarity."

Were the spirits I saw at Castle Blackthorn also victims of the Dullahan? Berengar wondered. Maybe the hag had summoned the Dullahan to collect souls for her. But if that was true, what was her purpose?

When they finished, Godfrey stopped to say a short prayer over both graves before starting on the return journey to Alúine. It was well into the day by the time they reached the village. So far he'd found lodging for his stay and learned more about the headless rider, but there was much left to do, and each passing hour brought him closer to the fulfillment of the hag's curse. He accompanied Godfrey to the home of Donald's sister, where the friar broke the news of her brother's demise. Though Godfrey wisely omitted the grisly details of their deaths at the hand of the Dullahan, the woman was heartbroken nonetheless to learn of Donald's sad fate.

As they departed, Berengar counted the forty copper coins he'd received as payment. Perhaps Iain would have a lead on a horse when he returned to the inn. He stopped short when he noticed a familiar face among the crowd of villagers.

"What is it?" Godfrey asked.

"It's the boy I saved from the Dullahan." *He survived.* At least his ill-fated duel with the Dullahan hadn't been for naught.

The boy accompanied a woman who had just filled a bucket with water from the well. Judging from the way they interacted, Berengar guessed she was his mother, which meant the child came from Alúine all along.

"You," Berengar said. "What were you doing at the bog on your own?"

When she noticed Berengar, the boy's mother quickly averted her gaze. "Come along, Lucas."

"It's him," Lucas said to his mother. "The bear man. I told you he saved me."

At the mention of the word *bear*, recognition flooded Friar Godfrey's expression. The boy's mother, however, simply grabbed her son and prodded him along. "Your father will be home soon, and he'll want to know where you've been."

Berengar followed them to their home. "Wait. I have questions."

The woman ushered her son in through the door. "I'm sorry. We can't talk to you." She was scared, but did she fear him, or someone else?

She shut the door in his face, though not before Berengar saw Lucas start to open his mouth to speak, as if he had something to say.

"Blast it," he muttered. "That boy is the only person who could have told us more about the Dullahan."

Godfrey only stared. "I thought there was something familiar about you. You're him, aren't you? The Bear Warden?"

Berengar pulled him aside, away from prying ears. "Not that I'm who you say I am, but I suggest you keep that name to yourself."

"That explains what you were doing at Castle Black-thorn. Laird Margolin sent you here to deal with the ogre, didn't he?"

"That was before I got sidetracked by the Dullahan

and the Hag of Móin Alúin. I have unfinished business with both."

"I may know of someone who can help with the Dullahan," Godfrey said. "A bard who passed through the village not long ago. You might have met her at Blackthorn —her name is Saroise."

Great. Berengar remembered his last encounter with Saroise, who wasn't exactly fond of him. Still, bards were masters of lore. If anyone knew about a creature of legend and myth, she was his best bet.

"I will send her a message," the friar continued. "And I will keep your secret, but the people of Alúine are not fools. You can't hide the truth forever. They will realize who you are soon enough—perhaps sooner than you think."

CHAPTER SIX

BERENGAR OPENED the sack and dumped its contents onto the table.

Avery—the tanner—looked down at the leather armor in astonishment. "I've never seen its like before." He ran a hand along the armor's surface, and his fingers found their way to the tears left by the Dullahan's whip. "Who did you say you were again?"

"I didn't." Berengar folded his arms across his chest. "Can you mend it or not?"

Avery stared at the armor for a moment longer before nodding at last. "Aye. Can't say it'll be good as new, but I can get the job done well enough."

"Good. I want it by tomorrow."

Avery regarded him as if he had lost his mind. "Something like this would take me the entire night to fix. Why on earth would you need it so urgently?"

"That's my business," Berengar snapped, irritated. He didn't like people that asked too many questions, and the tanner had a meddlesome look. "Just tell me how much it will cost."

"Thirty copper coins." Avery clearly wasn't looking forward to the task ahead.

Berengar laid fifteen coins on the table. "Half now—half when you finish."

Faolán pawed at the doorway to get his attention. Outside, a pair of villagers were conversing just outside Avery's shop.

"The goblins stole my horse," said a voice he recognized. It was Rose, the woman who rescued him from Móin Alúin. She sounded upset.

"Don't worry," replied her companion. "I'll put you up for the night at the inn, and tomorrow I'll take you home."

Evander, Berengar realized. *The huntsman.* Iain had suggested Evander was the only man around who could help him navigate the bog.

He cast a final glance back at Avery. "I'll be back tomorrow." With the matter of his armor settled, he left the shop in search of Rose and Evander. *They can't have gone far.* The temperature steadily dropped in anticipation of night's descent. Between the journey to Alúine, the subsequent goblin attack, and his misadventure with Friar Godfrey, he'd accomplished far less than he'd hoped.

"You don't understand," Rose protested. "I can't stay in the village tonight."

"It would be dark before you reached the farm, and you know what's out there." Evander reached for her, but she pushed his hand away.

"I've told you I can look after myself." Rose stormed off, leaving a baffled-looking Evander standing alone.

Before he could pursue her, he noticed Berengar approaching. "You again. What do you want with Rose?"

"Actually, it's you I want to talk to. I'm told you know your way around Móin Alúin."

Evander seemed to relax with the understanding

79

Berengar wasn't after Rose, and his tone immediately became friendlier. "Better than most. Why do you ask?"

"I'm looking for a guide. I have business there."

Evander shook his head. "You would do well to stay away from there. The bog is treacherous. A powerful witch dwells somewhere within, and an ogre has its hunting ground nearby. Many who venture in never return."

"It's the ogre I'm planning to kill. I need your help to retrieve the weapons I left behind."

Evander's expression shifted to surprise, and he studied Berengar with new eyes. "Who are you?"

"Someone with a score to settle, and let's leave it at that. I understand there's a hefty bounty for the ogre's head. I can't pay you up front, but I'll split the reward with you in exchange for your help."

Evander took a moment to consider the offer. His clothes were less raggedy than many of the other villagers', but it was clear he needed the money. "The guards have hired me to track the goblins for them. Help me with the job, and I'll aid you in your hunt."

"Agreed." If anything, Evander was doing him a favor, since Berengar had already agreed to help the guards with the goblins as a way to recover the stolen thunder rune.

Evander offered his hand, which Berengar shook. "We set out at nightfall."

"I'll be waiting. You can find me at the inn."

That was some progress, at least. With any luck, he would retrieve the thunder rune before the night was through. After that, he would recover his weapons and slay the ogre in the morning, which left him two days to deal with the Dullahan and the Hag of Móin Alúin. Then again, considering the way his luck was running lately, it was probably best not to get ahead of himself.

Night was fast approaching, and he didn't intend to go

hunting for goblins without eating beforehand. He started on the path to the inn, a decision his stomach welcomed with a growl of approval. The place was more crowded than when he left. Iain and Silas were hard at work tending to their patrons, most of whom sought to unwind after another day's labors. Despite the warmth of the burning fire, there was something cold about the hall. Many of the villagers kept to themselves, nursing drinks in solitude or chattering in small groups. On his way to the bar, he overheard snippets of conversations about the goblin raid or speculation on when the ogre might strike next.

"Did you hear?" one man asked of his friend. "Young Lucas has been running around the village telling everyone he was rescued from a headless rider by a bear!" The man laughed, but his friend didn't seem as amused. Given all the recent happenings, it was likely the villagers knew something was going on, even if they didn't know what.

Berengar averted his gaze to prevent the men from noticing his scars. Friar Godfrey was right. It wouldn't be long before someone deduced his identity. A loud crash came from the bar, where a familiar-looking man kicked away a barstool and staggered to his feet. Berengar recognized him as the drunk who'd been slumped over the bar earlier in the day. From the look of things, the man—Iain called him Duncan—hadn't moved much in that time, which suggested he'd been so inebriated at the time of the goblin raid he'd slept right through it.

Silence fell over the hall as the drunk pounded the counter with his fists in anger.

"I'll say when I've had enough," Duncan shouted at Silas. "Give me another."

Despite the disparity in their sizes—Duncan was stocky but much shorter than the bartender—Silas seemed unable to form a response, and his forcible attempts only resulted in a string of incomprehensible stuttering. He finally shook his head to indicate his refusal to pour another drink.

Iain made his way to the bar in a show of solidarity with Silas. His friendly expression was gone. "This is my establishment. Go home and sleep it off, Duncan."

"How dare you," Duncan slurred, projecting spittle with each word. "I'm a veteran of the Shadow Wars. I'll not be ordered about by the likes of you." He gave Iain a shove, and the innkeeper nearly lost his balance.

"That's enough," Berengar said. He grabbed Duncan and slammed him against the bar. "You heard the man."

Duncan struggled vainly to free himself. "Let me go, you bastard."

Berengar pinned the man's arm behind his back to restrain him. "Say one more word and I'll break it." He released his hold on Duncan's arm and tossed him toward the door. "Get out of here. Now."

Duncan landed on the floor and glared up at Berengar, only to find himself face-to-face with Faolán, who growled and showed him her teeth. He scrambled to his feet, pushed a pair of patrons out of his way, and hurried outside.

Berengar turned his back and took a seat at the bar. "Smells good. I'll have some of whatever you've got cooking." He slid some copper coins across the counter, and the patrons returned to their activities.

Silas went into the kitchen and returned with a bowl full of venison stew and a plate of hot soda bread.

"It's good," he said, stuffing his mouth with a sizable piece of bread.

Silas beamed at the praise.

"Duncan's always been trouble," Iain muttered. "It seems we're in your debt yet again. If I had the coin, I'd hire you on full-time. Unfortunately, between the vice tax on spirits and all the strange goings-on, business has suffered since the start of the year. Many travelers or merchants would rather take a longer route to Dún Aulin and avoid this area entirely. Can't say I blame them, either. From what I hear, people have been going missing all across Laird Margolin's territory. Of course, Margolin has something of a reputation himself."

"What do you mean?"

"The man rules with an iron fist." Iain looked around the room—as if to make sure neither of the guards was present—and lowered his voice before continuing. "There was a time when Margolin was one of the most influential lords in the realm, until he was banished from court. Some said it was on account of his barbarity during the Shadow Wars, though there were rumors the church suspected him of heresy."

That explains what Margolin's doing in a place like Blackthorn, Berengar thought. "Heresy?"

"Aye—that he held with the old ways."

The rumors seemed consistent with the absence of a church or chapel at the castle, a rare occurrence in pious Leinster. Berengar, who came from the north—where worship of the elder gods was widespread—didn't see it as cause for concern, but he could see how Margolin's subjects might hold such beliefs against him.

"Laird Margolin claims the rumors are all lies spread by his enemies, and there are few left who would dare challenge him on the subject. Margolin has killed or imprisoned most of his rivals over the years." Iain's eyes grew distant, as if recalling a memory from long ago. "It wasn't always so. Laird Cairrigan once held dominion over Alúine, before Margolin made war against him. Margolin murdered Cairrigan and all his heirs and claimed his territories for his own." The innkeeper reached across the bar and poured himself a drink. "When he slew Cairrigan, only the goblins were left to oppose him. Soon they too will be gone from these lands."

"What about the brigands who live in the forest?" Berengar asked. "Friar Godfrey told me they aren't friendly to Margolin."

Iain chuckled. "I'd say not. Most are former subjects or servants of Laird Cairrigan, although word has it a fair number come from Alúine and neighboring settlements. They tried rebelling against Margolin after the war and even attempted to assassinate him on more than one occasion."

Berengar recalled the scars across Margolin's throat.

"Margolin crushed the rebellion and slaughtered all the rebels he could find. Those who remain are little more than outlaws. They make trouble from time to time, but they're no longer a threat to him. Few can withstand the wrath of lords."

Berengar frowned. Margolin's ruthlessness had been readily apparent from the moment they'd met, but this was something else. He'd been forced into a pact with a devil, and now there was little recourse but to see it through to the end. It was the price to be paid for the death of Skinner Kane.

Iain left to attend to other patrons, and Berengar continued eating in silence.

"I've got a lead on that horse you asked about," the innkeeper said when he returned. "A friend of mine needs the money. Fifty copper coins is what he's asking."

The door to the inn opened, and in walked Evander, accompanied by Phineas and Tuck.

"Tell him I'll have the money by tomorrow." Berengar finished the last of his stew, set the bowl aside, and followed the others outside.

The sky slowly darkened as Berengar and the others made their way to the outskirts of the village. Phineas—clearly the man in charge—discussed the plan while Tuck outfitted Berengar with a club and passed around torches. The guards had rigged up a seemingly abandoned wagon not far from the forest's entrance. According to Phineas, the sacks of grain in the back of the wagon were sure to attract the attention of goblin scouts patrolling the forest. When the goblins came, they'd capture one and force it to reveal the location of their lair. The plan sounded simple enough, but Berengar knew from experience goblins were clever creatures. If they smelled a trap, the hunters might become the hunted, and goblins weren't the only creatures lurking about.

The company started on the road to the forest with night unfurling around them. The full moon emerged to cast a bright glow across the trees.

Phineas waved to the others with his torch. "This way."

Evander took the lead. In addition to his bow, the huntsman carried a dagger strapped to his waist. Faolán held her nose to the ground, sniffing out scents on the forest floor while the two guards brought up the rear. Unlike the dense hedges that made it difficult to navigate the area around Castle Blackthorn, the forest's trees were widely spaced. A dirt path was visible underfoot, though masked by overgrowth, as if neglected for quite some time. The air was cold, though at least there was no trace of the mist that obscured the road to Móin Alúin.

Evander pointed out a set of prints. "Look."

"You've got good eyes," Berengar replied.

Evander knelt in the mud to inspect the prints. "My parents died of the plague when I was a lad. I had to fend for myself, or else I didn't eat."

"Is it the goblins?" Phineas asked, keeping a lookout.

Even in the dim light, it was obvious from Evander's expression that something troubled him. "No."

Berengar crouched beside the huntsman and examined the tracks. "No goblin left these—they're too large." The strange prints reminded him of those of a hound or wolf, but much bigger. Was there another monster stalking the countryside besides the ogre and the Dullahan?

When Faolán sniffed the tracks, she let out a soft whine. Berengar heard a twig snap nearby and raised his torch, but when he peered into the darkness past the brush, there was nothing there.

"We should keep moving," Evander said. He waited until the others were out of earshot before speaking to Berengar in a hushed tone. "I've seen prints like these before, left by the beast that killed Rose's father."

"What sort of beast?"

"I never saw it. Things were different in those days. Rose and I were to be married. Then one night I went away on a hunt, and when I returned, the old man was dead. He'd been ripped to shreds."

"Was Rose injured in the attack?"

"No, but she was never the same after that. She wanted to be a healer. Lord knows the village needs one, and she was good at it, too. When her father fell ill, the priest said there was nothing to be done. Rose wouldn't hear of it, and she nursed the old man back to health herself. Then the beast killed him, and everything changed."

"It sounds like she took her father's death hard," Berengar said.

"That's the truth of it. She broke off our engagement and gave up healing. She hardly comes into the village anymore. Still, I'll never give up on her. I'll find a way to kill the beast and avenge her father, and with the reward for the ogre, we can have the life we've always wanted."

Although the sentiment struck Berengar as foolishly naive, he chose to let the remark pass unanswered. He'd learned the hard way that life rarely doled out happy endings, and even more rarely for commoners—who were far more likely to succumb to disease or a robber's knife than death of old age. Either way, death always won in the end, which meant life was really about surviving as long as possible. The High Queen had a different outlook, but while Berengar respected Nora's well-meaning optimism, he didn't share it. Evander was young. He had plenty of time to see the world as it really was.

Suddenly, he noticed a man-sized figure just off the path. Long, unruly willow branches surrounded the darkened figure like a shroud, cutting it off from the moonlight. When Berengar tightened his grip around the club's handle and rushed forward, crows fled the tree's branches, and the torchlight revealed lifeless gray stone.

It's a statue. He reached out and pulled vines away from the figure's head, exposing a monstrous face. Like Berengar, it too had only one good eye.

Evander, following behind, lowered his bow when he saw the statue. "I see you've found Balor. There aren't many of these old shrines left. The church ordered them destroyed."

Balor. Anyone with knowledge of the elder gods or the old ways knew that name, and with good reason. Balor, also known as the Deadly One and Balor of the Evil Eye, was the Fomorian King—a god of death, plague, and pestilence. Worship of such a monstrous entity was unusual but not unheard of. In the days of old, there were entire sects and cults led by druids or magicians who sought the Fomorians' blessing, often to disastrous effect.

Phineas beckoned to them from the path. "Come along. The wagon isn't far from here."

A short time later, the company reached a bend in the path, where a wagon lay bathed in moonlight.

Berengar caught a glimpse of movement on the other side of the wagon and lowered his voice to a whisper. "We're not alone."

Evander nocked an arrow, the guards eased their swords from their sheaths, and the group silently advanced toward the wagon. Berengar half-expected a goblin scout to jump over the wagon and attack. Instead, he heard the sound of teeth and claws tearing into flesh. As he drew closer, he noticed green blood pooled across the ground, where a mangled goblin corpse lay twisted and broken. Something else had found the scout first. Berengar's gaze fell on a creature making a meal of the goblin's limbs, and suddenly he knew exactly what had killed Rose's father.

The wind shifted, and the creature stopped what it was doing and sniffed the air before slowly turning around. The werewolf's fangs glistened in the moonlight. Long claws sprouted from its hands. Although it stood on two legs like a man, its limbs and torso were covered in thick, dark fur.

Berengar stared down the creature, which regarded the companions with a set of predatory amber eyes. Were-wolves were extremely difficult to kill. In addition to their supernatural strength, speed, and senses, most varieties could only be seriously injured by silver. True, he carried a silver dagger, but without his axe, there was little chance he'd get close enough to use it.

"Run," he said.

Unlike Phineas and Tuck—who had already fled down the path—Evander stood his ground and trained his bow on the creature. "I have you now, monster."

"What are you doing?" Berengar demanded. The arrows wouldn't do a thing but make the werewolf mad.

Evander ignored him and fired an arrow, which struck the creature in the heart. Evander fired a second arrow, which also found its mark.

The werewolf howled in pain and leapt at Evander, but Berengar pushed him out of the way at the last second.

"Idiot. You're no match for a werewolf. We have to go—now."

While Evander hesitated, the werewolf landed gracefully and spun around to face them. It pounced on Berengar, who struggled to free himself as the werewolf's jaws inched closer to his face. Twin arrows hit the creature in the side, and Berengar managed to free his hand and strike the werewolf with his club as Faolán jumped on its back, biting and clawing. The werewolf tossed Faolán aside as if she were weightless, and the wolfhound crashed into a tree with a yelp.

Berengar lunged forward, grabbed his fallen torch, and jabbed it into the werewolf's face. There was a sizzle and a pop, and the werewolf let out a pained cry and clawed the air blindly.

"Get out of here," he shouted to Evander.

They took off running deeper into the forest. A howl echoed through the night behind them, and Berengar heard the werewolf moving through the forest. The blasted thing had their scent. He ran until his legs burned and his sides ached. Somewhere along the way, he lost sight of Evander and found himself alone in the unfamiliar forest. Or was he? Something moved in the brush nearby—something too small to be the werewolf.

Berengar reached into the brush and grabbed hold of something that thrashed about in his grip. He tightened his hold and pulled a goblin from the brush. The goblin bit his hand and broke free, but Berengar tackled the creature before it could scramble up a tree.

"You." He recognized the creature's shoddy armor. It was the leader of the raiding party that attacked Alúine. "You took something from me, and I want it back. Where are the others?"

The creature merely hissed in response.

Berengar tore off the creature's helmet. "I'm done playing games." He frowned, surprised by the face looking back at him underneath. "You're not a goblin."

The creature was male. His skin was a pale yellow. Rounded teeth protruded from his lips, and his ears and nose were much longer and pointier than those of ordinary goblins. Coupled with his stature—short even by goblin standards—it was clear Berengar was looking at an altogether different creature entirely.

"You're a hobgoblin, aren't you?"

The discovery didn't make any sense. If their leader was a hobgoblin, so were the others who had raided the village. Although they were known to be playful and mischievous, hobgoblins weren't dangerous like their cousins. If anything, they were known to be extremely shy around humans. That accounted for why no one was killed in any of the attacks, but it didn't explain why hobgoblins would pose as goblins in the first place.

The werewolf's howl reverberated through the night before the hobgoblin could answer. When Berengar glanced toward the source of the sound, the hobgoblin wriggled free of his grip and scurried up a tree. At that moment, the werewolf burst free of the thicket and brandished its bloodstained claws. It crouched to jump, as if expecting him to flee. Berengar charged it instead, catching it off guard, and the two met in a violent clash. He reached for the silver dagger, but the werewolf overpowered him and opened its jaws to devour him.

Without warning, a black arrow sailed through the

night and pierced the werewolf's throat, allowing Berengar to grab the dagger and plunge it deep into the creature's side. The werewolf reacted even more violently to the silver than the arrow in its throat. It writhed in agony, steam rising from the wound. Above, the hobgoblin watched from the tree, a bow in his hands. He jumped to another branch and vanished into the darkness.

Berengar found his footing and tore through the forest, the werewolf hot on his trail. He stumbled through a thicket and emerged into a clearing, where the ruins of an abandoned structure loomed under the moonlight. The structure—which might have been a castle or fort at one time—had largely been reclaimed by nature in the absence of human occupants. Scorch marks marred its blackened stone surface and crumbling walls.

As he ran through the open clearing, Berengar spotted an open door partially hidden by moss and vines. He glanced over his shoulder and saw the werewolf close behind, gaining on him with each step. At the last moment, he threw himself across the threshold and slammed and bolted the door shut. The frame shuddered when the were-wolf crashed against the door, and for a moment he thought it might come off its hinges, but the door held firm.

Berengar continued pressing his weight against the door until the pounding finally ceased. He was alone, at least for the moment. Still, the structure was expansive enough that the werewolf might find another way inside, and he needed somewhere safer to wait out the night. He turned and advanced through forgotten hallways, unsure what he might find.

CHAPTER SEVEN

MOONBEAMS SPILLED in through gaps in the ceiling, illuminating the path ahead. His footsteps echoed faintly as he wandered along an empty corridor. When he neared the end of the passage, he noticed a hint of firelight in an adjoining chamber. He crept toward the partially open door and heard a soft tune coming from within the room. He had company.

Careful not to make a sound, Berengar inched forward with the silver dagger in hand and cracked open the door. Tuck sat inside, warming himself by a fire and muttering the words of a lullaby. An open flask rested at his side.

Berengar lowered the dagger and emerged from the shadows.

"You made it." Tuck's voice was distant. "Shut the door, will you? I don't think it can get to us in here."

Berengar did as he said and sat opposite him. "How did you find this place?"

His companion merely shrugged. "Phineas left me. Can't say I blame him. I'm always slowing him down—

slowing everyone down, really. That's why the captain sent me to Alúine. At least here I'm out of the way."

Tuck was old for a guard. Though his hair was not yet entirely white, scant black remained among the gray. He'd probably been a fighter his whole life. It was doubtful he knew another path. Berengar could relate. When one spent a life killing men, it was difficult to find another profession. For many, it was all they knew how to do.

He surveyed the expansive chamber in the firelight. Apart from dust and cobwebs, the room was mostly barren. Based on what he'd seen so far, the whole place had been ransacked. Anything of value had been taken a long time ago. "What is this place?"

"Laird Cairrigan's castle, it was." Tuck took another drink of whatever was in his flask. "I never wanted to see the place again. Funny sense of humor life has, doesn't it?"

"What happened here?"

Tuck stared into the flames with a vacant expression, as if a thousand miles away. "It was the only way to win the war. That's what they told us. The moon was full, like tonight. Laird Margolin paid a man inside to open the gates to us. I was just following orders, wasn't I?" His eyes grew misty. "Old Cairrigan begged us to let his family live, even after we filled his belly with steel. When his eldest daughter tried to run, we killed her next. I still remember the look in his wife's eyes before I slit her throat. Not a day goes by that I don't remember it." He shivered. "After that, it was a mess. Servants running about, the tower ablaze… and then I saw him. Cairrigan's youngest son. He was dressed as a peasant, but the likeness was unmistakable. I looked at him, he looked at me…and I couldn't do it. I let him go. That counts for something, doesn't it? Doesn't it?" He lowered his head into his hands and sobbed.

Berengar crossed the room and snatched the flask from

the ground. "That's enough. Get a grip on yourself. Right now, we have other things to worry about, unless you've forgotten the monster on the prowl outside these walls. Got it?"

Tuck wiped his eyes and nodded weakly. "Aye. You're right. It's the drink. It makes me say things I shouldn't."

"Good. We'll keep watch in shifts and make our way back to the village in the morning. I'll take first watch. Try to get some rest."

His companion quickly fell into a deep slumber—which, given the amount of alcohol he'd likely consumed, wasn't exactly surprising. If Laird Cairrigan and his family were indeed butchered by Margolin's soldiers, it was easy to see why the brigands chose to rebel against his rule. The truth was, more often than not men like Margolin prevailed, no matter how many bodies they left in their wake. Berengar understood that as well as anyone. He held his hands just short of the flames and listened, waiting as one second slid into the next.

S hadows crept in as the flames died low. Something whispered to him in the darkness. Berengar looked around the room. Tuck remained fast asleep. There was no hint of another presence. He sat up and reached for the dagger, only to find himself staring into the hag's eyes. The blade fell limply at his side, and the hag leaned forward to whisper into his ear.

"Bring me the sacrifice. You have two days."

Berengar felt a hand on his shoulder. Suddenly, the hag was gone. In her place stood Tuck, who stared at him with concern.

"Are you all right? You were mumbling in your sleep."

"I'm fine," Berengar said tersely. Sunlight streamed in

through cracks in the walls. It was morning. The werewolf, if it remained in the area, would have returned to human form. "Let's go." He'd already lost one day; he couldn't afford to lose another. "Can you find your way back to the village from here?"

"I think so." Tuck looked as if he was still suffering the aftereffects of a night spent drinking.

Together, they made their way to the abandoned castle's entrance. Berengar opened the door and saw notches embedded deep in the wood where the werewolf's claws left their mark. Although the sun was fully visible outside, clouds lurked on the horizon, a reminder the rains in Leinster were never far away. Something stirred in the thicket at their approach, and Faolán emerged. When she reached his side, she immediately began licking his hand affectionately.

"It's good to see you too. I owe you." Berengar patted her head and looked her over to make sure she hadn't been seriously injured. Fortunately, she appeared unharmed. Their reunion was interrupted by a woman's scream. Berengar glanced up alertly. "That came from nearby."

Faolán sprinted toward the scream's source, and Berengar followed close behind, leaving Tuck trying his best to keep up. Whistling sounded through the trees ahead, and Berengar slowed his pace. He stole closer and glimpsed three rough-looking men surrounding a woman whose back was to him. Each man carried a rusty or beat-up weapon.

The brigands. He held a finger to his lips to warn Tuck to keep quiet.

"Look what we have here, lads," the whistling brigand said to the woman. "What are you doing all the way out here, lass?"

"Leave me be."

Berengar recognized her voice at once. It was Rose. She had lost her cloak, and her hands were stained with dirt.

The brigand grinned at his companions. "She's the right age—and a pretty one too." He turned his gaze back to Rose. "You're a long way from Blackthorn, my lady."

They think she's Imogen. But why were they looking for *her*? Hadn't Margolin's niece been taken by the ogre?

He heard grass trampled underfoot, and two more brigands appeared with a familiar prisoner in tow: the hobgoblin Berengar encountered the night before. The creature's hands were bound, and a rope was tied around his neck to prevent him from fleeing.

"We caught this one by the stream," said a brigand who gave the hobgoblin a push, causing the creature to land on the ground. When he tried to rise, the brigand kicked him in the side, and the others roared with laughter.

As the hobgoblin's eyes flitted around the faces of his captors, the brigands inched toward Rose, slowly tightening the circle.

She took a step back, but there was nowhere to go. "I don't know what you want, but my name is Rose. I have a farm near Móin Alúin."

"She doesn't sound like no lady," another of the brigands said. "Maybe she's not who we're looking for."

The first man stopped whistling and studied Rose carefully. "That still doesn't explain what she's doing out here. You lot heard those howls as well as I did. You know what's out there. What's to say she's not the beast? Let's take them both back with us and be done with it."

Before any man could take another step toward Rose, Berengar left the trees to face them, the dagger hidden behind his back. "That's enough. Let her go—now. The hobgoblin too. Before I lose my temper."

"Well, this is a surprise," the whistling brigand said, looking past him to Tuck. "You know what we do to Laird Margolin's men in our woods."

"I told you once," Berengar said, his size drawing the group's collective attention. "I won't ask again."

"You may be a monster of a man, but there are five of us, and only one sword between the two of you. I say we—"

Berengar drove the dagger through his throat before he finished speaking, and Faolán mauled an archer attempting to take aim. When another brigand swung a sword at him, Berengar caught the man's forearm, snapped it, and used him as a shield to avoid a stab from another swordsman. The swordsman's blade lodged itself in the abdomen of his companion, who dropped to his knees as blood stained his tunic. Berengar caught the swordsman before he could flee and bashed his head into a tree until he finally stopped jerking.

The final brigand—a younger man barely out of adolescence—tripped over his own boots in a panic, landed next to the hobgoblin, and dropped his weapon in the process. Tuck, whose sword hung uselessly to one side, stared at the scene in apparent disbelief.

"Thanks for the help," Berengar muttered with unrestrained sarcasm as he stooped to retrieve his dagger.

"You saved me," Rose said in gratitude.

"Consider us even." He started toward the last remaining brigand.

"I surrender!" The young man scrambled backward over the wet earth. "Please don't hurt me."

Berengar grabbed him by the neck. The men would have killed him and Tuck without another thought—not to mention what they might have done to Rose. Anger coursed through his veins, and the world was replaced by a

97

wave of red. In the next moment the brigand lay dead on the ground as the silver dagger dripped with his blood.

"You killed him in cold blood," Rose said.

"You think he and his friends would have shown you mercy if I hadn't come along?"

"That's not the point. What gives you the right?"

"This dagger gives me the right." He wiped the blade and returned it to his boot. As a warden, he could pronounce judgment as he saw fit—a power he exercised freely over the years. He'd spent enough time dealing with murderers and thieves to know who was deserving of punishment when he saw them. If he'd shown the brigand mercy, the man would have simply run back to his hideaway, gathered his companions, and returned.

Rose put her hands on her hips in a show of disapproval. "Just because you can kill someone doesn't mean you should."

Before he could form a response, a searing pain shot through his hand and traveled the length of his arm up to his shoulder. Violent spasms racked his muscles, and his hand involuntarily closed into a fist, refusing to open in response to his will.

Rose noticed his pained expression. "It's your hand, isn't it? Let me see it—maybe I can help."

Berengar pulled the hand away from her. "Those men had a point. What *were* you doing out here?"

She hesitated, seemingly thrown off balance by the question. "I heard Evander went off in search of goblins. I wanted to make sure he was safe, but a beast chased me through the forest—the same beast that killed my father. I'm sure of it. Evander must have gone after it. I need to know if he's all right."

Her concern seemed genuine enough, which surprised him, given how she'd distanced herself from Evander in the village. Still, that didn't mean she *wasn't* the werewolf. "Take off that scarf and let me have a look at you."

"What?"

"You heard me. I want to make sure you're not the werewolf we encountered last night. If you don't have a scar from where you were turned, you have nothing to fear."

"As you wish." Rose raised her sleeves, allowing him to check her for bite marks.

"She's clean," he said to Tuck, who still looked fairly squeamish. *Good.* He hadn't looked forward to the alternative, especially since she'd rescued him from the bog.

Rose shot him a rueful expression. "You didn't answer my question. Iain told me that Evander went with you and the guards. What happened to him?"

"I don't know. We were pursued by the werewolf and I lost sight of him." Berengar grabbed the hobgoblin and forced the creature onto his feet. "You're coming with us."

The hobgoblin did as he asked without resistance. The reward for the creature's capture would be enough to cover his obligations.

"We should return to the village," Tuck suggested. "If Phineas and Evander survived, that's where they'll be."

They'd better be, Berengar thought. Otherwise, he had lost his guide to the bog.

While his companions started in the direction of Alúine, Berengar lingered behind to inspect his injured hand. Though the pain again subsided, his fingers remained tightly clenched. He pried back the bandages to find that the skin around the rusted nail had turned black. The surrounding gray area now extended beyond his palm and up his forearm. The underlying muscles were stiff to his touch—almost like stone. The wound was unmistakably worse, a sign the witch's curse was taking hold.

He grunted in discomfort and returned to the trail before the others took note of his absence. Tuck, who held the hobgoblin's leash to prevent the creature from fleeing, followed Faolán north. The hobgoblin briefly caught Berengar's eye and held his gaze, as if reminding the warden of his help against the werewolf. As far as Berengar was concerned, he'd returned the favor by rescuing the hobgoblin from the brigands, though in truth the creature wasn't likely to receive better treatment at the hands of Margolin's guards. Still, the hobgoblin knew where to find the stolen thunder rune, and Berengar was determined to recover it—no matter what.

His thoughts turned to the mention of Lady Imogen. The brigands weren't searching for her by accident. Was it possible she was still alive? If that was true, killing the ogre was only half the job. He had promised to discover Imogen's fate, and the ogre's lair was the best place to start. His stay in Alúine continued to raise new questions. Given the presence of the ogre, the werewolf, the Dullahan, and the hag, why hadn't Margolin hired one of the church's monster hunters, or at least paid a mercenary to do the job? Instead, he'd sent Berengar to kill the ogre and retrieve his niece. Something didn't add up. At least the Dullahan hadn't shown up again. Berengar thought again of his conversation with Godfrey and wondered if Godfrey had any more information to share with him. Perhaps the friar knew something about the hag that would aid in the removal of her curse.

Ahead, Rose kept to herself, looking downcast. Berengar wasn't sure if it was her run-in with the brigands or Evander's whereabouts that troubled her. In either event, he supposed his behavior hadn't helped. When many might have left him in the bog, she had lent him aid and asked for nothing in return. He let out a sigh of regret and quickened his pace. "Sorry about back there. I didn't mean to frighten you. I was only trying to keep you safe."

When she turned to face him, the anger was gone from her face, replaced by an expression of resignation and unexpected weariness. "I've treated soldiers before. I know what kind of world this is. I've seen enough death, that's all."

"Evander told me you trained to become a healer. That explains why you did such a good job patching me up."

For the first time, she smiled a little. "It was my dream. I wanted to make a difference. Things were difficult here even back then."

"Still are," Berengar remarked. "From what I've seen, there are plenty of people in Alúine who could use your help."

"You sound like Evander. I hope he's safe."

"He's brave," Berengar replied, which was about the highest praise he could offer. "He stayed and fought the beast when others would have fled."

Rose shook her head. "He thinks killing the creature will make everything like it was."

"Evander told me what happened to your father. He also said you were to be married. I can see that you care for him. Otherwise, you wouldn't have risked going into the forest to find him."

"Aye, I loved him—love him still. But there are other concerns. What does it matter to you?"

Berengar shrugged. "The pain of losing someone never really goes away. I know what that feels like. But you have someone who loves you. That kind of thing doesn't come along that often, and it doesn't last forever. Take it from someone who knows."

Rose's brow arched in surprise, and she started to reply, but Faolán interrupted her with a loud bark.

"Look," Tuck said as Phineas and Evander approached through the forest.

When Evander saw Rose, his eyes widened in shock. "Rose? What are you doing here?" He ran to her side and embraced her, and this time she did not push him away.

"I went looking for you—to make sure you were safe."

"We ran into some brigands on the way," Berengar said to Phineas. "I took care of them."

"And look what you brought back with you." The guard's eyes lingered on their captive with visible delight. "Where are the rest of your kind?"

The hobgoblin stared up at him in a show of defiance.

Phineas spit at the creature's feet. "We'll see if we can't make you talk after we throw you in a cell to rot." He returned his attention to Berengar. "Well done. I'll see to it that you're properly compensated when we reach the village." He motioned for the others to follow. "Let's go. It's a short way to Alúine from here."

His words proved correct, and they reached the edge of the woods a short time later. The spasms in Berengar's left arm slowly subsided as they approached Alúine, and by the time they reached the village he was able to unclench his fist.

A shout sounded somewhere in the distance, and the guards looked at each other in alarm. A group of villagers had congregated around the well, where one of their number addressed the others using sweeping, animated gestures. It was Hirum, the man who had berated Silas when Berengar first arrived in Alúine.

"Let us through," Phineas said, pushing his way into the center of the assembly. "What is it? What's happened?"

"It's my daughter," Hirum said. "It's Leona. She's dead."

CHAPTER EIGHT

THE VILLAGERS REACTED to the news with considerable alarm.

"Quiet, you lot," Phineas ordered the crowd. "Haven't you got work to do?"

Rather than risk drawing the guards' ire, those gathered around the well dispersed, speculating about what had caused Leona's death as they returned to their affairs.

"I'll handle this," Phineas said to Tuck. "Throw our captive in a cell. We'll deal with the slime later."

Tuck nodded obediently and prodded the hobgoblin along. "Come on, you."

Another killing, Berengar thought. From what he'd seen so far, the people of Alúine had endured more than their share of hardships. He turned his attention to Leona's father. Hirum was flustered and agitated, which wasn't surprising, considering the circumstances.

Phineas demonstrated uncharacteristic concern for Hirum's well-being. "Are you all right? What happened?"

Hirum sucked in a deep breath and wiped a bead of sweat from his eyes. "This morning, I found Leona missing from her room. She must have gone out alone last night without telling me. I searched for her and…" Hirum's voice caught in his chest, as the horror of his discovery dawned on him for the first time. "I was too late. When I found her, she was dead—killed." His expression of grief quickly gave way to anger. "Well? What are you waiting for? I want my daughter's killer brought to justice."

Berengar expected Phineas to bristle at Hirum's criticism, but instead he acted in an almost deferential manner. "Show us the body. Come along, huntsman. We may require your assistance."

Evander and Rose started after him, and Berengar followed, for once unnoticed by others. Leona was roughly the same age as the young woman whose lost spirit he'd encountered with Friar Godfrey. If her death was also the Dullahan's doing, it might hold a clue to the reason for the monster's presence in Alúine.

Hirum led them west, toward Móin Alúin. Leona's body lay at the foot of the great hill that looked over Alúine. Only a day before, the girl was young and full of life. Now she was cold and dead, her corpse covered in mud and blood. She had not died peacefully.

Hirum's hard expression faltered as he gazed upon his daughter's lifeless form, and his voice broke as he spoke. "She was all I had." He quickly recovered his composure and made no move to approach the body.

"Go on," Phineas said to Evander. "Tell me what you see."

Evander nodded grimly and crouched low to inspect the body. Tears marred Leona's bloodstained dress, and puncture wounds were visible across her abdomen.

"Was it the beast?" Rose seemed barely able to look at the grisly scene, perhaps reminded of her father's death.

"Or perhaps the ogre," Phineas muttered. "The bog isn't far from here."

Berengar interrupted for the first time. "No. The ogre would have crushed its victim. Does it look like Leona's bones are broken to you? Besides, the ogre wouldn't have left her here, and certainly not in one piece. The werewolf didn't do it either."

"If those monsters didn't kill my daughter, what did?" Hirum demanded.

"Let me take a closer look." Berengar knelt beside the body and gestured to Phineas. "Hand me your drinking horn." When the guard complied, Berengar used the water to clean away the blood. "These aren't fang or claw marks —they're stab wounds. This wasn't some random killing, either. It was murder. Look at these wounds. Leona was stabbed multiple times up close, which suggests she knew her attacker—maybe even trusted them. Whoever killed her probably left her here hoping she would be mistaken for another of the beast's victims."

Phineas was clearly unhappy at being upstaged. "That tells us nothing." He reached down and snatched the empty water horn from Berengar. "This is Alúine. Everyone knows everyone in this godforsaken hellhole. Anyone could have killed her."

Berengar pushed himself to his feet. "It's your job to find the killer, not mine. I'll say this—it was clearly a crime of passion. Whoever killed her was full of rage."

"How can you possibly know that?" Phineas asked with a derisive laugh.

"I've seen wounds like these before," Berengar said in a tone that warned the guard from pressing the subject. "It shouldn't be too hard to find whoever's responsible. You find the weapon and you'll find your culprit. I'd guess it's a dagger, or else a cook's knife. Hirum, you said she went out alone. Do you have any idea why?"

Hirum shook his head. "Leona was a good girl. None of this makes any sense."

"I'd start there, if I were you," Berengar told Phineas.

The guard's expression darkened, and he took a step toward Berengar. "I don't care how big you are—I wouldn't go giving orders if I were you. In case you've forgotten, I'm in charge around here."

Berengar merely stared back at him with a cold expression until Rose laid a hand on his shoulder, presumably to defuse the tension. "We should get the body back to the village before the crows find her. It's the least we can do for her now."

Phineas averted his gaze. "Get to it, then." He started toward Alúine, leaving Berengar and Evander to lift the body.

When they reached the village, Evander removed his cloak and used it to shield Leona from curious passersby. They carried the body to the church, where Hirum and Phineas conversed briefly in hushed tones.

"I'll fetch Father Godfrey," Hirum finally said. "We'll be needing a coffin."

"What are you still doing here?" Phineas asked Berengar.

"There's still the matter of my pay."

"I suppose you did help us catch that goblin," Phineas said, as if he had suddenly realized it would be unwise to renege on his word. "Very well. Wait for me at the jail, and I'll see to it that you're properly compensated."

Berengar turned away without a reply and walked over to Evander and Rose. "I did what you asked. Time to uphold your end of the bargain."

"Of course. After what you did for Rose…"

"Good. I'm going to collect my pay and see about a horse. Meet me at the inn in half an hour."

The jail wasn't difficult to find, as most of the villagers made sure to keep a safe distance. The people had no love for Laird Margolin or his guards, even if they clearly feared both. Still, in Berengar's experience, fear was usually enough for any despot's purposes. There was no sign of Tuck inside the jail. Given what he'd witnessed the previous night, the guard was probably holed up somewhere with a bottle in his hand. It was little wonder Alúine was overrun, considering the quality of its guards.

Something stirred in a corner on the other side of the iron bars. The hobgoblin wrapped his hands around the bars and stared at him, prompting Faolán to show her teeth in warning.

"Quiet," Berengar ordered the wolfhound. "What's your name?"

The creature made no reply.

"Fine. You can rot in here for all I care. I just want the thunder rune back. Where is it?"

Again the hobgoblin gave no answer.

"Why did you help me?" Berengar asked. "You could have left me to the werewolf."

Finally, the hobgoblin spoke. "We're only monsters to your eyes, human."

Berengar leaned closer. "Then why attack the village? Why disguise yourselves as goblins girded for war?"

A soft, non-threatening hissing noise almost like a sigh came from the back of the goblin's throat. "There are few of us left now. The soldiers have hunted us almost to extinction."

"Margolin's men?"

The hobgoblin nodded. "I am Gnish. Mine is the last of the tribes. I have done my best to keep the others safe.

We take food and medicine—only what we need to survive. It is not in our nature to harm others, even if we must fight to stay alive."

That fit with what he knew about the shy creatures. "How many are left?"

"Thirteen," Gnish answered. "And two goblin younglings we are raising as our own. There are only five fighting males among us. The others are females or younglings."

No wonder they have to pose as goblins. Without their masks or armor, hobgoblins weren't threatening-looking in the slightest. Goblins, on the other hand, were hated and despised far and wide. Berengar wasn't immune to anti-goblin sentiment. He'd killed more than his share in battle over the years. Still, they weren't all hostile, and humans bore more than their share of blame for relations between the species. He'd learned to tell good from evil long ago, and Gnish didn't fit in the latter category.

"Why not leave? Munster isn't far from here. The people there are far more tolerant of nonhuman creatures than those who live here. There are goblin smiths in Cashel with forges of their own. Perhaps your tribe could find peace there."

"This is our home. Our ancestors lived here, and theirs before them."

"The fairies once thought this land belonged to them. Where are they now?"

While there were many areas of Fál where magic and magical creatures remained common—particularly in the north—times were changing. Even before the purges that followed the Shadow Wars, other races were left with smaller and smaller territories to call their own as human cities and settlements spread across the land. In the past, human magicians and druids often mediated between species, but now they too were almost nonexistent. Although the High Queen had declared most peaceful magical races under her protection, such proclamations were largely left to the monarch of each realm to enforce —and no realm had more antipathy for nonhuman creatures than Leinster.

"Just tell me where I can find the thunder rune, and I give you my word no harm will come to your tribe." Even as he said the words, he remembered promising to let the scholar live before running him through. It wasn't a promise he could keep.

"I will die before betraying my kin."

"Have it your way, then," Berengar said through clenched teeth, fighting back his anger. "I expect the guards will put your resolve to the test." He felt sympathy for Gnish, but there was nothing he could do. One way or another, the end would be the same.

As if on cue, the door opened. Phineas entered and immediately aimed a kick at Gnish. "Don't worry, you filth. I haven't forgotten about you."

The hobgoblin retreated into a corner, and Phineas motioned for Berengar to follow him outside, where he reached into a pouch and produced a number of silver and copper coins.

"For your efforts. That ought to cover it, I think."

Berengar counted the coins and tucked them away. Although it wasn't an overly generous reward, the amount was more than enough to cover the cost of a horse.

"Wait," Phineas said when Berengar turned to go. "I have my hands full with this murder at the moment, but I'll need good men by my side when we find the goblin encampment."

"His name is Gnish," Berengar said. "He's a hobgoblin. He and the others are the last of their kind. They're only thieving because your lord and his soldiers have made it impossible for them to survive otherwise."

"Goblin, hobgoblin—they're all the same. Can I count on you when the time comes?"

Berengar hesitated. The hobgoblins weren't monsters, and they hadn't actually hurt anyone. He didn't care for Phineas, whose greed and hatred of goblins didn't bode well for Gnish and his kind, but he couldn't allow the thunder rune to remain in their hands. It was too dangerous.

"Aye. I'm with you."

"Good. It's better to have a fighting man with us. Learn to mind that tongue of yours, and you might have a place at our side when Laird Margolin rewards us for stamping out the goblin threat."

It wasn't unusual for people who saw the warden's size and scars to assume he was some mindless brawler or the like. By the time they realized their mistake, it was usually too late. Berengar was no scholar, but he was clever in his own right. More importantly, he understood people. It was better to let Phineas think he could be of use, at least for the moment. He didn't want the man getting in his way, and he certainly didn't want to have to kill one of Margolin's guards.

Berengar returned to the inn with his new funds. Iain proved good on his word, and after a quick exchange of coins, Berengar purchased a dapple-gray stallion. Although the horse was accustomed to the plow rather than the heat of battle, it was well built and suitable enough for his purposes. With the matter of the horse settled, Berengar visited Avery's shop to collect his armor, but the tanner was nowhere to be found.

An icy cold wind rushed down from the ominous sky. *Rain's coming.* He returned to the inn and retrieved his cloak. Evander was waiting for him outside when he emerged. "Ready?"

"Aye. Are you sure about this?"

Berengar stared at him hard. "Having second thoughts?"

"No. I gave you my word, and that means something to me."

"Good. Let's go."

Once astride their steeds, the pair left Alúine behind and traveled west until they neared the bog.

Evander brought his horse to a halt. "There it is. Móin Alúin."

Even in the daylight, there was something eerie about the bog. Most of the trees were crooked and bent, deformed by some unseen hand. In contrast to the surrounding fields, the grasses and plants were a sickly pale color.

Evander slid from the saddle and motioned for Berengar to do the same. "Horses grow restless this close to the bog. We go on foot from here."

Berengar dismounted, and they hitched their horses to trees at the edge of Móin Alúin. Fog clung to the path ahead as the pair advanced into the bog. It was dark inside, but enough light made it through the trees that the way forward was visible without the need for torchlight.

Evander nocked an arrow and held his bow at the ready, clearly aware of the dangers lurking within. "There aren't many men brave enough to go hunting ogres, even for coin. Why are you really doing this?"

"The ogre abducted a young woman from Laird Margolin's castle. Keep an eye out for any signs of her when we reach the ogre's lair."

Evander regarded him curiously. "Lady Imogen? What's your interest in her?"

Evidently, word of Imogen's disappearance had spread beyond Blackthorn.

"Margolin sent me to kill the ogre and learn the where-abouts of his niece. She's probably dead already, but the brigands we met seemed convinced otherwise."

He peered through the fog, searching along the path for a sign of his missing weapons. Suddenly, he saw the hag among the shadows, watching him with the same malevolent smile he remembered from his dreams. Berengar's left hand throbbed with pain. *Not again,* he thought, wincing.

"What is it?"

When Berengar looked again at the place where the hag stood, she was gone. "It's nothing."

Evander held out his hand to prevent Berengar from taking another step forward. "We can't go that way. It leads to the swamp, which is too close to the witch's dwelling." He led Berengar through unfamiliar surroundings until they came to a tree where the ground had been recently disturbed.

"There are two sets of prints here," Evander said, looking over the area. "Something was dragged through here—something big."

"My horse, most likely," Berengar muttered, the memory of his battle with the Dullahan fresh in his mind. He saw the marks the Dullahan's whip had left behind on a tree and the impact his stallion made when it landed in the mud. Judging by the trail on the ground leading away from the spot, the ogre had dragged it away.

There it is, he thought as his gaze fell on the place where his battleaxe rested. *Finally.*

He picked up the axe and ran a hand along its surface, as if greeting an old friend. He'd wielded it for so long it felt like a part of him. There were few weapons feared more in the whole of Fál. His sword, a storied blade in its own right, lay a short distance away. The feel of the blade only further stoked his thirst for vengeance.

"Show us the way, Faolán."

Howling winds faded behind them as the wolfhound led them deeper into the bog. The sky continued to darken until storm clouds eclipsed the sun. A foul odor lingered nearby, growing stronger with each step they took.

Berengar eased his sword from its sheath and lowered his voice. "We're close."

Weeds and tall grasses gave way to a clearing ahead, where bones—human and otherwise—blanketed the muddy earth. The scene was vaguely reminiscent of the stories Berengar's mother told him about the dens of greedy cave dragons, but instead of gold and treasure, common trinkets and keepsakes from victims littered the ogre's lair.

The ogre's club lay outside a shallow cavern that extended into the rocky hillside. A charred animal corpse lay beside the soot and ash of a recent fire. The presence of the saddle and saddlebags nearby told him he was looking at what remained of his horse. Berengar scanned the area but saw nothing to indicate Lady Imogen's presence. None of the human remains, which were fully decomposed, could have belonged to Margolin's niece, as she'd vanished only days ago.

The ground shook without warning. The ogre lumbered from the cavern's entrance, and Evander took aim with his bow.

"Not yet." Berengar stepped into the clearing, his axe in one hand and his sword in the other. "Time to finish what we started." He was ready for a fight, even without his armor, and more or less recovered from the beating sustained in his fight with the Dullahan.

The ogre growled—a deep, menacing sound that

would have sent most men running. "You should not have come." Its voice was deep and gravelly, as if carved from the stones jutting out from the hill. A scab ran the length of its forearm where Berengar had wounded it with his axe.

"Where's the girl? What did you do with her?"

The ogre's protruding brow furrowed. "What girl?"

She's not here, Berengar realized. *Maybe she never was.* Imogen's absence raised a new set of questions. If the ogre didn't abduct her, where did she go—and why? Berengar swore and shook his head in anger. Any questions would have to wait for later.

The ogre charged, its club held high. The fury of battle took him, and Berengar rushed to meet it with an angry shout. He slashed across the ogre's side with his sword, ducked under the ogre's club, emerged behind the creature, and lodged his battleaxe deep in its back before ripping the weapon free. The ogre let out a shriek of pain and stumbled. When it spun around to face him, their eyes met, and Berengar grinned at his foe, causing the creature's face to tighten with rage.

The ogre wrapped an oversized hand around a tree and uprooted it from the ground, wielding the club in one hand and the tree in the other. Berengar countered the club with his battleaxe, but the tree caught him squarely across the chest, and he hit the ground hard and tasted blood. When an arrow streaked through the air and hit the ogre in the neck, the ogre hurled the tree at Evander, who was forced to dive away to avoid being struck.

Berengar, already on his feet, threw himself at the monster before it could reach Evander. The ogre was the bigger of the two, but Berengar was angrier, and that anger gave him a mad strength. He attacked in furious tandem with Faolán, cutting and clawing the ogre in turn. He did not relent, and he did not give ground.

His sword found its mark, and the fingers of the ogre's right hand fell away, taking the club with them. The creature dropped to its knees, clutching its mangled hand, and Berengar smote it across the face with his battleaxe, sending skin and blood flying.

"How do you like that, you ugly bastard?" Berengar said, overcome by hate. "It's not so easy when someone hits back, is it?" He hit it again, drawing a fountain of blood from its nostrils. "Stay down, you dumb brute."

As he raised the sword to deliver the killing blow, the muscles in his left arm and hand locked up again. *Not now.* Intense, burning pain shot up his shoulder to his jaw, and the blade dropped from his hand.

The ogre seized the opportunity to tackle him off his feet, and they struggled over possession of his axe's handle until a second arrow from Evander caught the creature in the chest. The ogre staggered toward Evander, who tried and failed to nock another arrow in the time it took the ogre to close the distance between them. It seized Evander and threw him against the cavern's entrance, but before it could bash him against the rocks, Faolán weaved under the creature's legs and ripped out a tendon from its heel. The creature shrieked and dropped Evander, who slid to the ground, unconscious.

Berengar shifted his axe to both hands. "Let's end this."

The ogre turned to face him, and the two sprinted at each other as the ground shook beneath them. They met in a final, violent clash, and Berengar split the ogre's belly in half with his axe, spilling the contents of its abdomen across the mud.

The ogre staggered away and collapsed, blood gushing

from its mouth. Berengar stepped over the dying creature, which dragged itself to the cavern's entrance to die alone, and made his way over to Evander.

"Get back," he said to Faolán, who sniffed at the huntsman's body. "Wake up."

Evander's eyes slowly opened. "What happened?"

"It's over." Berengar stuck out his hand and helped Evander to his feet. "Good work."

Evander's gaze fell on where the ogre had finally fallen still at the cavern's entrance. "You did it." He sounded impressed.

"Easier than killing a troll," Berengar muttered, retrieving his sword. The muscles in his arms had relaxed again, but for how long? If he couldn't find a way to get the hag's curse under control, it would only continue to spread. He heaved his recovered saddle over his shoulders and carried the saddlebags in his arms. "Let's go. Imogen's not here."

Evander looked over his shoulder at the ogre's corpse. "We'll need its head to claim the reward."

One stroke of Berengar's axe cleaved the ogre's head from its body. With his weapons recovered and the ogre slain, one task was complete, but he still needed to learn what had happened to Lady Imogen and deal with the hag's curse. Distant lightning flashed as the riders emerged from Móin Alúin, and for a brief moment, he thought he saw the hag watching him from the bog's entrance.

"Come on." He swung himself onto the saddle, and the pair started on the way back to Alúine.

CHAPTER NINE

SCREAMS GREETED their return to the village.

"What's going on?" Berengar jerked back on the reins, and the stallion readily came to a stop.

"I don't know," Evander replied. "Do you think it's another goblin attack?"

Someone called out for help, and Berengar spotted Iain near the inn, surrounded by a crowd. He recognized several familiar faces among the villagers.

Guess I'd better see what this is about. He slid from the saddle and started toward the inn with Faolán.

Phineas approached the stables and banged on the door. "This is your last chance, Silas! Open up."

"I told you it would come to this," Hirum told Iain. "I warned you to keep him away from my daughter, but no one listened."

Iain ignored him and instead focused his attention on the guards. "Don't do this. I beg of you."

"Fine," Phineas said to Tuck when the door remained closed. "We'll break it down."

Godfrey offered Iain his support. "Silas is not a

murderer. He's just frightened, and you're only making it worse."

"Stay out of this, friar," Phineas retorted, and together the two guards battered the barn door.

Iain noticed Berengar. "You. Thank heavens. It's Silas —they think he murdered Leona."

At that moment, the barn door came crashing down, and Silas fell hard on his backside and landed in the dirt. Blood oozed from a deep wound to his scalp, and his clothes were torn and stained with sweat.

Phineas drew his sword. "You shouldn't have run, halfwit. Now we have to make an example of you." He nodded to Tuck, who seemed to draw his sword only with reluctance.

Silas pleaded for mercy, but his panicked words were barely comprehensible. His malformed arm hung limply at his side while he attempted to use the other as a shield. Even with his handicap, a man of Silas' size might have easily defended himself if he was the brute the others believed he was.

"Stop," Berengar said, drawing the crowd's attention.

"You again," Phineas muttered. "What do you want?"

Berengar trained his gaze on Silas. "Did you hurt Leona?"

Silas shook his head emphatically. "No. She was nice to me. She was my friend."

Berengar remembered the flower Silas had offered Leona when he first arrived in Alúine—a gesture that drew her father's ire. "I know you liked her. Maybe it was an accident. Maybe you wanted to be more than friends and lost your temper."

"I didn't," Silas sputtered, struggling with his words. "I wouldn't."

Berengar stared into his eyes and nodded. "He's telling the truth."

"And I suppose we're to take your word for it, then?" Phineas demanded. "Who the hell do you think you are?"

"I am Esben Berengar, Warden of Fál, here at Laird Margolin's request."

The pronouncement was followed by a few utterances of *the Bear Warden* and *the High Queen's monster* from alarmed villagers in the vicinity. Even those who hadn't recognized him had heard the stories of his deeds.

Phineas' expression wavered as his gaze swept over Berengar's cloak and weapons, though he remained defiant. "I don't believe you. What is a Warden of Fál doing in Alúine?"

"I've just come from Móin Alúin, where I slew the ogre that's been harassing the village."

"I—" The guard's face whitened a shade when he noticed the ogre's head fixed to Berengar's horse's saddle. "In either event, this matter is none of your concern."

Berengar rested his hand on the hilt of his blade. "I'm making it my concern." It didn't surprise him the guards had rushed to judgment in their hurry to catch Leona's killer. He'd seen it many times before. The poor and oppressed had little recourse when it came to the justice meted out by their betters.

"We found a bloody knife among his things. When we tried to ask him about it, the fool fled. He'd been warned to keep away from Leona more than once. What more is there to say?"

"You heard them," Hirum said angrily. "That brute murdered my daughter. I demand justice!"

"No," Berengar replied, his voice almost a growl. "I won't let you put this man to death without evidence. Now put that sword away before I lose my temper." He and the guards faced each other in a tense standoff, with each man waiting to see if the other would back down.

Phineas looked to Tuck for support, but his companion averted his eyes. "You would let Leona's murderer go free?"

The matter of Leona's death was a distraction from the task at hand, and his time was short enough as it was. As always, the innocent suffered while the wicked prospered. It was the way of things. What was one more?

No, he told himself. He wouldn't stand by and let them execute an innocent man. "Fine. I'll find the killer on my own. If it turns out Silas did it, I'll help you hang him myself."

"You should do as he says," Godfrey urged Phineas. "Laird Margolin would be displeased if you killed the wrong man in his name. Just imagine the effect it would have on local morale."

In the face of no support, Phineas was left with no recourse but to put his sword away, though it was more than evident he hated having to back down. "Have it your way. In the meantime, Silas will remain in our custody. You have until the end of the day to find the killer—otherwise, the brute hangs."

"You can't be serious." Hirum trained his anger on the guards. "This is an outrage." He glared at Berengar before storming away.

"It's going to be all right, my friend," Iain said to Silas after helping him from the ground.

Rose inspected Silas' bloody scalp. "This wound needs to be stitched. His ribs are broken. He needs care."

"You can tend to him at the jail," Phineas informed her. "Take him, Tuck."

"Wait," Berengar said before the guards left with their prisoner in tow. "I didn't kill the ogre alone." He gestured to Evander. "He helped. I expect he'll be fairly compensated for it."

"Take it up with Laird Margolin," Phineas said. "We don't have that kind of gold on hand."

"Then find some," Berengar insisted. "Or I'll make sure Margolin hears of it."

"As you wish," Phineas replied through clenched teeth. "Come with us, huntsman, and we'll see to your reward."

"What about your share?" Evander asked Berengar.

"I'm not doing this for coin. Take my share and give it to Rose as thanks for her help when she found me in the bog."

Evander held out his hand as a sign of friendship. "Thank you."

Berengar hesitated before shaking his hand, and Evander went after Rose and the guards.

"We'd better go inside," said Iain, watching the crowd.

The inn lay empty, and Berengar guessed the patrons had been drawn outside by the commotion.

"I can't believe I had Warden Berengar under my nose this whole time and didn't recognize him." Iain shook his head at the thought. "The tales they tell about you…"

Berengar cut him off. He knew the stories better than anyone, and he wasn't particularly fond of them. "Tell me what happened."

Iain sat at one of the tables, and Berengar settled across from him. "There's not much to tell. The guards came to talk to Silas and go through his things. I'd wager Hirum put them up to it. When they found the knife, Silas panicked and ran. I swear to you, he never laid a hand on the girl."

"Then where did the knife come from?"

Iain shrugged. "It looked like an ordinary kitchen knife to me. It wasn't one of ours—I'm sure of it. Silas and I have been in and out all morning. Anyone could have hidden it among his things in that time. It was no secret Silas was smitten with Leona. She was a kind girl. I don't know why anyone would hurt her."

Berengar always found such sentiments naive. People hurt others for all sorts of reasons, and sometimes no reason at all. "I don't suppose you can vouch for his whereabouts last night? It would make my job a lot easier."

"I'm afraid not. I turned in early and left him to sweep up after me."

"Then I'll ask around and see what I can find out. If Leona's killer entered the inn to plant the knife among Silas' things, someone might have seen."

Iain let out a sigh of relief. "It appears I am in your debt yet again. If Hirum had his way, the guards would have hanged Silas without another thought."

"Phineas doesn't seem like a man who likes taking orders, yet he hangs on Hirum's every word. Why?"

"Hirum is a wealthy man—by our standards, at least. He's wealthy enough to influence the guards, at any rate. His wife died some years back, leaving him an angry and bitter man."

"What was his relationship with his daughter like?" Berengar asked. "When I saw them together, he acted possessive."

"He had a reputation for being strict with her, yes. Hirum rarely let Leona out of his sight. Still, whatever his faults, he cared for his daughter."

Berengar pushed away from the table. "That's enough for now. I should get started." He reached for the door when a thought occurred to him. "In the meantime, there's another way you might be able to help me."

"Name it," Iain said.

"Laird Margolin sent me to the bog to find his niece. I

thought the ogre abducted her, but now I'm not so sure. The brigands I met earlier certainly seemed interested in her. Do you know anything on the subject?"

A puzzled expression came over the innkeeper's face. "Lady Imogen? Come to think of it, I have heard rumors she vanished from Blackthorn, but nothing beyond that. Although…" He trailed off, deep in thought.

"What?" Berengar asked, interested.

"Varun O'Shiridan, one of the village elders, does a fair amount of trade at the castle. I believe he's had dealings with Lady Imogen in the past. You might want to hurry if you plan to speak with him. When he was in here last night, I heard him say he'd be leaving for Blackthorn earlier than usual on account of the weather."

"Thanks." It wasn't much, but at least it was a start.

Thunder sounded for the first time as he departed the inn. The crowd that had assembled to watch Silas' arrest had already dispersed. Everywhere he looked, villagers worked to finish their chores and tasks before the impending storm. Some hurriedly plucked dry garments from clotheslines while others herded animals into pens and barns, all while the wind howled and raged with the promise of worse to come.

Berengar led his horse to the stables and secured it in a stall before delving into the saddlebags and withdrawing a piece of parchment, on which he hastily scrawled a brief letter to accompany the ogre's head to Laird Margolin.

I trust you'll find this gift to your liking.
The ogre didn't take your niece. If she lives, I'll find her.

. . .

"That was noble of you," Father Godfrey said when he emerged from the stables. "What you did for Silas. You're not the man I imagined you would be, Warden Berengar."

"You don't know a thing about me." Berengar started on his way, leaving Godfrey to follow.

"Perhaps not. We aren't always what we appear—I should know that better than most." Godfrey chuckled, as if amused by some private joke. "I wanted to offer my help with your investigation."

Berengar fought the urge to laugh. "You're unusual for a friar, I'll give you that."

"Don't confuse us with priests," Godfrey said. "I care about people, not just souls. This world can be a hell of its own, and we all must do our part to make it a better place."

"If you really want to help, you can start by telling me what you've learned of the Dullahan."

"Not much. Even folk who know the stories don't like to speak of him, as they fear he will overhear. Hopefully, Saroise will be able to tell us more. I'm sending word to her with Varun O'Shiridan."

"That's the man I'm headed to see," Berengar said. "You can show me the way."

Godfrey raised an eyebrow but chose not to pry. "From what I'm told, with the exception of Lucas—the boy you rescued at Móin Alúin—all the missing are young women. Perhaps Leona was yet another of these victims."

"It wasn't the Dullahan. Leona knew her killer. It was a crime of passion."

Godfrey's brow furrowed. Something clearly troubled him. "Perhaps I can help after all. You see, Leona was to be married."

"Married?"

"Aye. To Maddox, the blacksmith's son."

Berengar searched the friar's face for answers. "How do you know of this?"

"Leona asked me to perform the ceremony. She was afraid her father wouldn't approve of the match, so she wanted it kept secret."

"What happened?"

"She came to me in tears to cancel the wedding. She wouldn't tell me why."

That explains why she looked so sad when I first saw her, Berengar thought. "How well do you know her intended?"

"Only by reputation, though the lad seems to be well-liked. Why?"

"Maybe he didn't take rejection well. Maybe he tried to persuade Leona to change her mind and things got heated. After we finish with Varun, we'll find him and get to the truth of it."

Godfrey stopped in front of a modest hut near the heart of the village. From the look of things, they'd arrived just in time, as a loaded wagon was waiting outside. It was a sign of just how frightened the villagers were by Laird Margolin that Varun would risk traveling through the approaching tempest to reach Blackthorn. Godfrey knocked on the door with his wooden hand, and hushed voices came from inside. For a moment no one answered. As Godfrey raised his hand to knock again, the door slowly cracked open, revealing a rotund man with a round face and a long, flowing beard.

"Come back later." When Varun caught sight of Godfrey, his expression brightened immediately. "Oh, Friar Godfrey—it's just you."

"It's good to see you again, Varun. This is Warden

Berengar. He's come to Alúine at Laird Margolin's request."

Varun's smile faded immediately at the mention of Margolin, and he stared intently at Berengar with obvious unease. "Where are my manners? Do come inside, the both of you."

"Wait here," Berengar ordered Faolán before entering.

The floorboards groaned under their host's considerable weight. Candles illuminated the interior of Varun's home in the absence of sunlight. Each window was shuttered to keep out wind and rain.

"Coleen, bring our guests something to drink," Varun called to his wife. He reached for his cloak, which hung nearby on a chair, and fastened it around his shoulders. "What can I do for you? I'm leaving for Castle Blackthorn soon, but I'll help you if I'm able."

There was something awkward in Varun's manner that suggested he was uncomfortable with Berengar's presence in his house. Such behavior wasn't all that unusual— Berengar was often an unwelcome guest—but worth noting nonetheless.

Godfrey reached into his satchel and passed Varun a rolled-up piece of parchment. "When you arrive at the castle, I'd like you to deliver this message to Saroise the bard. It's for her eyes only."

"Understood," Varun said as his wife poured water from a pitcher into two cups. "And you, Warden Berengar?"

When Berengar took a cup from Coleen, he noticed two girls spying from the next room. The younger of the pair was barely on the cusp of adolescence, but the other —a fair-haired girl who watched him keenly—was an adult in her own right. It occurred to Berengar that perhaps the family had another reason for keeping their windows shuttered, given that the young woman was roughly the same age as the others who went missing.

Varun followed his gaze. "These are my daughters, Keely and Oriana. You'll have to forgive them for prying. It's not every day a Warden of Fál walks through our door. Tell me, does your business have something to do with Laird Margolin?"

Berengar, more than used to a few stares on account of his face, turned his attention back to Varun. "Aye. Margolin believed an ogre abducted his niece. I tracked the beast to Móin Alúin and killed it."

"I don't understand," Varun said, confused.

"I didn't find Imogen at the ogre's lair. I think she's still out there somewhere. The innkeeper at the Green Flagon tells me you're acquainted with her."

"I am. Lady Imogen has been good to us." Varun gestured to his daughter Keely. "When my youngest fell ill, Lady Imogen had the castle alchemist tend to her. Keely would have died if not for Imogen's generosity."

Like many of Margolin's subjects, Varun was clearly loyal to Imogen. If she was in trouble, she might seek out someone who could be trusted to help her. "Have you seen or heard of her recently? It's important I find her soon. I think she's mixed up in danger of some kind."

Varun looked at him for a prolonged interval before shaking his head. "Wherever she is, it isn't here. If Lady Imogen was in Alúine, someone would have seen her. A noble lady would attract attention in a place like this." He glanced quickly in his daughters' direction before looking away. "What do you want with her?"

"Laird Margolin asked me to bring her back to Black-thorn, and that's what I intend to do." Berengar set the empty cup aside, and Godfrey did the same.

"As I've said, I haven't seen her." Varun started toward the door, leaving them to follow him outside.

It was appearing more likely than ever Imogen was still alive, a prospect raising even more questions. If the ogre didn't take her, what happened to her? Whatever the truth, if Imogen was out there somewhere, he needed to find her before the brigands did.

"Is there anything else I can help you with?" asked Varun, who was loading the wagon with his back to them. "I really must be going soon."

"Aye," Berengar answered as Varun's daughter Oriana emerged from the hut. "I want you to take the ogre's head with you to the castle."

Although he doubted Margolin would be satisfied until his niece was returned, the head might at least persuade him to uphold his side of their bargain and keep what happened in Kildare quiet. He hadn't forgotten why he was doing Margolin's bidding in the first place.

Varun winced at the mention of the ogre, as if superstitious that traveling with a monster's head might bring misfortune.

"I assure you, you'll be well compensated for your efforts," Berengar said.

"I can help him, father," Oriana volunteered. "I've never seen an ogre before."

Varun looked at her with hesitation, appearing reluctant to leave her in Berengar's company unattended, before finally relenting. "Very well. But hurry—the storm's coming soon."

"If it's all right with you, I'd like to discuss something with Varun in private," Godfrey said.

Berengar merely shrugged in response.

Oriana followed him back to the stables. "How did one

of the High Queen's wardens come to be in the employ of Laird Margolin?"

Berengar kept walking. "Hasn't your father told you it's impolite to pry into the affairs of strangers?"

Oriana ignored the remark. "Whatever Margolin's promised you, you can't trust him."

Berengar unstrapped the ogre's head from the saddle and stuffed it into a sack. "What would a girl like yourself know of Margolin?"

"I've accompanied my father to Castle Blackthorn many times before. Laird Margolin is an evil man. You would do well to be wary of him."

He dusted off his hands and looked at her. There was something bolder about her than the other villagers he'd encountered. "I'll take it under advisement." He expected that to settle the matter, but still he felt the weight of her gaze upon him. "Got something else on your mind?"

She accepted the bloody sack without reluctance. "When you were at the castle, did you encounter Saroise?"

"Aye."

"Did you speak with her? Was she safe?" Though conversational, her tone betrayed worry.

"She was. Is she a friend of yours?"

"Saroise did me a great service." Oriana stopped speaking and looked around suddenly, as if mindful of being observed. "I just remembered I have errands father asked me to attend to before his departure. I must go."

Berengar followed her gaze and saw Avery watching them intently from across the road. "Wait." He delved into his cloak and handed her the message he'd written earlier. "Give this to your father. Tell him to deliver it to Laird Margolin for me."

Oriana took the message and hurried off without another word.

"Warden Berengar," Avery called out as he approached. "I finished mending your armor. I should have known armor of its quality could only belong to someone with a famous name."

"Word travels fast." He took the armor and looked it over. "Good work." For a humble village tanner, Avery had done an admirable job at repairing it.

"I was Laird Cairrigan's tanner before the castle fell. Iain tells me you're searching for Lady Imogen. Any luck finding her?"

Berengar narrowed his gaze. Avery was curious for a simple tanner. "Not yet. Why so interested?"

"I heard a rumor a stranger showed up at the church a few nights back. Well, not just any stranger—a woman, and a noble at that."

"What happened to her?"

"That's just it—no one knows what happened to her after that."

Godfrey. Did the friar know more than he was telling?

He peered through the thinning crowd and saw Oriana stop outside the baker's shop, still carrying the letter he gave her. She checked to make sure no one was looking before unfurling his letter to Margolin and reading its contents. Berengar frowned. Apart from a man of the cloth like Godfrey, he doubted there were more than a handful of literate villagers in the whole of Alúine, if that. It seemed strange that Varun's daughter would be among them.

As he watched, Oriana tore the letter to shreds, lifted her hood, and went on her way.

CHAPTER TEN

CLAD IN ARMOR ONCE MORE, Berengar trekked down the dirt road that led through Alúine. Most of the villagers had already taken refuge indoors. Storm clouds from Móin Alúin descended on the village, leaving the darkening sky caught somewhere between gray and black. He needed to solve Leona's murder quickly so he could return his attention to other matters.

At least the shops and stands were mostly clustered together, so he didn't have to go far. It was always easier to find someone in a rural settlement than in a city, where it might take him half an hour just to walk from one district to the next. He didn't like people much to begin with, and a smaller population was just one reason he preferred towns and villages to cities, even if he favored the road over both. Berengar had come of age in a village not unlike Alúine. It wasn't a place he ever planned to return to. Sometimes the past was better left in the past.

"Keep up."

"Right behind you," Godfrey muttered, hurrying to match his pace. "That's it, just ahead."

Although Berengar could have found the blacksmith's forge on his own, he wanted to keep a close eye on Godfrey. He hadn't yet confronted the friar with what he'd learned from Avery. Berengar made it a habit not to trust anyone, no matter how they appeared. He'd sensed from the beginning Godfrey was a man with secrets. If Avery's story was true, it was possible the friar was somehow involved in Lady Imogen's disappearance, but to what end?

"You there," he said to the blacksmith. Warmth radiated off the cooling forge. "I want to talk to you."

The blacksmith scowled at the sight of him. "We're closed on account of the storm. You'll have to come back later."

"It's not your business I'm interested in. It's your son, Maddox."

The blacksmith wiped sweat from his brow with a cloth and crossed his arms. "What do you want with him?"

"I understand he was close to Leona."

"What of it?" the blacksmith snapped. "Working for Hirum, are you? If you've come to tell me that a blacksmith's boy wasn't good enough for his precious daughter, you can bugger off."

"I'm looking into Leona's murder on behalf of the guards."

"Maddox is a good boy. He's done nothing wrong."

"Where is he? I don't want to have to ask again."

"He's not here," the blacksmith said. "I haven't seen him all day. He's probably grieving somewhere."

He's protecting him. Berengar put his hand on the hilt of his blade. "You sure about that?"

The blacksmith's gaze darted to the door to his shop. The glance only lasted an instant, but it was enough to tell Berengar where the son was hiding. He pushed the blacksmith out of the way in a sudden motion. The door fell open under his weight, and he barged inside, sword drawn. Faolán barked loudly, alerting him to another presence as a young man climbed out the window before Berengar could intercept him.

"Blast it. After him, Faolán!"

Having failed to notice Friar Godfrey waiting outside, Maddox didn't get far. Godfrey struck him across the chest with his walking stick, and he went down hard. Faolán pinned him to the ground before he could recover his footing.

The blacksmith grasped at Berengar's cloak. "Stop. He's my son."

Berengar shoved him aside and seized Maddox by his long leather apron. "Talk."

"I'd do as he says, if I were you," Godfrey said in a jovial tone. "This one tends to get his way." He aimed a wink in Berengar's direction.

"Leona," Berengar demanded. "Did you kill her?"

Maddox stopped struggling at once, and all the fight went out of him. "You think I murdered her? I loved her, you bastard."

"If you're so innocent, why run?"

Maddox stared at him with contempt. "After what happened to Silas? Everyone knows he didn't do it, including the guards."

Berengar tossed him to the ground. "If you didn't kill her, who did?"

"If I knew that, I'd kill the man that did it myself."

"Word is you and Leona were to be married."

Maddox bowed his head, and his lip quivered. "Aye."

"But she called it off—why?"

Maddox allowed his father to help him into a sitting position. "On account of her father. We tried to keep our engagement a secret, but somehow Hirum found out about us and forced her to cancel the wedding."

"Leona left her home to meet someone the night she was killed," Berengar said. "Was it you?"

"No. Hirum wouldn't even let me talk to her. I never even got to say goodbye." By the last words, the young man's eyes were red and misty. "Are you going to kill me or not?"

Berengar returned his sword to its sheath. "Not yet. If I find out you've lied to me, or if you try to run again, I'll break both your legs—and that's just for starters." He whistled to Faolán and gestured for Godfrey to follow. "We're finished here."

"Where to now?"

"The jail. I still have a few more questions that need answering."

"Only a few?" Godfrey didn't bother hiding his confusion.

"Maddox told me what I wanted to know." Berengar kept his answer intentionally vague. He had his suspicions as to the identity of Leona's killer, but he needed to be sure.

They walked in solitude, though Berengar caught more than a few villagers watching from their windows as he passed. Varun's wagon had vanished, suggesting the man was on his way to Blackthorn. It was obvious that Varun had been hiding something from him during their discussion of Imogen. He thought again of Varun's mysterious daughter, Oriana, and her peculiar interest in Laird Margolin's affairs. Try as he might, he couldn't think of a reason why she had torn up his letter to Margolin.

The whole blasted village is full of secrets, he mused. He should have forced Varun to talk when he had the chance.

The guards were busy delivering a beating to Gnish outside the jail. Gnish hissed and thrashed about, but stripped of his armor, the hobgoblin appeared rather small and helpless. Tuck held him fast as Phineas struck the captive across the face. After several successive strikes, Gnish's strength gave way, and his knees buckled. Scrapes and bruises covered his skin, and his right eye was nearly swollen shut.

"Scum." Phineas spat on the hobgoblin and kicked him in the side for good measure.

"What the hell are you doing?" Godfrey demanded. His habitual smile faded, lost to anger.

Phineas wiped the hobgoblin's blood from his fist. "What's it look like?"

Godfrey hurried to Gnish's side and propped him up. "For God's sake, you're killing him!"

Phineas scoffed at him. "Not until he tells us where the others are hiding, and maybe not even then. Laird Margolin might want to play with him first."

Godfrey ignored the guard and reached into his satchel to retrieve his drinking horn. He pried the top from the horn and lifted it to Gnish's bloodied lips. "Here. Drink this." It was an unusual act, as few men of the cloth would deign to allow a nonhuman creature to share their water. According to the Church of Leinster, such creatures were lesser beings. "Monsters, the lot of you. And the man you serve."

"That thing is the monster, in case you've forgotten," Phineas retorted. "And friar or not, I'd be careful who you insult."

Tuck winced uncomfortably at the threat and took a swig from his flask.

Gnish gagged on the water, which spilled down his chin. His eyes remained fixed on Berengar, and his voice came out as a hoarse croak. "You're him. Berengar Goblin-Bane. I should have let you die."

It wasn't surprising that Gnish had recognized him, now that he was again outfitted with his cloak and weapons. Berengar had a bloody reputation across Fál, but nowhere more so than with goblins and their kin. Goblins were more plentiful in the north, and he fought them often in his youth. He'd killed so many over the years he'd lost count. There wasn't a goblin across the five realms that hadn't heard his name.

"They're just doing their job," he said to Godfrey. "It's the way the world works."

Godfrey just glared at him. "For men like you, perhaps."

Berengar turned away and pulled Phineas aside. "A word." He lowered his voice to keep from being overheard. "This isn't working. This one will die before he turns on his tribe."

"What's it to you?" Phineas asked. "I thought you had your hands full at the moment."

"The hobgoblins took something of mine, and I want it back. I can help you find their encampment, but you have to do it my way."

Phineas regarded him shrewdly. "What exactly are you proposing?"

"Let him escape. My wolfhound has the hobgoblin's scent. Throw the creature back into his cell, but give him the means to free himself. When he goes to rejoin his kin, we'll track him to the others."

Phineas nodded in approval of the plan. "Agreed. I'll assemble a larger force to subdue them. I'm sure the huntsman will be up for it." He held out his hand, which Berengar ignored.

"There's something else. I want the knife you found among Silas' belongings."

"What for?" Puzzle showed on the guard's face.

"Leona's killer."

"Fine. Speak in riddles if it suits you, as long as I can count on you against the rest of those vermin." Phineas led him indoors, leaving Godfrey to follow.

Inside the jail, Rose had almost finished tending to Silas' injuries while Evander waited at her side. A pouch of coins hung from his belt—likely his reward for the ogre's death.

"How is he?" Godfrey asked when Phineas went to retrieve the knife.

Rose glowered at Phineas behind his back. "He's just lucky the guards didn't bash his brains in."

Godfrey examined Silas' bandaged ribs. "This is fine work. Are you a healer?"

She lowered her gaze. "Not anymore."

"There are several villagers suffering from plague in need of care," Godfrey said. "There is little I can do for them, but perhaps you…"

"I'm sorry. I've been away too long as it is. I must return home."

"You shouldn't ride out in this weather," Evander said. "What's one more day?"

"I implore you," Godfrey said. "Even if you could only ease their passage."

Rose shook her head and let out a resigned sigh. "Fine, but you'll have to gather the herbs and ingredients I require." When she turned to Berengar, her expression softened. "Silas told me that you gave him the coins to buy a new horse for me. Thank you."

"I owed you. As far as I'm concerned, we're square."

Phineas returned with the knife and handed it to Berengar. He took it and turned it over in his hand. The weapon, which was still stained with Leona's blood, wasn't some dagger made for killing. Instead, it had the look of an ordinary kitchen knife. He pocketed the knife and started toward the door.

"And just where are you going?" Phineas called after him.

"There's something I need to see to. Alone. Wait for my return."

Berengar left the guards to their interrogation and set out on the path from the jail with only Faolán for company. He made his way to a home on the outskirts of Alúine, far removed from the huts packed near the village's heart.

Hirum answered when he knocked on the door. "You again. What's this about?"

"I'm just here to talk about your daughter." Berengar glanced over his shoulder as a flash of lightning shot through the heavens. "Mind if I come inside? Storm could hit at any minute."

Hirum hesitated before allowing him entrance. "Very well. Just make it quick, and leave that hound outside."

Faint candlelight revealed an abundance of well-made furniture.

Iain wasn't lying when he spoke of Hirum's wealth. "This is an impressive home, especially for a place like Alúine."

"Can I offer you bread and wine?" Hirum's tone wasn't particularly cordial, but whatever else he was, he was a man of Leinster, where tradition dictated showing hospitality to one's guests.

"Aye. I haven't had time to eat since killing that ogre. I've been too busy tracking down leads."

Hirum led him to a spacious dining hall. "Have a seat."

Berengar took his place at the table, and his host disappeared into the next room before returning with a goblet, which he promptly filled with wine before setting a plate of bread before him.

"Are you any closer to finding my daughter's killer? Assuming the halfwit didn't do it, that is."

"I believe I am. There were a few more questions I wanted to ask you first."

"I've already told you everything I know," Hirum said with barely restrained anger. "I tire of being made to relive my daughter's death. Do you know what it's like to lose your only child? Of course you don't."

Berengar stared hard at him, stone-faced. "You said Leona went out alone the night she was killed. Do you have any idea where she went?"

"No—as I said before."

"Was she acting strangely in the days before her death? Worried by something, perhaps?"

"Not to my knowledge."

"I understand Leona wished to wed Maddox, the blacksmith's son," Berengar said. "Was it possible that was who she was planning to meet?"

"You don't think that he killed her, do you? I wouldn't put it past him. The lad has a greedy look about him."

"But you did put a stop to the union. Why?"

Hirum slammed his fist down hard, rattling the table. "Do you think I would allow her to throw her future away on some lowly blacksmith's boy? My girl? Leona was my daughter—mine." The anger seemed to fade away as quickly as it had manifested, and he put his head in his hands. "Now I've lost her too."

"From all accounts, Leona was a good and kind girl. I can see why you cared for her so deeply."

"When my wife died, she was all I had left."

Berengar reached for the bread. "A knife, if you will—to cut the bread." He continued speaking after his host went into the next room to fetch the knife. "That's why you prevented her marriage, wasn't it?"

"I don't catch your meaning."

"It's why you were angered when anyone showed interest in her. You were afraid she would leave you, and you'd be alone. It's why you killed her."

He heard Hirum stop moving, and silence fell over the room.

"She tried to leave, but you wouldn't let her. You probably didn't mean to hurt her, but you lost your temper. She was dead before you realized you had stabbed her, again and again."

Hirum's voice was quiet. "You're mad."

"You thought you could take advantage of all the missing girls to cover your tracks. Hell, you probably didn't need the guards in your pocket to convince them she was killed in a monster attack, when really it was just an old-fashioned murder."

"Get out of my home."

Berengar remained where he sat, with his back to Hirum, even as his host's footsteps sounded behind him. "It was easy to pin the crime on Silas, although if I had to guess, I'd say someone spotted you entering or leaving the Green Flagon."

Hirum's voice came from directly behind him. "You shouldn't have poked your nose in my business."

Berengar's hand shot up and seized Hirum's forearm, pinning it like a vise. A knife like the one used to kill Leona fell from Hirum's grip as Berengar's chair crashed to the floorboards. He clamped a hand over Hirum's mouth and slammed him against the wall.

"I already killed an ogre today. Did you really think I'd be afraid of you?"

Hirum broke down. "I didn't mean to. It was the hag—

she made me do it. She came to me in my dreams every night, telling me Leona was going to leave me. I couldn't take it anymore."

Berengar frowned. "The hag?"

"Aye." Hirum started to sob. "I made a deal with her years ago. She promised to make me rich. I even sacrificed my wife to her in return, but it wasn't enough. She wanted more."

Berengar stared at the wretched man across from him with contempt. The hag might have influenced him, but it was Hirum's hand that held the knife. The anger took hold of him again, and he threw Hirum across the room.

"You murdered your own daughter, you piece of filth."

Hirum pleaded with him with his eyes. "Do it. Kill me."

Berengar shook his head. "No. Killing you would be an act of mercy. I'm not feeling merciful at the moment. You killed your daughter. Now live with it." Ignoring the throbbing pain in his left hand, Berengar reached into his pocket, withdrew the knife Hirum had used to commit the murder, and dropped the bloody knife on the floor at Hirum's feet. "Or don't. The choice is yours."

Hirum slowly reached for the knife. Berengar left the man to his fate and went outside, where Friar Godfrey approached with Lucas, the boy he'd rescued from the Dullahan.

CHAPTER ELEVEN

"WHAT HAPPENED IN THERE?" Godfrey asked, unease written across his face.

Before Berengar could answer, his fist and arm seized up with spasms so intense he thought his bones might break. He tried his best to hide his discomfort, but the pain spread across his chest, and his heartbeat slowed.

Godfrey lowered his voice. "Are you all right?"

"I'll be fine." Berengar gritted his teeth and waited for the pain to subside as it had before. The attacks were becoming more frequent, which wasn't a good sign. "Leona's killer is dead."

Godfrey glanced past him to Hirum's open door. "You mean to say…"

"Aye."

A light rain began falling from above.

"There's nothing to see here," Berengar told an observer. "Go back to your home."

The man refused to leave. "You killed him, didn't you? Murderer."

"Go and fetch the guards then," Berengar replied.

"The murderer is the one they'll find inside. You might tell them to release Silas while you're at it." Berengar returned to Godfrey. "Let's get out of the rain."

They walked to the stables and took refuge from the elements.

"What's with the lad?" Berengar asked.

"Lucas sought me out at the church," Godfrey answered on behalf of the lad, who clung to his robes. "He said he wanted to help."

"No need to be afraid," Berengar said to Lucas. "I helped you before, remember?" There was no sign of the lad's protective mother, who had prevented them from talking with him the day before.

"Does your mother know you're here?"

Lucas shook his head.

"Speak up, lad. Tell me about the headless rider. What did he want with you?"

"I don't know," Lucas said shyly.

Godfrey crouched low and smiled to reassure the boy. "Why don't we start at the beginning? What were you doing at the bog?"

Lucas looked away, refusing to meet either man's gaze. "I ran away."

"There are better places than a cursed bog to run to," Berengar said.

"I went to the hill first," Lucas explained. "I thought I could hide there. That was when I saw them."

Berengar exchanged a glance with Godfrey. "Saw who?"

Thunder bellowed louder than before, and Lucas shuddered, frightened. "The girl the bad man hurt."

"What bad man?" Berengar asked. "What did he look like?"

"I didn't see his face. It was covered by a hood."

Godfrey laid a comforting hand on Lucas' shoulder. "I know you're afraid, but do you think you can show us where you saw this man? It's very important. Besides, the warden won't let anything happen to you."

Lucas trained his gaze on Berengar, as if unsure whether or not to trust him. "Promise?"

"Aye. I give you my word." Whatever other oaths he had made, that one at least he planned to keep.

The pledge was enough for Lucas. After saddling his horse, Berengar borrowed Evander's mare, which occupied the next stall, for the friar's use. They emerged from the stables on horseback, with Lucas riding with Godfrey. The rains intensified as they set out from Alúine, but the horses remained steady despite the raging storm. To the west loomed the great hill, illuminated by flashes of lightning. At Lucas' direction, they steered their horses uphill, past the place where Hirum had concealed Leona's body.

Once the horses reached the peak, the riders dismounted to explore the area on foot. Crows watched from their perches as Berengar and the others pushed their way through the brush. There was something unsettling about the hill. He felt it in his bones. He sensed that the answers to his questions about the events that transpired the night he came to Móin Alúin were close.

Lucas kept to Berengar's shadow, unwilling to stray beyond their sight. Whatever the lad encountered previously had spooked him, and it wasn't just the headless rider.

"What was that back there?" Godfrey asked him. "With your arm?"

"I told you before. It's nothing."

"And I suppose those veins on your neck are nothing too."

Berengar peeled back his armor to discover the gray

and black discoloration had spread across his torso and now crept up his neck. He swore under his breath and showed Godfrey the nail lodged in his left hand. "It's a curse—the hag's doing." He tried again to pry the nail free, but the hag's magic anchored it in place.

"What sort of curse? I've heard a great deal from the villagers about the hag and her curses. Perhaps yours can be lifted."

Berengar briefly recounted the symptoms he'd been experiencing and relayed everything he remembered about his encounter with the hag. He could almost hear the hag's distorted voice in his ear.

Your heart is stone, and stone you will become.

"She wants a sacrifice of some sort. If I don't find it before tomorrow night, the curse will claim my life."

Godfrey took a moment to consider his words. "Have you tried finding a magician to break the curse?"

"There are no magicians left in Leinster. The purges saw to that."

"There's one in Munster, to the south. King Mór's court magician is said to be young, but the kingdom boasts one of the most impressive libraries in Fál. Cashel is far from here, but you might make it in time."

Berengar had no intention of running. "I have unfinished business here."

"You could also attempt to bring the hag what she's asked for, though there's nothing to say she'll live up to her end of the bargain. The way I see it, your only other recourse is to kill her, and I'd wager she's not so easily killed." Godfrey hesitated, as if a new idea occurred to him. "The hag said you are ruled by rage and hate. It might be that giving in to either brings on these attacks. The next time you're faced with such a choice, why not prove her wrong? Maybe it would forestall the spread of the curse."

Berengar chose his path a long time ago and had walked it ever since. "I hurt people. It's what I do." He felt no shame in it. Fál needed men like him, who weren't afraid to make the hard choices and dirty their hands so others could live in peace. Besides, anger was all he had. If he let it go, there would be nothing but hollowness in its place.

Lucas pointed out a grove ahead. "There."

"Stay behind me." Berengar advanced with his sword drawn, just in case.

The trees bore the brunt of the storm, shielding them from the worst of the wind and rain. Branches waved at them in the weak light, inviting their entrance. They were alone, at least as far as Berengar could tell. Ash and soot licked his boots, carried by a stream of rainwater. He followed the stream to where a stack of kindling lay beside the remains of a fire. *Someone was here.*

He noticed a series of strange markings etched into the trees. "You recognize these?"

Godfrey traced the carving with his hand. "They look like pagan symbols to me."

Berengar spotted a stone pillar through the rain, just past the trees. Beneath the pillar rested a weathered slab with markings similar to those carved on the trees. Lightning flashed when Berengar put a hand on the wet stone, and the illumination revealed blood smeared across the surface. He knelt down and picked up a frayed rope from the muddy earth. *Someone was bound here.* "Lucas, you said there was a girl?"

Lucas held Godfrey's hand for reassurance. "She was tied to the table. The bad man had a dagger in his hand."

The man in the hood. "Tell me about this man."

"I didn't understand what he said. He spoke in a strange tongue. When I tried to get a better look, he saw me and sent the headless rider after me. I ran to the bog, but it followed."

Faolán barked from beside a charred set of skeletal remains a short distance away.

This isn't a table, he realized. *It's an altar.* The killing had all the markings of a ritual sacrifice.

"Do you remember the murdered couple we found at the farm?" Godfrey asked. "I think we know what became of their daughter after the Dullahan abducted her. He brought her here to be sacrificed. Probably the other girls too."

"Aye, but who's sacrificing them, and why?"

Berengar had assumed the hag controlled the Dullahan. Instead, it appeared the Dullahan answered to the mysterious individual in the hood. The hag was aware of the sacrifices, since she'd asked him to bring one to her, but her involvement with the hooded figure was unclear.

Godfrey studied the pillar after another flash of lightning. Another mark was etched into the stone. "Or to whom. Look at this."

"I recognize this symbol." It matched one he'd seen on the forest shrine during the goblin hunt.

"It's the mark of Balor, King of the Fomorians. Whoever commands the Dullahan must be sacrificing the girls' souls to him."

That must be where the sluagh come from. The poor things were cursed to wander the land in search of their souls.

"There was a cult of Balor here, but it was stamped out long ago," Godfrey said.

"Perhaps someone is trying to revive it."

For a friar who claimed to wander Leinster, Godfrey seemed to know a lot about the immediate area and its history. Godfrey, dressed in friar's robes, also wore a hood. There was clearly more to him than there appeared on the surface. That didn't make him a killer, but he bore watching nonetheless.

"We should leave," Godfrey said. "The boy is frightened."

Berengar agreed. There was nothing more the hill could tell them, and he had other matters to attend to.

G odfrey volunteered to show Lucas home when they arrived in Alúine. After returning the horses to their stalls, Berengar made his way to the jail, where the guards waited with a group of villagers armed for battle. The door to Gnish's cell lay ajar, and the hobgoblin was nowhere in sight. Silas too was gone. The guards must have realized their mistake when they discovered Hirum's self-inflicted wounds.

"Where's Evander?" he asked, surprised the huntsman was not among them.

"He said he has somewhere else to be tonight," Phineas explained. "We've enough men for the job without him, especially with the Bloody Red Bear fighting alongside us."

It struck him as odd that Evander would turn down the chance to earn more coin. Then again, when he borrowed Evander's horse earlier, he had noticed some supplies in the stall. *Maybe he's going somewhere.* Had Rose finally agreed to start a new life with him, or did Evander have another destination in mind? In the end, it didn't matter. Evander's plans weren't his concern. It was time to reclaim the stolen thunder rune before it fell into more dangerous hands. He lingered at the back of the room as Phineas addressed the hunting party.

"The goblins and their kin have plagued our lands for

too long. They've raided our towns and villages, stolen our cattle and horses, and murdered our friends and families. Even Laird Margolin's niece lost her parents to the vermin.

"Tonight, we strike a blow for Leinster! Tonight, we show the monsters that only humanity has the divine right to rule! In the name of Laird Margolin—in the name of the church—we will stamp out the race of goblins in Leinster once and for all!"

Berengar's arms remained folded across his chest as the men raised their weapons and cheered, ready for blood. "Follow the scent, Faolán."

Faolán sniffed the hobgoblin's cell, bolted from the jail, and sprinted south. The others marched toward the forest, their oil-soaked torches glowing amid the downpour. The wolfhound led them ever deeper into the dense forest, until at last the trail turned north and stopped at a ledge looking over the land below. Rain trickled down Berengar's hood as he stared down at the hobgoblins' hideaway, which lay just beyond the forest, far removed from civilization.

The encampment slid into view as they crept toward the treeline. The storm masked their movements. The full extent of the hobgoblins' desperation was readily apparent, and it soon became clear conditions in the camp were even worse than Gnish suggested. The hobgoblins were bone-thin and emaciated, and most wore ragged clothes or no clothes at all. Some were clearly ill, a sign the outbreak of plague had not confined itself to the human race. Aside from Rose's horse, there were no animals or livestock in the camp, suggesting the hobgoblins had eaten them to avoid starvation. The few huts and tents were shoddy enough that some had been blown down by the storm. Yet despite the sense of hopelessness and fear that hung about the camp, the hobgoblins clung to each other for support. As Berengar watched, it was evident hardship had forged these last survivors into a family.

Phineas gave the nod, and the men emerged from the forest's edge and ran into the camp. Screams spread through the camp as creatures attempted to flee in a blind panic. Caught unawares, the hobgoblins were too late to mount a defense. One managed to reach his bow only to be impaled by a spear before he could nock an arrow. The struggle was over within minutes. Most of those remaining were females or younglings who cowered in fear, left with nowhere to run.

Two villagers dragged Gnish—kicking and biting—before Phineas.

"Stupid goblin. So much for protecting your kin. You led us right here." He smacked Gnish across the face, drawing blood. "Put him and the others in chains—a gift for Laird Margolin." Malice gleamed in his eyes, and his lips curled into a thin smile. "Of course, there's no reason why we can't have a little fun first. He doesn't need *all* of them."

While men looted the camp, taking what few possessions the hobgoblins had as their spoils, Berengar searched for the thunder rune, which he found tucked away inside a wooden chest in one of the tents. He made sure no one was looking before securing the stone. When he rejoined the group, the men were doling out goblin-mead among themselves. Phineas looked on from a log under a tent's entrance, where he had taken refuge from the rain. The men laughed as they took turns beating various goblins—all except Tuck, who drank alone.

When Berengar approached, Phineas raised a tankard in his direction.

"You—Bear Warden. Are you not pleased?"

Berengar just stared at him and returned his attention

to the hobgoblins' suffering. A throaty wail came from nearby, where two men dragged a hobgoblin away from two green-skinned goblin younglings.

Gnish spat at Phineas' feet, and the guard struck him hard across the face.

"Someone take this scum and execute him."

Two eager-looking men started toward Gnish with their swords in hand, but Berengar blocked their path.

"I'll do it." He dragged Gnish away from the camp, out of sight, and took out his battleaxe. "On your knees."

Gnish bowed his head and sank onto the mud as the rain fell around them both. "Do what you want to me, but don't let the others suffer. I beg you."

"Shut up." He stood over Gnish and looked him in the eyes. "Goblins used to raid the northern villages when I was a child. I was taught to hate them before I was old enough to swing a sword. I killed scores in war—hundreds, even." More screams came from the village, but he ignored them. "I remember one that almost got the best of me. We hurt each other pretty bad before we realized we'd stumbled onto a troll's hunting ground. Bastard was the biggest one I'd ever seen. It took the both of us to bring him down. You learn things about someone after doing something like that. The goblin was doing his best to survive to get back to his family, same as me."

"Why tell me this?" Gnish asked, confused.

"That was when I understood that all goblins aren't evil, any more than all people are." Lightning flashed again, and Berengar raised the axe high. The axe cut the chains binding Gnish's hands, freeing him, and Berengar held out his hand to the hobgoblin. "Free the rest. I'll handle the guards."

He trudged through the mud back to camp without another word.

"You took long enough," Phineas called out. "Is it done?"

Berengar didn't reply. He merely stood there, axe in hand, as the storm washed over him. Phineas' leering grin faltered in response to his harsh expression. One by one, the others stopped what they were doing and exchanged worried glances.

He struck the first man in the face with the axe's handle. Blood spurted from the man's nose, and he slipped and lost his footing. Berengar stepped over him, picked up another villager, and threw him against a stack of firewood.

"I wouldn't do that if I were you," he said when an archer took aim with his bow, blocking his path to Phineas.

Faolán snarled, ready to pounce at the archer, and Berengar resumed his course. The archer lowered his bow, and the remaining villagers scattered at his approach.

"What are you doing?" Phineas shouted. "I demand you—"

Berengar kicked him, and Phineas toppled backward over the log. Tuck started toward him, but when Berengar warned him away with a shake of his head, the guard eased his hand off the hilt of his blade and backed away.

Phineas scrambled to his feet, drew his sword, and trained it on the warden.

Berengar ignored the blade. "They haven't hurt anyone. I won't let you slaughter them."

"The famous Warden Berengar." Phineas looked past him to Gnish, who was busy liberating the remaining hobgoblins. He spat at Berengar's feet and waved his sword in the hobgoblin's direction. "You butcher men like cattle, but you would defend *them*? You dare court Laird Margolin's wrath?"

"I am a Warden of Fál," Berengar said. "I fear no lord."

Phineas rushed forward and swung his sword at him, but Berengar sidestepped the blade and hit Phineas in the gut with his axe's handle. Phineas landed at his feet, and Berengar crushed the guard's sword hand under his boot.

"Besides—without you to tell him, Laird Margolin will assume the hobgoblins killed you." He raised his axe to deliver the killing blow.

"Wait," Phineas cried. "I know you've been looking into the girls' disappearances."

"What of it?" Berengar said. "Speak up, before I lose my patience."

"You don't understand what's really going on here. I can tell you, but only if you let me live."

Berengar crouched beside him. "Understand this. If you're lying to me, your death will be slow and painful." He struck Phineas in the head with his fist, and the guard slumped to the ground, unconscious.

When he emerged from the tent, the hobgoblins clung together, still uncertain of his intent.

Berengar turned to face Gnish. "Laird Margolin won't stop. It might not be today, it might not be tomorrow, but more men will come. If you stay here, you will die. Take your tribe and leave. Go somewhere else, far from here, where you will be safe."

"We have nothing. Where can we go?"

Berengar hesitated. *He's right.* They wouldn't last long on their own, especially without resources. He stared at the hobgoblins for a long moment before reaching into his cloak to retrieve the thunder rune, which he offered to Gnish. "This should fetch a steep enough price for your tribe to start a new life. Just don't sell it to anyone shady. I don't want it falling into the wrong hands, understand?"

Reclaiming the rune was the reason he'd joined the raid in the first place, but now that he saw the hobgoblins posed no threat, it didn't seem as dangerous to leave it in their possession.

Gnish accepted the thunder rune with a mixture of gratitude and surprise. "I will not forget what you've done for us this day. We'll tell of your deeds to all we meet."

Berengar doubted anyone would believe such a story, especially one told about him. He cast a parting glance at the hobgoblins, slung Phineas over Rose's stolen horse, and turned his back.

CHAPTER TWELVE

THE RETURN JOURNEY left him cold, hungry, and wet—
and those were the least of his worries. The hag's curse
weighed heavily on his mind. Berengar did his best to bite
back his anger. It wasn't an easy task.

No good deed goes unpunished. He had saved the hobgoblins
from further bloodshed, but at the cost of jeopardizing his
agreement with Laird Margolin. Phineas' claims of
conspiracy probably amounted to nothing more than an
attempt to save his own skin, and he would undoubtedly
report Berengar's actions to Blackthorn the moment he
was free to do so. Then there was the matter of Lady
Imogen, who was almost certainly still alive, even if the
reasons for her disappearance remained hidden.

Every time he tried to do the right thing, it resulted in
one headache after another. Despite his efforts, it remained
more likely than not that the hobgoblins would never leave
Leinster alive. Most of Leinster's human inhabitants would
just as soon kill anything related to a goblin as look at it,
even without the promise of reward. Then all his actions

would be for nothing. He shook the rain from his hood. Alúine was close.

He glanced back at Phineas, who showed no signs of stirring. The silence was one thing to be grateful for, provided he hadn't accidentally hit Phineas hard enough to kill him. It wouldn't be the first time. He checked to make sure Phineas was still breathing before continuing on. Once the members of the hunting party reached the village, they were sure to spread the news of what happened. Few villagers would look well on him for siding with the creatures that raided them. Berengar was long past caring what anyone else thought of him. Finishing the job was the only thing that mattered. That, and staying alive long enough to settle accounts with the hag.

The storm relented just before he reached the forest's edge, and pale light again broke through the clouds. It wouldn't be long before sunset, after which he would have only one day left to lift the curse. Mud caked his boots by the time he entered Alúine, where some villagers had emerged from their homes to inspect the damage left behind by the storm. Most were smart enough to look the other way and avoid mention of the unconscious guard when they saw him coming.

A savory aroma greeted him outside the Green Flagon. He found Iain and Silas finishing repairs to the stable door.

"There you are," Iain said when he noticed him. "We were wondering when you'd turn up again. Please, come inside and warm yourself by the fire while we fetch you food and drink. After what you did for Silas, it's the least we can do to thank you."

The thought of food and drink was appealing, though in truth, he would prefer to make use of the room he had yet to sleep in.

"Maybe in a minute." Berengar ignored Silas' heartfelt

utterances of thanks. There'd be plenty of time to rest when he was dead. "There's something I need your help with first." He hitched the horse to a stall door and dumped Phineas on the ground.

Iain's smile faltered at the sight of Phineas.

"I need a place to keep him out of sight until he comes to," Berengar explained.

Despite his obvious reluctance, Iain motioned for him to follow him to the inn. "Bring him inside."

Fortunately, the storm had driven all patrons from the inn. Berengar and Silas carried Phineas into a storeroom while Iain stood watch. He bound Phineas' arms and legs with rope and gagged him for good measure before returning to the bar.

"I'll take that drink now."

Iain set a tankard before him, clearly uneasy at the idea of holding one of the village guards captive inside his establishment. "You don't look so good, if you don't mind my saying so."

"More than usual?"

Iain and Silas appeared uncertain how best to answer the question.

The hag's words returned to him. *Stone you will become.* More than ever, his body was showing the effects of the curse.

He lifted the tankard and drank deeply of its contents before Silas returned with a plate of bread and stew. When he started to eat, the muscles in his jaw tightened with painful spasms, causing his teeth to grind against each other. Even after the spell passed, his jaw remained sore. Unable to eat, Berengar pushed the food away.

"I'm going out. Keep an eye on our guest, will you?"

He left the inn, retrieved Rose's horse, and started on the road to the church. Again the anger rose within him.

He had thought sparing the hobgoblins might have relieved the curse's symptoms. He'd followed Godfrey's suggestion and resisted his darker impulses, hadn't he? Then again, maybe it was already too late. His heart was too black, and a few good deeds couldn't change that.

This is what comes from meddling in the affairs of witches. It was just another reminder of why he hated magic. He'd rather fight a fully-grown troll than a mage. Even so, he had yet to find something his axe couldn't handle. If it came down to it, he would kill the hag or die trying.

Still—his aversion to magic notwithstanding—a magician would have come in handy, if the blasted purges hadn't driven the survivors into hiding or the arms of powerful patrons. There hadn't been a truly great magician in Fál since Thane Ramsay of Connacht. In the days of King Áed, when Nora was only a girl, Ramsay delivered the land from more evils than perhaps even Padraig himself. Those evils returned with a vengeance after Áed's fall, and with none to stand against them, chaos reigned in the years leading up to the Shadow Wars.

A sob cut short his path to the church. Was he being watched? Berengar stopped to listen and quickly heard it again. He searched the abandoned street for the source of the sound and saw nothing.

"Faolán. We're not alone."

The wolfhound stared at two barrels nestled against a hut only a short space away. Something hid behind them. Whatever it was, it was too small to be an adult.

"Who's there?"

The sobbing stopped abruptly at the sound of his approach.

He looked behind the barrels, where a boy fit into the narrow space between the barrels and the hut. "Lucas?" *Godfrey was supposed to take him home.* "Come out from there."

Lucas cast a fleeting glance at the hut, and Berengar saw the boy's face was bruised and bloodied.

"What happened? Who did this to you?"

Lucas just stared at him, as if he'd lost his voice.

He's terrified.

A woman's scream came from the hut. The door crashed open, and Lucas went stiff as a board as two figures emerged. One was Lucas' mother, herself bruised and battered.

"Don't hurt him," she pleaded with her husband.

The man knocked her aside and turned his attention to Lucas. "There you are. Did you think I wouldn't find out where you'd been?" His temple pulsed with anger. "Look at me when I'm talking to you, you sniveling brat."

Unable to meet his father's gaze, Lucas stood rooted to the spot.

Incensed, the man started toward him.

Berengar's voice was almost a hiss. "You. You're Lucas' father."

It was Duncan, the drunk he'd ejected from the Green Flagon.

Iain said Duncan mistreated his wife and son. He finally understood why Lucas ran away from home on the night he encountered the Dullahan. He was fleeing from his father's abuse.

"What's it to you?" Duncan snapped at him. As before, his eyes were bloodshot, and he reeked of alcohol. "Get back inside, boy."

Lucas' mother clutched at her husband's boots until a callous kick from him caused her to collapse with a whimper.

Berengar stepped in front of Lucas, blocking Duncan's path.

"I'm the man of this house," Duncan said. "What I do with my family is no business of yours."

Berengar didn't budge. "I'm making it my business."

Most people wouldn't have gotten involved—much less one of the High Queen's wardens, who were usually preoccupied with some great quest or another. There wasn't always time to concern oneself with the affairs of the common folk when the fate of an entire kingdom was at stake. Besides, in many parts of Fál, a man's family was his property. Easier to look the other way. That was what most people did.

Berengar wasn't most people. He understood the brokenness in Lucas' eyes only too well, and he wasn't about to let custom or tradition stand in his way. His rage built as he remembered the pain of his father's fists, a hurt he knew only too well. Monsters didn't go away until someone put a stop to them. Whispers of warning ran through his head, reminding him of the curse, only to fall aside in the face of iron-hot anger.

When Duncan started toward Lucas, Berengar stopped holding back. The first punch broke Duncan's nose, and only Berengar's grip held him upright. Berengar hit him a second time, and a third. It wasn't long before Duncan was gurgling blood.

"Not so tough now, are you? It's not so much fun against someone who can hit back, is it?"

Although no one emerged to try to stop him, he knew they were watching. Perhaps the villagers thought Duncan had it coming, or perhaps they were simply afraid of the warden's wrath. He held Duncan in place, hitting him again and again until at last the man no longer put up a struggle. The pain from the curse was excruciating, but he wouldn't let it stop him. He was going to do for Lucas what no one did for him, and nothing could stay his hand.

"Stop," Lucas said. "You're killing him."

Berengar's bloodied knuckles stopped short of a final blow. Duncan's face was now nearly unrecognizable. "You know what he is—what he's capable of. He'll never stop hurting you, or your mother."

"He's my father."

Berengar threw Duncan to the ground and shook his head in disgust. "He doesn't care about you. All he knows is bitterness and anger, and he won't stop until you end up just like him." He pulled out his dagger and pointed it at Duncan, who coughed up blood and phlegm, still speaking to Lucas. "Do you know what it's like? Watching your mother die, and wishing you could have saved her? I can spare you that. I can make it so you never have to be afraid of him again."

He grabbed Duncan by the collar, pulled him close, and pressed the blade against his throat. Duncan stared up at him through swollen eyes, barely conscious. The pain from the curse threatened to overwhelm him, but he had strength enough to deliver the killing blow.

Then he glanced at Lucas, who stared back at him in horror, and his hand faltered. Berengar wrestled with himself, torn between his anger and the look on the boy's face. Duncan deserved to suffer. It would be so easy to do it. Unlike the killing of Skinner Kane at St. Brigid's altar, the death of an insignificant drunk would go unnoticed. Nora would never know. Still, no matter how much he wanted to, he couldn't kill the man in front of his son.

He lowered the dagger and pulled Duncan closer. "I know what it's like to be an orphan. I won't make one of him. I'll be gone from here soon, but I swear to you now— one day I will return. When that day comes, if I learn you've laid a finger on either of them, I'll finish what we started here today."

He released Duncan and left him lying in the dirt.

"Thank you," Lucas said.

A look passed between them, and he went on his way. Although the pain improved, and some flexibility returned to his joints, he felt no relief at having spared Duncan— only a sense of defeat. He had saved Lucas from the Dullahan, only for the boy to return to the monster who lived at home.

It was always the same. Despite all the enemies he'd killed, the world never seemed to get any better. Maybe it was even worse. For every threat he dealt with, two more took its place. He'd been fighting all his life. In the end, had any of his actions ever made a difference? He suddenly felt tired—and not from the hag's curse.

When this is all over, I'm going to find a tavern somewhere in the middle of nowhere and drink myself into a stupor.

Never one to ruminate on such matters for long, Berengar put the thoughts out of his mind. There were other things to worry about at the moment.

He waded through the mud and made his way to the church. The place was as deserted as ever. In his time in Alúine, he hadn't observed any villagers around the church, which struck him as unusual. Such a sight would have been in keeping in the north—where worship of the elder gods dominated that of the Lord of Hosts—or in prosperous Munster to the south, where the church played a lesser, ceremonial role. Leinster's culture was steeped in religion, but Berengar couldn't remember seeing a cross other than the one Godfrey wore. While rural areas often held onto customs and traditions left over from the old ways, people often sought the comfort of religion in times of hardship. If the villagers hadn't turned to the Lord of Hosts, where had they turned? The images of the pagan shrine and sacrifices haunted his thoughts.

The bell tower cast a tall shadow across the ground with evening's approach. Water cascaded down the surface of moss-covered stone, draining into puddles left by the storm. He heard muffled voices carrying from inside the church. Perhaps it wasn't so deserted after all. Berengar hesitated on the steps and used water from one of the puddles to scrub Duncan's blood from his hands before venturing inside. Candles illuminated the dimly lit interior.

He found the sanctuary empty. The voices seemed to be coming from the chapel.

"I've done everything I can," a familiar voice said. "The girl might pull through. As for the others...I did my best to make them comfortable."

"Thank you, Rose," replied the voice of Friar Godfrey. "May the Lord bless you and keep you."

Berengar quietly made his way through the sanctuary, hoping for a word with Godfrey. When two figures suddenly entered the room, he stopped and remained in the shadows, just out of sight.

"You're not leaving, are you?" Evander asked Rose. "What about the others?"

"I showed Friar Godfrey how to tend to them properly. I have to go, Evander. It'll be dark soon."

"Then why not stay? They need you—I need you." Evander put his hands on her shoulders. "I'm leaving the village soon. I was trying to find a way to tell you before. Friar Godfrey's given me a task, and it needs doing soon. When I return, why don't we leave Alúine together, for good this time? With the reward money from the ogre we'll have enough to start a new life." He lowered his face toward hers, and the pair shared a brief kiss until Rose pulled away suddenly.

"I'm sorry, Evander. I can't." She briskly walked toward the doors.

"Wait," he called after her. "I don't understand. I thought you felt the same."

"I did. I do. It's just…we can't be together. It's not safe for me here." With that, she hurried from the sanctuary.

What did she mean by that? Berengar's gaze moved to Evander, who lingered a moment longer before departing. As he had guessed, the huntsman was going on a journey of some sort. But where was he going, and what was so important about his task that it needed to be done so quickly?

He found Godfrey at prayer inside the chapel. "Have you made anything of the pagan symbols we found?"

Godfrey gave a grim nod and climbed to his feet. "There is an evil power at work in Alúine. The Dullahan, the sluagh… I believe they're all connected to the cult of Balor, and I'm afraid the worst is yet to come."

Berengar followed him into the sanctuary. "What do you mean?"

"Tomorrow night is the Festival of the Blood Moon. It's one of the oldest rites observed by followers of the Fomorians. The moon represents the eye of Balor, which is thought to open during the festival. I believe all those lost souls have been building up to something—a final sacrifice."

Tomorrow night. That's when the hag wants me to bring the sacrifice to her. Even if there was such a final sacrifice, he still didn't know who she was, or where. "Who else knows about this?"

Godfrey shrugged. "I'm not sure. When I arrived in Alúine, I worked hard to gain the people's trust, but I've long sensed they've been hiding something from me."

"You're not without secrets of your own. Avery told me about the woman who came to the church seeking aid around the same time Laird Margolin's niece went missing. Is there something you want to tell me?"

"I don't know where the girl is. Maybe Avery just wanted to learn what you knew about Imogen's whereabouts."

"Then tell me what it is you've got Evander doing."

Godfrey's surprise was evident, though he quickly attempted to hide it. "I can't do that."

"You can't, or you won't? I'm not fond of games."

"I swear to you it's nothing sinister. Why would I lie to you? I'm a man of the cloth."

"If you were an honest priest, you'd be the first one I've met." With that, Berengar started for the doors.

"You don't know what you're up against," Godfrey warned. "Be careful."

"It's too late for that. I've got Phineas tied up at the inn. He says he knows what's behind the killings."

He left the church still unsure if Godfrey was telling the truth. Given his knowledge of the ancient ways, it was still possible the friar was the man in the hood seen by Lucas. He needed to interrogate Phineas to know for sure. Fortunately, the guard had almost certainly regained consciousness in the interim.

An eerie silence settled over Alúine in the storm's aftermath. The rains had ended, but the clouds remained. A light fog covered the abandoned streets. With night's impending arrival, the villagers remained in the safety of their homes, hoping to endure another night among the monsters roaming the land.

Hushed voices broke the quiet, and Berengar caught a glimpse of four figures through the fog. He recognized Evander, accompanied by Varun's wife and daughters. Berengar approached the hut, careful to remain unseen. The women conversed in hushed tones as Evander loaded two horses' saddlebags with supplies. Varun's daughters were dressed for the road. Whatever they were up to, having waited until nightfall, they obviously wished to do it in secrecy.

So this is what Godfrey has Evander doing. He's taking the girls somewhere. Considering the friendliness with which Varun greeted Godfrey when they arrived at his door, it was likely Varun was aware of the plan. If anything, Varun's journey to Blackthorn was a ruse to allow his daughters to slip away unnoticed.

Before he could pursue the matter further, he spotted another figure leaving the village on foot. Berengar frowned as he watched the figure head south, toward the forest. Given the dangers lurking about, why would she approach the forest alone? It occurred to him she might be the next sacrifice, trapped under some sort of spell or enchantment. Evander and the others would have to wait. Berengar turned away from Varun's hut and followed the stranger.

When she neared the forest, the wind shifted, and the woman stopped to sniff at the air. She glanced around, as if suddenly aware of being followed, and Berengar crouched low to avoid being noticed. It was too dark to get a good look at her face. He needed to get closer. The fog thinned at the forest's edge, where the woman slipped past the trees and out of his sight.

Berengar waited a safe interval before following. She hadn't gone far. He found her foraging through the brush, looking for herbs with her back to him. Faolán growled, causing the woman to stiffen instantly.

"Who's there?"

When she turned around, he recognized her instantly. It was Rose.

"You shouldn't be here."

"I could say the same of you." His gaze moved to her fist, in which she attempted to hide the herbs she'd collected. *Wolfsbane*. "It's you. You're the werewolf."

"I don't know what you're talking about." Her voice betrayed her fear.

The reason she lived alone, the absence of animals on her farm, Faolán's instant distaste for her—suddenly, it all made sense.

"It wasn't an accident, finding you in the forest—was it? You didn't come looking for Evander last night. You were there because you wanted a place where you could transform away from the village."

Rose took a step back. "Don't come any closer. I don't want to hurt you."

"I should have known. But you didn't have a mark."

Her expression hardened instantly, all pretense abandoned. "That's because I wasn't bitten. I was cursed."

Berengar reached for his sword.

"Stop," a voice said at his back, where Evander trained a bow on him.

He must have noticed me outside Varun's hut, Berengar realized.

Rose's eyes filled with alarm. "Evander, you have to go. The transformation could happen at any moment, and I won't be able to control it when it happens."

"So it's true," Evander said.

Rose glanced away, as if unable to meet his gaze. "I wanted to tell you, Evander, but I couldn't."

"How? How did this happen?"

"My father was sick. He was dying, and I couldn't save him. So I went to the hag. She told me she could help, but what she wanted in return…" She shuddered, as if the mere memory was abhorrent. "I stole one of her healing draughts instead and used it to cure my father. Everything

167

went back to the way it was before. I thought I had escaped retribution, but then came the first full moon.

"I killed him, Evander—my own father. That's why I kept you away. It was to keep you safe. I've tried my best to find a way to lift the curse, but nothing's worked. Wolfsbane is the only thing that helps with the transformations."

Berengar looked from one to the other, mindful of the bow trained on him. "She has to die, Evander."

"Shut up."

"I never meant for any of this to happen," Rose said. "You have to believe me. I never wanted to hurt anyone."

"It doesn't matter what you want," Berengar said. "You'll kill again and again until you're stopped. You can't control it. You're a monster—it's what you do."

"Let me go," Rose pleaded. "Before it's too late."

The clouds parted above before she could reply, and the light of the moon washed over her.

It's already too late.

"Run," Rose said, and her eyes turned dark amber.

CHAPTER THIRTEEN

ROSE'S PAINED cry deepened and became a howl as fangs sprouted in place of her teeth. Her fingers twitched and elongated into claws, and patches of fur appeared over her skin. With Evander's attention otherwise occupied, Berengar drew his sword and sprinted forward. Rose was defenseless at the moment, but a full-fledged werewolf would be much harder to stop. He had to finish her before the change was complete. A few hits with his sword would leave her vulnerable enough for his silver dagger to finish the job.

She stared at him with an almost pitiable expression, her face still half-recognizable despite the change. Berengar left no room for pity. Compassion was a weakness he couldn't afford. It didn't matter that Rose wasn't in control of her actions, or that she was a kind and decent person when the beast didn't hold sway. If he let her live, she would only continue to kill. Berengar refused to let that happen. If that meant taking one life to save dozens more, so be it.

Evander slammed into Berengar before he reached

Rose, and the two rolled across the wet earth. He tossed the huntsman off him with ease, but by the time he recovered his footing, it was too late. Rose, now a fully transformed werewolf, opened her jaws and let out a bestial roar. Evander looked on in horror at the sight. There was no humanity left in her eyes. Under the moon's light, only the monster remained.

Rose's gaze moved to the sword in Berengar's hand.

"Come on," he said to taunt her. Werewolf or not, this time he had his weapons, and he was ready for battle.

She moved with supernatural speed, leaving him with no time to react. Fortunately, she was so focused on him, she forgot to pay attention to Faolán, who jumped out of the darkness and onto her back. Rose's momentum carried her forward, leaving Berengar free to dodge her attack and slash across her flank with his sword.

He started to go for the dagger, but again Evander threw himself in the way, and they struggled for possession of the blade. Rose, having reached a stop, looked down at her bleeding side and let out an angry howl. She crouched, as if to pounce, and Berengar pushed Evander out of the way. However, instead of attacking, Rose leapt over their heads and took to all fours, vanishing into the fog.

Blast it. She's headed toward the village. Berengar swore and picked up his sword. "Let's go, Faolán. We have to find her before she hurts someone."

Evander barred his path, once more training the bow on him.

"Get out of my way," Berengar said.

"I won't let you hurt her."

Berengar's expression darkened. "Let me guess. You think your love will save her."

"I'll find a way to lift the curse. I know I can. Please, let me help her. I can take her away from here—somewhere safe."

Berengar shook his head. "You don't get it, do you? There's nowhere safe for you. There's no happy ending for the two of you. Even if you ran, eventually, she would kill you."

"You're wrong about her," Evander said with the brash, naïve confidence of someone in love.

Faolán ran at Evander, drawing his attention long enough for Berengar to hit the bow with his sword, and the arrow careened into the darkness. Berengar ripped the bow away and quickly subdued the huntsman.

"Enough." He trained his sword on Evander. "Don't make me use this."

Evander struggled to rise to his feet. "So you're just going to put her down, like a mad dog? You really are a monster."

Berengar kicked him in the side. "Stay down." He headed for the village and whistled for Faolán to follow, leaving Evander behind. Evander didn't see it, but he was doing him a favor. By killing Rose, he was saving Evander from having to do the job himself.

Berengar sheathed his sword and took out his axe. Now that Rose had fully transformed, inflicting significant damage was more important than speed. Most werewolves possessed enhanced healing, and it was likely the wounds he'd inflicted earlier were already healed. He needed to do enough damage to immobilize her so he could get within range with the silver dagger without having to worry about her fangs and claws—an unenviable task by any measure.

Alúine lay peaceful, oblivious to the werewolf's presence. With Phineas tied up and Tuck probably off drinking somewhere, there come no guards to patrol the village's abandoned streets. Berengar searched through the fog for a glimpse of the beast. He heard movement at his back and spun around, half-expecting a pair of glowing eyes waiting for him. Instead of the werewolf, he saw only a harmless cat watching him from its perch atop the well.

The wind shifted, and Faolán's fur bristled in response to the werewolf's scent. She led Berengar down a lonely path that took them past the inn, where the moonlight revealed a trail of blue blood along the ground. The trail ended outside a rundown barn. Berengar stopped to inspect a partial footprint in the mud before staring past the barn doors, which hung ajar. He rose and advanced into the darkness within, steeling himself for what waited inside.

Apart from the creaking of wooden beams under the breeze, the barn was quiet. A musty odor lingered in the air. Moonlight filtered in through gaps in the beams. Although there was no sign of the werewolf, he felt her presence nearby.

She's close.

A drop of blue blood fell and landed on the ground at his feet. Berengar turned his gaze upward, where the werewolf hung from the rafters. Her amber eyes gleamed in the shadows, and her jaws widened to reveal a set of monstrous fangs. He brought his axe up to defend himself, but Rose leapt on him from above. The impact carried them through the rotten wall and into the night.

Rose was on him in an instant, clawing and snapping at him. Berengar used his axe's handle to keep her at bay long enough for Faolán to intervene. The respite was over in an instant. Rose swatted Faolán aside, and the hound slammed against the side of the barn with a whimper.

Berengar pushed himself up and swung his axe with all the force he could muster, and blood spurted from a fresh gash across her chest. Before he could bring the axe around again, Rose retaliated by lifting him off the ground as if he were weightless and pinning him against a neighboring hut. Her claws pierced his armor, digging into his flesh as he strained to keep her fangs away from his neck. He wrenched his hand free at the last second and brought the axe down, which allowed him to roll away mostly unharmed.

The wound only served to further enrage her, and she rounded on him again, attacking in a frenzy. Her claws raked along his forearm, forcing him to drop the axe.

I can't keep this up much longer.

Berengar did his best to hold his ground, but strong as he was, going toe-to-toe with a werewolf was a deadly proposition. He felt the curse's effects slowing his movements, and with each blow, his strength ebbed. With few options, he went for his sword. Rose seized the opportunity to pounce, and they met in a violent collision.

The sword slipped from his grip, and he hit the ground hard. Rose landed across from him, bleeding from another wound. Berengar's gaze settled on his axe, which lay just out of reach. Battered and bruised, he spat out a mouthful of blood and crawled toward the axe. A monstrous shadow loomed over him before his fingers grasped the handle, and when he looked back, he found himself staring into a mouthful of fangs.

The beast stopped without warning and staggered back. Clouds obscured the moon from view, and the werewolf slowly shrank in size as it returned to its human form. Berengar let out a weary sigh, grabbed the axe, and staggered to his feet.

"It's over," he said as Rose scrambled backward at his approach. "There's nowhere to go."

She stared at him with defiance. "I could have let you die of your wounds, but I helped you. This is how you

173

repay my kindness? If I'm a monster, so are you. I hadn't hurt anyone until you came along. I kept to the farm, away from everyone else."

Berengar ignored her pleas. She was a monster, and she had to die. It was as simple as that. Darragh would have probably found some way to break the curse, but Berengar was the Bloody Red Bear, and he did not show mercy.

"You're a killer. You'll always be a killer." He raised the axe to strike.

Searing pain tore through his chest before he could deliver the final blow. Unlike before, the agony spread across his entire body, as if he were on fire. Every muscle tightened at once with uncontrollable spasms. The axe fell from his hands, and he landed on his back, where he lay paralyzed. His jaw clamped shut with such force he was unable even to speak, and every shallow breath was a struggle.

Rose's eyes fell on the bandage she'd wrapped around his hand. "We're both cursed, it seems." Her gaze moved to his sword, which lay nearby. Berengar could only watch, helpless, as she retrieved the blade and held it over him.

"If I were the monster you believe me to be, I'd kill you right now without a thought." Rose threw away the sword, which slid across the ground. "But I'm not a murderer. Remember this, Warden Berengar—that a monster showed mercy where you did not." She took a fleeting glance at the sky and hurried away while the moon remained concealed by clouds.

Then several things happened at once.

Berengar heard the screams first. He tried to crane his neck to see their source, but his body refused to obey. Instead, the spasms racking his body only intensified, forcibly arching his back. His labored breaths were rendered visible as the temperature plummeted and frost crept along the ground. A chorus of otherworldly whispers carried through the night, and frightened villagers emerged from their homes to investigate.

Then all hell broke loose.

Villagers scattered as chaos consumed the whole of Alúine. From his position on the ground, Berengar couldn't get a good look at what they were running from, but he knew it wasn't anything good. Crazed animals broke free from their pens and enclosures in their terror. No one took notice of him in all the confusion, and he was nearly trampled more than once. He managed to roll over onto his side, where he finally saw the source of the commotion: a humanoid, corpse-like figure wreathed in shadow.

The spirit, nearly identical to the sluagh Berengar encountered at the ransacked farm, advanced—or rather, glided—toward the nearest villagers, grasping at them with a withered hand. More of the restless spirits followed. The sluagh roamed Alúine, moving from home to home as if searching for something. His gaze fell on Varun's daughters, who were hiding under a wagon nearby. They were close enough that he could hear them over the confusion. Berengar tried reaching out to them, but they failed to notice him. The elder daughter held out her hand, and the girls emerged from cover and fled Alúine as Berengar looked on.

Hooves sounded just outside the village, where a pair of riders approached. One wore a black robe, and a hood covered his face. Beside him sat a rider with no head.

The Dullahan. Berengar struggled in vain to move, but unlike before, the curse did not relent.

The riders stopped just short of where he lay and surveyed the chaos.

"Find her," the hooded rider commanded the Dullahan.

The Dullahan dismounted without question, and his boots hit the ground with a thud.

The hooded rider's gaze fell on Berengar's fallen sword. "The warden. He's here."

The Dullahan stopped, awaiting orders. Berengar lay helpless off to one side of the road, just out of their sight and hidden by darkness. It was only a matter of time before they found him lying there. Suddenly, a hand grabbed him from behind, and he felt himself dragged into the barn.

It was Godfrey.

"Quiet," the friar said, unaware he couldn't speak.

Berengar watched from the barn as the Dullahan strode past them. The hooded man lingered a while longer before turning his horse around and riding into the fog.

Time passed, and Berengar drifted in and out of consciousness. Godfrey left to help the villagers and failed to return. For all Berengar knew, he might be dead.

Even without the added effect of the curse, he was weary from his battle with Rose. The pain only fed his rage, but the angrier he grew, the more he felt the curse take hold. He longed to move, to take up his arms and fight something—*anything*. Instead, he was trapped, alone with his own thoughts.

Evander's words came back to him. *You really are a monster.*

Berengar remembered the fear in Rose's eyes when he drew near. When he told her she would always be a killer, he might just as easily have been referring to himself. It was something he'd accepted a long time ago. It was a path he walked without wavering, and yet, for the first time, he felt a seed of doubt. Rose spared his life when she could have killed him. He had always believed he could recognize evil when he saw it, but what if he was wrong? What if his heart had hardened to the point he could no longer recognize evil even in himself?

Sometime in the night—he wasn't quite sure when—the screams finally stopped. Intermittent sobs from beyond the barn punctuated the silence. The Dullahan and the sluagh were gone, though he didn't know where to.

They were searching for someone, Berengar realized. The next sacrifice, most likely. With the Festival of the Blood Moon fast approaching, the hooded rider needed one of the young women from the village. But who? There was nothing out of the ordinary about the girls abducted so far. What was so special about the final sacrifice?

The man in the hood controlled the Dullahan—that much was clear—as well as the sluagh. He was probably a spiritist or dark magician, and a powerful one at that. There was also something vaguely familiar about the man's voice that Berengar couldn't place.

A pair of eyes gleamed from the shadows that clung to the rafters, and he became aware of another presence in the barn. At first, he thought his eye was playing tricks on him, until a grotesque face slowly emerged from the barn's dark recesses. The hag's mouth twisted into a cruel, pitiless smile.

"Look how you have fallen, man of stone—brought low by your own rage." She vanished almost as soon as she appeared.

Berengar's sense of relief was short-lived, as he heard her breathing behind him. He tried to call for Faolán, but no sound escaped his mouth.

She put her lips to his ear. "No one will come. You are

all alone. You care for no one, Berengar One-Eye, and no one cares for you." The sound of her mocking laughter filled the barn. "Fear not. Soon your pain will end, and the death you long for will come at last." Her voice changed, becoming a harsh, angry hiss. "But first you must bring her to me."

Who, blast it? Berengar thought.

"You know who she is," the hag said, as if in response to his thoughts. "You have always known. You have sought her all along, unknowing. But your time grows short, and I must have her before the spiritist. Find her before the sun sets and bring her to me. You will find me waiting in the bog. You have one day."

With that, she was gone. Berengar's eyes grew heavy, and despite his efforts to remain conscious, sleep took him.

I t was morning when he woke. Weak sunlight filtered into the barn, which still bore the marks of his battle with the werewolf. His body ached in more places than he could count. Berengar unclenched his jaw and sucked in a deep breath. Although the curse had abated enough for him to move, its effects continued to weigh him down, and considerable soreness and stiffness lingered in his joints and muscles.

Faolán lay curled up beside him, as if to ward against evil. While he was sure she found him sometime in the night, Berengar had no memory of it. Everything following the hag's visitation remained a blur. Upon seeing him stir, Faolán uttered a tired yawn and licked his face, and Berengar sat up and patted her head. She seemed no worse for wear, despite her run-in with Rose. Like him, Faolán wasn't so easily killed.

"We're not done just yet." The residual tightness in his jaw left his words muffled.

They were alone. Godfrey had failed to return, which wasn't an encouraging sign. Berengar used the wall to steady himself and staggered to his feet. There were questions that needed answers, and he wouldn't find them sitting on his backside. He emerged from the barn unsure of what waited outside.

Alúine was still standing, for the most part. The Dullahan and the sluagh had moved on, but not without leaving their mark. Many villagers were hard at work inspecting or repairing the damage left behind in the aftermath of the attack. Most appeared to have survived, suggesting the hooded man was indeed searching for a specific individual. Whether or not he found her was another matter entirely. An ominous mood hung over the village, and with good cause. Whatever had happened the previous night wasn't over.

On his way to retrieve his weapons, Berengar sidestepped a frustrated man attempting to round up a herd of escaped pigs. He made his way to the well, where a group of villagers were discussing what to do about the water, which had taken on a sickly green color, as if befouled by the presence of supernatural evil. A few doused Tuck with a bucket of water in hopes of awakening the sleeping guard, who had likely fallen into a drunken stupor prior to the attack and slumbered through it all.

When Berengar stopped to inquire about the events of the previous night, each villager remained strangely silent on the topic. The looks he received were even more hostile than usual, probably on account of his appearance. Gray discoloration had spread across his hardened outer layer of skin, covering his entire body. Even his heartbeat was nearly imperceptible, as if his heart too had almost finished turning to stone.

The hag told him the sacrifice was someone he knew—someone he'd been seeking all along. Laird Margolin's niece was the only person who matched that description, but he was no closer to finding her than he was when he first arrived at Móin Alúin. He thought again of the mysterious individual in the hood. If the hag wasn't behind the killings and the Dullahan, then who was?

Fortunately, there was one person who could provide him with the answers he sought. Berengar started toward the inn, where a number of villagers had gathered.

"I tell you, it was Rose," said a villager addressing the crowd. "She transformed into the beast. I always thought there was something odd about the way she stayed at that farm after her father died. She probably killed him herself, come to think of it."

Iain shook his head. "Absurd. I've known Rose since she was a child. She's no monster. After last night, we have troubles enough of our own without you making up tales."

"It's no tale, Iain," another said. "I saw it with my own eyes. In a fight with the warden, she was—around the time everything went south."

A round of intense murmurs greeted this proclamation, and Berengar knew it would not be long before the rumors spread throughout the village.

"Poor girl," Iain muttered. "Did he kill her?"

"She fled the village just before the spirits invaded," the first man said. "I say we round up the men and find her before the blood moon." He stopped short when he noticed Berengar.

"I'd like a word," Berengar said to Iain, ignoring the others.

The crowd dispersed at the sight of him, no doubt to discuss their plans to go after Rose elsewhere. It was something else he'd have to deal with. Werewolf or not, he wasn't about to let them lynch her in the center of the village—not while she was still human. Then again, he'd been willing to kill Rose prior to her transformation, so was he really any better? The hag's curse couldn't have taken hold unless his heart was already hardened. Maybe she was right about him.

He decided to forget about Rose and focus on the final sacrifice before the hooded figure or his minions found her first. No matter what he ultimately decided, he wouldn't harm her during the day, while she was in control of her actions.

The moment he set foot inside the inn, his gaze fell on the door to the storeroom, which had been left open. The room was empty.

"Where's Phineas?"

Iain and Silas exchanged a pained glance before the innkeeper finally cleared his throat and spoke up. "I'm afraid he managed to escape amid all the confusion."

Berengar brought his fist down on the nearest table in a fit of rage. "Blast it!" By now the pain had become so familiar it hardly bothered him anymore. He doubted that meant anything good.

He's probably on his way to Margolin this very moment. Events were quickly spinning out of his control.

"Are you sure you're all right? I don't mean to speak out of turn, but you look even worse than you did the last time I saw you."

"Never mind that," Berengar muttered. "Tell me what happened here last night."

"Everything happened so quickly, it's hard to say. We heard the screams and went to see what the fuss was about." Iain shuddered involuntarily. "That was when I saw them, heaven help me. What were those things?"

"Sluagh. The lost souls of those who've gone missing. They're under the control of some kind of spiritist—the same man responsible for all the disappearances." Berengar thought back to the familiar quality of the man's voice. He'd heard it somewhere before, even if he couldn't remember where. "Did either of you get a good look at him?"

Silas opened his mouth to speak, but Iain elbowed him in the ribs, and he fell silent.

"I'm afraid not," the innkeeper volunteered. "We hid behind the bar until the danger passed." He averted his gaze when he spoke, like he had something to hide.

The behavior seemed unusual for the innkeeper, piquing Berengar's interest.

"They came here looking for someone, and if they find her, they'll kill her. Are you sure there's nothing you can tell me about what happened here?"

Again Iain looked away. "No."

He's either lying, or he's afraid of something. Maybe both.

"Not everyone is accounted for," Iain said, as if aware of the warden's suspicions. "Friar Godfrey was looking for Evander earlier, and Avery was asking after a pair of girls this morning."

"Avery?" Berengar hadn't forgotten how the tanner had spied on him during his conversation with Oriana, or the man's peculiar interest in Lady Imogen. "Let me guess— he was searching for Varun's daughters."

Iain's brow knotted in confusion. "Daughters, you say?"

Berengar frowned. "Aye. Keely and Oriana." His words seemed to trouble the innkeeper. "What is it?"

"Keely is Varun's only child. There's no one from the

village by the name of Oriana. Trust me, I'd know if there was."

Berengar's mind raced at the revelation. *If Oriana isn't Varun's daughter, then who is she?*

Then it hit him.

I've been a fool. There was no Oriana, and there never had been. She was Imogen.

CHAPTER FOURTEEN

MARGOLIN'S NIECE was right under his nose the whole time.

All the pieces fit. After her mysterious disappearance from Castle Blackthorn, Imogen came to Alúine, and Varun, who owed her for saving his daughter's life, took her in. She then assumed the identity of Oriana when Berengar came looking for her.

Avery was telling the truth. Imogen sought aid at the church after her arrival in the village, which meant Varun's family wasn't the only party involved in the deception.

"Godfrey," he said under his breath. The corner of his mouth twitched in anger. Godfrey might have rescued him from the Dullahan, but it didn't absolve the friar of lying to him. Still, now he finally knew where to find answers.

Berengar left a befuddled-looking Iain behind and set out from the Green Flagon. He wasted no time making his way to the church. A small number of parishioners lingered around the church. He guessed some had taken refuge on holy ground while the sluagh wandered the village.

The villagers glowered or looked away as he approached. Those inside appeared equally uncomfortable. Berengar was used to being the cause of such discomfort, but to his surprise, they almost seemed to ignore him. Something else had them on edge, though whatever it was, the people refused to speak of it in his presence.

"We need to talk," he said when he found the friar.

The events of the previous night seemed to have had no effect on Godfrey's cheerful disposition. "It's good to see you're still in one piece, Warden Berengar. I was planning to check on you, but as you can see, I'm rather busy at the moment—something you can help me with, perhaps."

"Where is she?" Berengar asked, his meaning plain.

Godfrey glanced at those at prayer and lowered his voice. "Outside."

"Fine." Berengar waited until they were out of earshot before continuing. "You knew I was looking for Imogen, and you kept her from me."

"You're cleverer than you appear." Godfrey sounded amused. "Aye—I lied to you."

"Most men who do that come to regret it."

Godfrey only smiled. For a man of the cloth, he wasn't easily frightened. That, coupled with his wooden hand and readiness to fight, again hinted at an unusual past.

"We're on the same side, my friend—or at least I think we are."

"I'm not your friend," Berengar snapped. "And you have exactly three seconds to tell me what's going on before I lose my temper."

"Although Varun agreed to give Lady Imogen shelter, it was only a matter of time before someone recognized her. She came to me for help, and I arranged for Evander to spirit her away to someplace safe, far from here. Imogen made me pledge not to reveal her identity or intentions, and I kept my word."

"A lot of good your word did her," Berengar replied, still bitter at having so narrowly missed out on the woman he'd been searching for. "I would have protected her and kept her safe. Now she's missing again."

A rider approached the village from the north. The horse galloped into Alúine at full speed on its way to the church. Its rider, a golden-haired woman with a thoughtful face, jerked back on the reins and brought her mount to an abrupt stop just short of them.

"I received your message," she told Godfrey. "I came as fast as I could."

"You," Berengar said. It was Saroise, the bard he'd encountered at Castle Blackthorn. "I should have known you were mixed up in this somehow."

It was to Saroise that Godfrey had written about the Dullahan, and Oriana—or rather Imogen—had specifically asked Berengar about the bard, who had supposedly done her a great service.

Saroise eyed him warily, a sign her chilly attitude toward him had not warmed since their last encounter. "What are you doing here?"

"My job." Under the circumstances, he was in no mood for another quarrel. "I'm here for the girl."

"He knows the truth," Godfrey told her. "Or enough of it, at any rate."

Saroise took the news in stride as she dismounted. "Do you trust him?"

Godfrey regarded Berengar for a quick moment. "I believe he wants to find Imogen. More than that, I cannot say."

Saroise sighed and put her hands on her hips. "I suppose that will have to be enough for now." She looked around and spoke in a hushed tone, clearly mindful of observers. "We don't have much time. Is she safe?"

Godfrey quickly recounted the events of the previous night.

"This bodes ill," Saroise muttered. "The blood moon is tonight. We must find her first, unless the Dullahan has done so already."

"Imogen fled the village with Keely, Varun's daughter," Berengar said. "They were headed for the forest."

Saroise started toward her horse and looked back at them with one foot in the stirrup. "Well? What are you waiting for? We should leave at once."

"I'm not going anywhere without answers," Berengar said. "You still haven't told me how you're involved in all this, or what the Dullahan wants with Imogen."

"Help us save Imogen, and I'll tell you whatever you desire."

She doesn't trust me. Then again, he hadn't exactly given her a reason to.

A scream rang out before he could press the matter further. Berengar tensed and reached for his sword but eased his hand off the blade when he noticed a young woman hurry into the village. "It's Keely." *She must have come from the forest.* She was alone. Where was Imogen?

Keely stumbled and lost her footing, and a crowd quickly formed in response to her cries. Berengar went to investigate and pushed his way through the throng of villagers.

"They've taken Lady Imogen," Keely said through her tears. "You have to help her."

The revelation of Imogen's presence in Alúine, coupled with her possible abduction, touched off a new round of speculation on the part of the villagers, only causing the girl further distress.

"Who's taken her?" asked Saroise, who knelt beside Keely to comfort her.

Keely wiped her eyes and stifled a sob. "It was Avery. He led the brigands to us."

That explains Avery's interest in Imogen, Berengar thought. *I should have known.* The whole time he'd been searching for Imogen, Laird Margolin's enemies were doing the same. The role of village tanner was the perfect way for Avery to remain informed of happenings in the area without drawing undesired attention. He'd probably been feeding information to the brigands for years. "Do you know where they took her?"

Keely gave a weak nod. "They have a fort hidden in the woods. I followed them there."

"How many are there?"

"At least a dozen—maybe more."

Given the pronounced effects of the curse, those odds put him at a distinct disadvantage, but he didn't have much of a choice. "Can you show me the way?"

Her voice resonated with newfound resolve. "Aye. I can take you there."

Saroise addressed the crowd. "People of Alúine. Your lord's niece, Lady Imogen, has been taken prisoner by brigands. We aim to rescue her. Who here will stand with us?"

Most stared at their feet or averted their gaze.

Berengar spotted Tuck standing among the crowd. "You." As the village's sole remaining guard, recovering Imogen was his responsibility too. Besides, current events seemed to have sobered him, at least for the moment. "Time to earn your pay. You're coming with us."

Tuck merely nodded without argument and trudged through the ranks of villagers to join them.

"Is there no one else?" Saroise asked.

"These people have no love for Margolin," Godfrey said. "Some even support the rebels."

"How many times has Lady Imogen interceded on your behalf to convince her uncle to show mercy?" Saroise demanded of the crowd. "Will you abandon her now in her hour of need?"

Silas stepped forward. Although his disabilities might put him at a disadvantage, his impressive size might give the brigands pause.

"What about the men who accompanied us last night?" Berengar asked Tuck.

"They won't fight with you. Not after you stood against them to defend goblins."

That left him with a one-handed friar, a bard, a drunk, and a cripple. As usual, he'd have to do the heavy lifting himself. Berengar trudged toward the barn to collect his horse, leaving the others to follow after.

The brigands' fort was hidden deep in the forest, near the ruins of Laird Cairrigan's castle. It was a difficult journey, even on horseback. Berengar's stiffening muscles and seizing joints limited his mobility and made it difficult to remain in the saddle, though he took pains to conceal his discomfort from his companions.

He trailed behind the others, keeping an eye out for danger. Since Keely had escaped to carry word of Imogen's capture, the outlaws would be on the lookout, and they wouldn't let their prisoner go without a fight. Curse or not, with Imogen finally within his reach, Berengar wasn't leaving without her. He would cut down every man himself if need be.

Saroise fell behind the others and rode beside him.

"Is something bothering you?" Berengar asked, aware of her gaze.

"I asked you before what you would do if you found Imogen."

"My answer hasn't changed. I'm taking her back to her uncle."

"In return for Margolin's efforts to conceal your deeds at Kildare." There was a hard edge to her words. "Margolin is treacherous. He'll never uphold his side of your bargain." Her eyes lingered on his cursed skin. "Godfrey spoke of the curse the hag placed on you—that you'll turn to stone unless you bring Imogen to her."

Berengar returned his attention to the road. "What is it you want from me?"

"I know all the stories about you, Warden Berengar, and the man from those tales wouldn't hesitate to hand that girl over to the hag to save himself."

"Is that what you think? That I'm planning to rescue Imogen from the brigands just to give her over?"

"Sometimes stories are wrong. Those in our company give very different accounts about your time here. Did you really defend the goblins in these woods from the villagers?"

"What's it to you?"

"I'm trying to decide what kind of man you are."

"You might not like the answer to your question." He tried riding ahead, but Saroise persisted.

"Imogen wasn't abducted by the ogre," she offered. "She was running away from Blackthorn."

"How do you know?"

"I helped her escape. Margolin never cared about the ogre—he just wanted you to find his niece. That's why you can't bring her back to him."

"What was she running from?"

Saroise changed the subject abruptly. "How did a man like you come to enter the High Queen's service? I've never heard the tale."

The question surprised him, though it seemed only fitting a famous bard would want to know the story. He hesitated, considering her request. He rarely broached the subject, and not in many years.

"I'll tell you, but only if you swear never to speak of it to anyone—same goes for everything that's happened since the moment I set foot in Castle Blackthorn."

She raised her hand toward the heavens. "I swear by the elder gods, the Lord of Hosts, and any other powers there may be."

"Our paths crossed during the war," Berengar said. "I abducted Nora and rode north. My plan was to take her to Queen Scathach, who had placed a bounty on my head after the death of her son."

"You were going to turn her over to the Ice Queen to save your own skin?" Her tone conveyed disapproval.

"Nora thought the same. In truth, I wanted the chance to kill Scathach. Presenting her with a rival was the only way I could get close enough to do the job."

"A foolish plan. From what I've heard, you never would have left Dothrunvaggen alive."

"I didn't expect to. All I wanted was a chance to kill the queen."

"So much that you would risk your life?"

"My life wasn't worth much. Still isn't. I had my reasons for wanting Scathach dead, and we'll leave it at that."

Saroise seemed confused. "Seeing as Nora is High Queen and you're one of her wardens, it's clear you never reached Dothrunvaggen."

Berengar shook his head. "No. We never made it."

Saroise waited for him to elaborate.

"It probably goes without saying that Nora despised me at the time, and not just because I kidnapped her in the middle of the war. She thought I was a heartless killer, and she was right. I didn't care for her either. I hated the world. Not much has changed in that regard. I didn't believe Nora's talk of bringing peace to Fál. Why should she be any different from any other noble?

"But I underestimated her cunning. Nora escaped and took refuge in a small village. A band of mercenaries found her first. I already had something of a reputation in those days, and the mercenaries offered to cut me in on the reward if I threw in with them. I agreed.

"I still remember that night. It was winter, and snow filled the sky. Nora was bound, unable to help the villagers who had taken her in. She was far too valuable a prize for the mercenaries to harm, but they had no such reservations about the villagers.

"Sometime in the night, they dragged the village elder and his family into the square to make an example of them. The man had a granddaughter—eight, maybe nine years old. She carried a little doll. When they pried her away from her mother, the doll fell into the snow. The mercenaries were too busy reveling in their domination of the village to notice, but Nora did. She told me later I never took my eyes off the doll, like I recognized it from somewhere.

"I killed several mercenaries before the others knew what was happening, and then I cut down the rest. It wasn't easy. They were experienced and well trained, and Faolán and I were outnumbered. I took a few arrows and cuts but didn't stop until every last one was dead. Nora said it was like I was possessed by some dark power. She told me it was one of the only times she was truly afraid. When

I started toward the village elder, sword in hand, Nora thought I was going to kill him. Instead, I reached into the snow, picked up the doll, and handed it to the girl."

Saroise regarded him with a strange expression, as if despite the countless number of stories she'd heard as a bard, something about what he'd said nevertheless surprised her. "And you let Nora go?"

"I cut her free and resumed the journey to Dothrunvaggen. We were separated not long after. Nora saw something in me that night, and she's never given up on me since. She's the kind of person who believes in people and ideas. She thinks the world is worth fighting for."

"Do you?"

"No."

"Then what do you fight for?"

Berengar shrugged. "You asked for the story. Now it's your turn. Why did Imogen flee the castle?"

An arrow sailed past his head before Saroise could reply. Berengar tensed, expecting the brigands. Instead, Evander blocked their path forward.

"Where is she? Where's Rose?"

"I don't know where she is," Berengar replied.

The huntsman pulled back on the bow's drawstring. "Did you kill her?"

"No. Right now, we have other concerns. The brigands have taken Lady Imogen prisoner."

"I know." Evander pointed out a set of tracks. "When I couldn't find Rose, I went looking for Imogen. Her trail led me here."

"Unless we stop them, they'll kill her—or worse," Godfrey added. "We need your help."

Evander lowered his bow. "Very well. I will lend my aid, for Lady Imogen's sake. Don't think that means our business is finished, Warden Berengar."

Berengar nodded. Their truce, however temporary, would have to hold until the matter with Imogen was resolved.

They continued on in silence, careful to avoid alerting possible scouts to their presence. Again the weather turned sour, and a gloom settled over the forest. The trail led to a place where multiple sets of footprints marred the bare earth. Berengar noticed freshly trampled grass along a well-trodden path. *We're close.*

Faolán stared ahead, and her ears perked up in alert.

"This is the place," Keely said.

It wasn't long until the brigands' fort came into view, though the hideaway was only a fort in the loosest sense of the word. Even the crumbling goblin fortress to which Berengar had tracked the Black Hand made for a better defensive stronghold. An unimposing fence surrounded the inner encampment. The weathered spruce posts were warped and blemished from rain and insect infestations. A single watchtower peeked over the short fence; the forest had reclaimed a second such tower over time.

At their approach, a horn reverberated from the watchtower, where a sentry and two archers kept watch. Moments later, the gate opened to allow five brigands outside before closing again to bar entrance to the fort.

"What are you doing?" Saroise demanded when Berengar reached for his axe.

"Handling things."

"Is violence your only answer? Those men may be outlaws, but they aren't hardened killers. Perhaps we can reason with them."

"Sometimes there is no other way," Berengar told her. "Sometimes men have to die."

"What if you're wrong?"

"Have it your way," he muttered. "Just keep out of

range of those arrows."

Saroise led her mare to the head of the company, though she followed his advice and remained at a safe distance. The others fanned out to flank her on either side. The brigand foot soldiers seemed hardly equipped for battle. Most wore either threadbare or no armor, and their weapons were rusted and in need of repair.

"Come out and face us," Berengar called out. "We know you're holding Lady Imogen."

Saroise shot him a dark look before returning her gaze to the fort. "We only want to talk. We are not your enemies."

"Any friend to Laird Margolin is our enemy," Avery shouted down from the watchtower. "Margolin, who murdered good Lord Cairrigan and his family? Who befouled our land with arcane rituals and the worship of pagan devils? Who seized our property and crushed our people with heavy taxes?" He shook his head. "We will not submit. We will fight for our families and neighbors in the name of Laird Cairrigan. We will spill our blood until the tyrant is dead and our lands are liberated from his cruelty."

"Is that what this is about?" Godfrey asked, cutting short a cheer from the brigands. "Vengeance? Killing Lady Imogen won't further your cause."

Avery snarled. "We shall see. Laird Margolin must withdraw his forces from our towns and villages and end his oppressive taxation. If not, there are others who would pay a handsome price for her—coin enough to sustain ourselves and support our cause."

An archer fired an arrow that landed a few feet short of Saroise's horse.

"Begone," Avery said. "This is your only warning."

Enough of this, Berengar thought. *Time to do things my way.* "Can you draw their fire?" he whispered to Evander.

Evander nodded and deftly reached for one of the arrows in his quiver. Berengar took the reins in one hand and spurred his horse forward as Evander nocked and aimed an arrow, which he fired at the watchtower. Two enemy arrows streaked by, but Berengar lowered his head, gathering momentum as he charged the gate. The brigands scattered out of his way at the last moment, and the gate came crashing down.

Berengar was already on his feet, axe in hand, as the first cries of *warden* carried through the fort. He didn't bother waiting for the others to come to his aid. Brigands rushed to meet him, and the battle began. The curse slowed his movements considerably, and he took far more than his usual share of hits, but Faolán kept his enemies from overwhelming him. Stripped of his speed, Berengar relied on his superior strength to fight his way through the enemy ranks. Shouts rang out behind, where Tuck and Silas joined the battle under cover of Evander's arrows. Even Godfrey entered the fray, using his staff as a club while Saroise and Keely looked for Imogen.

A defender sprinted toward him, wildly swinging his sword. Rather than attempting to evade the blow, Berengar countered with his axe's handle. The force knocked the sword loose and sent the brigand stumbling back, and Berengar battered him to the ground with a backhanded strike. He raised his axe to deliver the killing blow but hesitated, remembering the unarmed man he'd killed in front of Rose.

Most of the brigands were thin and hungry-looking, their clothes soiled and ragged. These men weren't soldiers —just broken men fighting for a lost cause. It was something he understood better than most. Berengar stayed his hand and made his way to the camp's center.

There, Avery held a knife to Imogen's neck.

CHAPTER FIFTEEN

"THAT'S FAR ENOUGH," Avery said. "Don't come any closer."

When Berengar started toward him, Avery pressed the blade against Imogen's throat to warn him away.

"I mean it. Take one more step and I'll slit her throat."

Hushed silence fell over the fort as the fighting ceased. The others were too far away to intervene. Berengar looked to Faolán, who crouched nearby, waiting to strike. Their arrangement mirrored the positions they'd occupied when Berengar had confronted the scholar who wielded the thunder rune. Imogen was the only variable.

Tension mounted as both sides watched the standoff unfold. Berengar stared Avery down, weighing his options. The brigand leader was cornered with nowhere to run. One swing of his axe would do the job, but with the curse slowing him down, he wasn't sure he could close the distance between them in time.

He couldn't take the risk. Imogen would be dead before he reached her. Berengar pushed down his anger and lowered his axe. He'd have to find another way.

"It's over, Avery. Let the girl go."

Avery wore a venomous expression. "You're a Warden of Fál! You should be fighting with us! Laird Margolin bleeds these lands dry. The people cry out for help, but no one hears. So much for the High Queen's justice."

"We're running out of time," Saroise said. "Laird Margolin's soldiers are on their way to Alúine. I barely escaped the castle to bring word."

Her warning provoked a reaction from Imogen, who remained admirably calm despite the charged atmosphere. "Release me—I beg you. My uncle will raze the village to the ground to claim me."

Avery trembled with palpable rage. "You think I'm afraid to die? My brother and his family fell at Laird Cairrigan's castle, butchered by Laird Margolin's soldiers. I found their bodies, broken and bloodied."

Evander took aim with his bow, but Berengar shook his head to caution against the shot.

"Lady Imogen is not her uncle. His sins are not hers."

Avery returned his attention to him. "I've heard the tales of the Bloody Red Bear. I know what you did to the Ice Queen's son at the Fortress of Suffering. You terrorized the north in defiance of Scathach. How is this any different?"

"The tales are true," Berengar said. "See how your men tremble before me. They're right to be afraid. I could kill you all without breaking a sweat. Is this what you want people to see when they look at you? A monster?"

Friar Godfrey passed unharmed through the ranks of the brigands and came to stand beside him. "You're right. Laird Margolin's crimes have gone unanswered for far too long, but this is not the way." The friar's face showed sympathy and understanding. "You and your brother were

Laird Cairrigan's tanners, were you not? Do you think he would approve of what you have done in his name?"

Avery's eyes darted from Godfrey to Berengar and back again, as if expecting some sort of ploy. "What do you know of it, friar?"

"Laird Cairrigan was my father," Godfrey said. "So you see, I also lost my family when the castle fell."

Imogen and Saroise alone appeared unsurprised by Godfrey's revelation. No one was more taken aback than Tuck, who stared slack-jawed at the friar. Berengar remembered Tuck's drunken confession in the ruins of Cairrigan's castle, when the guard admitted to sparing Cairrigan's youngest son all those years ago. That son was Godfrey. Berengar felt a grudging sense of respect for the friar. Despite everything Margolin had taken from him, Godfrey had returned to help others, not for revenge, and renounced his claim to power in favor of a life of service.

Although a number of the brigands bowed in recognition of Laird Cairrigan's sole surviving heir, Avery refused to yield.

"Coward. We would have fought for you, but you abandoned us—left us to fight and die alone."

Godfrey held his wooden hand out to Avery. "Like you, my heart was once poisoned by revenge, but I let go of my earthly titles and possessions to follow a better path. Put the blade down and help heal these lands. If you kill her, you're no different from Margolin."

Avery's expression grew pained, and the knife wavered in his hand. No one spoke for a long moment, and at last he dropped the knife and released his hold on Imogen.

Instead of running to safety, Imogen turned to face her captor. "Thank you. I'm truly sorry for the pain my uncle has caused you." She glanced around the fort at the other outlaws. "All of you. You're not alone. This land has suffered under my uncle's cruelty for far too long."

"If you really mean that," Avery said, "be better than him."

"You have my word," Imogen told him. "I will make amends."

Saroise hurried to her side, and the two friends shared a brief embrace.

"You made it," Imogen said. "I owe you a debt I can never repay."

"Your uncle knows you're here," Saroise replied. "His men are on their way." She looked over her shoulder at the others. "We must get Lady Imogen to safety without delay."

Berengar blocked their path to the gate. "Not so fast." His gaze fell on Imogen. "I went through a lot of trouble on your account, and you're not going anywhere until you tell me what's really going on."

Imogen nodded. "Very well, Warden Berengar. If you want the truth, you shall have it. I suppose I owe you that much. You must be aware of my uncle's ruthlessness by now. The truth is far more terrible. He is a wicked man, willing to commit unspeakable evil to hold onto power. The church banished him from Dún Aulin for heretical worship of the elder gods, but he continued the practice in secret, delving further into the arcane arts. Some years ago, my uncle brought into his service a spiritist who claimed the power to commune with the Fomorian servants of old."

"The man in the hood," Berengar muttered.

"You might know him as Thaddeus, my uncle's chief adviser. Thaddeus knows of a ritual to wake Balor from his slumber—a ritual involving the sacrifice of souls at the Festival of the Blood Moon. Thaddeus bound the Dullahan to his will and sent him to collect enough souls to power the ritual, but a final blood sacrifice is needed—one of noble blood."

Margolin plans to sacrifice her, Berengar realized. *His own niece.*

"That is why I helped Lady Imogen flee the castle," Saroise said. "Laird Margolin's dark arts have already unleashed pestilence across the land. If he succeeds, Balor will rise again, and Fál will fall into utter ruin."

Berengar wasn't sure if he believed her. Magic was real enough, but that didn't mean the elder gods were real. The world was full of stories and tales that amounted to nothing more than superstition. Even if Balor was real, there was no guarantee the ritual would even work. Still, *Margolin* believed it, which meant Imogen's life was in danger nonetheless.

At last the true reason for Margolin's request stood revealed. The tale of the ogre was a ruse to trick him into delivering Imogen to her uncle, who was determined to recover her in time for the ritual. The hag probably thought she could harness Balor's power for herself, which explained why she wanted Imogen.

"Now that you know the truth, what do you plan to do?" Imogen asked.

None of his options were good. If he sided with Imogen, Margolin would refuse to uphold his side of their bargain. Word of his deeds at Kildare would reach the High Queen's ears. If he failed to bring Imogen to the hag, the curse would turn him to stone. He lost either way.

"We'll ride north, to Meath. There you will be beyond your uncle's reach." Whatever else he was, he was a Warden of Fál, and he would not give an innocent girl over to be murdered. He'd deal with the consequences later. "Don't think this means I'm getting involved in some struggle for the throne. I'll take you to safety, but that's as far as it goes."

"Thank you," she said.

They left the fort behind, and Berengar noticed Saroise regarding him with a curious expression as they made their way to the horses.

"What?"

"You let them live. You could have killed them, but you didn't."

Berengar shrugged. "They weren't worth the waste of energy."

The company mounted their horses and set off for Alúine. Once they reached the village, they'd only have a limited window to prepare for the journey to Meath before Margolin's soldiers arrived. Evander, who agreed to accompany them as far as the village, intended to go in search of Rose afterward.

Imogen convinced Berengar to take Keely and her mother with them in case Margolin attempted to exact retribution on Varun's family. Berengar acceded to her request, though he knew the company's number might attract unwanted attention on the road. He kept a close eye on Tuck, who had gone quiet following their departure from the fort. The guard appeared uneasy, and it wasn't hard to guess why. He probably had orders to bring Imogen back to Margolin, and the punishment for failing to deliver her would surely be severe. Whether he would let his fear or his conscience win out was an open question.

"How can we keep Lady Imogen safe from the Dullahan after reaching Meath?" Godfrey asked Saroise.

"As long as he remains enslaved to Margolin's will, there is nowhere she can go that the Dullahan will not follow," Saroise replied. "The head he carries is imbued with supernatural sight. Its eyes are always moving, searching for prey even in the blackest night."

"There has to be some way to stop him," Berengar said. "Even monsters have weaknesses."

"The Dullahan is no ordinary monster. He travels the land in search of lost souls, to guide them to the afterlife— a purpose Thaddeus has perverted for his own ends."

If that's true, killing Thaddeus might free the Dullahan from his control, Berengar reasoned. It was a difficult proposition at best, given the number of Margolin's soldiers and the spiritist's power over both the Dullahan and the sluagh. At the moment, he was better served getting Imogen out of harm's way before the Festival of the Blood Moon.

"Should we be so unfortunate as to find ourselves at his mercy, there is one thing that might work." Saroise held up a single gold coin. "The Dullahan is said to fear the sight of gold. In the songs, he flees when golden objects are placed in his path."

Berengar wasn't keen to trust his fate to another old wives' tale. If it came to it, he would rely on his axe. Although his previous encounter with the Dullahan hadn't gone in his favor, this time he would be ready.

The sun's warmth ebbed. Dark clouds rolled across the sky to cast looming shadows over the forest.

Blast it. Another storm was likely on its way. If the rains came, they'd lose precious time he didn't have. Even with night hours away, Berengar's time was short. Already the curse drained him of energy, sapping his strength. Saroise had praised him for sparing the outlaws, but he wasn't sure he could have taken them all in his weakened state. It wouldn't be long before the others took note.

As they neared the path's end, Faolán paused at the forest's border and glanced back at him, her eyes wide in alert. Berengar pulled back on the reins and signaled to the others, bringing the company to a halt.

"What is it?" Imogen asked.

Berengar didn't answer. "Stay here. I'll scout ahead."

He dismounted and stalked toward Faolán. When he reached the trees, he crouched low and peered past the forest's edge, and the source of Faolán's alarm became readily apparent.

Margolin's men had reached Alúine first.

Soldiers surrounded the villagers on three sides. Scouts rode past the village as the main force entered Alúine. Imogen's earlier prediction proved prescient. Now that Margolin's soldiers knew she was close, they'd tear the village apart to find her—by any means necessary.

"What is it?" Imogen whispered, approaching with Saroise on foot.

One of the scouts passed by, and Berengar held up a finger to warn her to keep quiet. Fortunately, they hadn't been spotted. As long as they remained unseen, they could slip through the forest and elude Margolin's forces.

A horn sounded behind them, causing the scout to turn around. Tuck raised the horn to his lips to sound the alarm a second time, and Godfrey used his walking stick to knock the guard from his horse.

Tuck scrambled to his feet and ran from the woods, shouting and waving his arms. "Over here!"

When the scout spotted Imogen at the forest's border, he called out to his companions, and horsemen diverted from Alúine and rode in their direction.

Saroise tugged at Berengar's arm. "We have to go."

He shook his head. "It's too late. We can't outrun them now that they've seen her."

"We have to do *something*," Saroise protested. "We can't just stand here."

Berengar didn't get the chance to respond. The approaching force stopped just short of the forest, where Tuck joined their ranks. Soldiers parted to clear the way for two riders. Berengar recognized each in turn. The first was Thaddeus, whom he remembered from his brief stay at Blackthorn. Beside him sat Phineas, who must have brought word to the castle after his escape.

Thaddeus' black robes rippled in the wind, giving him the appearance of a living shadow as he approached. He set his gaze on the forest. "Lady Imogen! There is nowhere left for you to hide. Come forth, or Alúine will burn."

Evander nocked an arrow, but Berengar shook his head to dissuade him. Thaddeus was right. They were trapped. There were too many soldiers to escape unscathed. Even if Evander's shot struck true, the remaining forces would kill everyone in their path.

Berengar seized Imogen's arm and started toward the forest's edge.

"I should have known," Saroise said angrily. "After everything, you're just going to hand her over."

"We can't fight them all. Not on our own. Listen to me —they can't kill Imogen until the blood moon. If I make good on my pledge and deliver Imogen to Margolin's men, I'll be welcomed into the castle with open arms."

"You mean to trick them," Saroise said, quickly catching on.

"Aye. Take the others and return to the brigands' fort. Tell them this is their chance to end Margolin's rule for good. I'll let everyone into the castle after dark, before Margolin can complete the ritual. We'll stop them there."

Thaddeus' voice again reverberated through the trees, and the soldiers began advancing toward the woods.

"You should do as he says," Imogen told Saroise.

"Once Thaddeus has me, he won't bother hunting the rest of you—and Alúine will be spared."

While Saroise and the others retreated to wait at a safe distance until Margolin's forces withdrew, Berengar helped Imogen onto his horse.

"You're playing a dangerous game, Warden Berengar," she whispered as they emerged from the forest.

It was true. Even if the brigands agreed to the plan and he managed to open the gates of Blackthorn, the odds were against them. They were vastly outnumbered, and Margolin had the Dullahan fighting for him. Still, it was too late to turn back. He'd made his choice, and there was nothing left to do but see it through to the end.

Berengar tightened his hold on Imogen, who put on a convincing display at resisting the show of force. The soldiers hesitated at the sight of them approaching, but Thaddeus held up a hand, and the men lowered their swords to grant them safe passage.

"Here she is. As promised." Berengar lowered Imogen to the ground and shoved her forward for good measure.

Thaddeus nodded to his men, who quickly took Imogen into their possession.

"I take it your master received the gift I sent him," Berengar said. "I've fulfilled my end of the bargain. It's time for Margolin to make good on his word."

The spiritist's lips pulled into a thin smile. "You've done well, Warden Berengar. Unfortunately, we can't risk word of these affairs reaching the High Queen's ears. Now that we have Lady Imogen, we no longer have need of you." He motioned to his men. "Kill him."

Berengar pulled back on the reins, but before he could turn his horse around, Margolin's archers fired on him.

The first arrow hit him in the shoulder.

The second struck him just above the heart.

CHAPTER SIXTEEN

THE REINS SLIPPED from his hands, and he slumped forward in the saddle. Berengar's horse bolted for the forest under a volley of arrows as more archers loosed their shafts. When he grabbed at one of the arrows in an effort to break off the shaft, his hand came back empty and smeared with blood.

I'm not dying here, he thought, fighting to remain conscious. *Not until I take a few of those bastards with me first.*

One arrow passed him by, and then another. Just as the forest seemed within reach, the flurry of arrows found his mount. Spurred on by the pain, the horse picked up speed despite its mortal wounds, moving erratically. Berengar found himself thrown from the saddle, but his boot remained caught in the stirrup. The horse dragged him along behind it into the woods before finally collapsing on top of him just after he freed the silver dagger from his boot.

"Find him," Thaddeus called to the foot soldiers. "If he lives, kill him. The rest of you, come with me. We have what we came for."

Margolin's forces were withdrawing from Alúine and leaving only a small contingent behind. At least he wouldn't have to fight the whole army on his own.

Ordinarily, easing his way out from under the horse would have been a simple task, his injuries notwithstanding. The curse, however, had stripped him of most of his former strength. Faolán tried dragging him free, but it was no use.

Footsteps sounded nearby. He didn't have long before Margolin's men found him. With a tremulous hand, Berengar attempted to cut himself free of the stirrup but dropped the blade, which landed out of his reach. When he looked up, he saw an archer and a swordsman standing over him. Berengar clenched his teeth and waited, but before the archer could release the bowstring, Rose hit the man from behind with a stone. Faolán charged the swordsman and left him a whimpering mess before making short work of the archer.

Rose's gaze lingered on the arrows extending from Berengar's armor. "You're hurt."

"What are you doing out here?"

"Hiding," she answered. "From you, actually. Bad place to do so, from the look of things." She dropped the stone and hesitated in front of the dagger. "If I help you, you aren't going to turn around and attack me, are you?"

"No. You have my word."

Rose picked up the dagger and cut him free from the stirrup. She helped him out from under the horse before rolling him onto his back and looking over his injuries.

"There'll be more of them soon," he told her as she worked to remove the arrows. "You should go." It was too late for him. The arrow was too close to his heart.

"Your wounds aren't fatal," Rose said. "Look."

Berengar looked again. The arrow should have pierced

his heart. Instead, his hardened, rock-like skin had blunted its point. The curse that was slowly killing him had just saved his life.

Not yet strong enough to stand, Berengar allowed Rose to help him into a sitting position. "Why help me?"

"I don't know. Maybe I'm just trying to prove to myself that I'm not a monster." Rose lowered herself to the ground and sat down next to him. "I would have killed Evander last night if you hadn't stopped me. You know what it's like to be cursed—to be betrayed by your own body."

Berengar grimaced at the sight of sinister black blood leaking from his chest and shoulder. "I do."

"I never wanted to hurt anyone."

"I know."

"As much as I don't want to admit it, maybe you're right. I can't control it—this darkness inside me. I'm so tired of trying. No matter what I do, everyone around me suffers, and now I have no one left."

The knowledge that at some point he might have to kill her afforded him a rare opportunity for honesty. "I understand. More than you know. Maybe we're both monsters, but unlike me, you didn't choose to become one. And you're wrong about one thing. You're not alone. Evander still cares for you."

"There was something in what you said before," she said after a moment. "You lost someone?"

"My wife. She died in childbirth, before the war." He let the cool breeze wash over him as his heartbeat grew fainter. "There's nothing I wouldn't do for another day with her. You still have that chance with Evander."

"If I were to transform at the wrong time, I could kill him."

"You could. It's for you to decide if you want to take that risk."

She eyed him suspiciously. "What about you? I thought you wanted to kill me."

Berengar shrugged. "I won't get a say in the matter. Now that Margolin has Imogen, there's nothing I can do to stave off the hag's curse." He held out his hand to her. "Now help me up. I only have a few hours left, and I'm not going to spend them waiting around to die."

Rose helped him to his feet, and together they made their way through the forest. Berengar killed four more soldiers with Faolán's assistance before returning to the place where he last saw the others. Although Saroise was gone, there was no sign of a struggle to indicate Margolin's men had discovered her. The fallout from his failed gambit with Imogen had probably drawn the soldiers' attention away long enough to allow her to escape. With any luck, Saroise was on her way to the brigands' hideaway to get help. Still, gaining entrance to Castle Blackthorn would be difficult without someone on the inside.

Faolán's tail straightened alertly, and Berengar turned around to find himself once again staring down Evander's bow.

"Get away from her," Evander said.

"Relax," Berengar told him. "She's not my problem—not while the sun's out, at any rate."

Evander looked skeptical, but before he could reply, Rose threw herself into his arms, and the two shared a passionate embrace.

"I'm so sorry, Evander. I could have killed you."

Evander stroked her hair. "It's all right. I'm here now."

"I should have told you the truth, but I worried you would take it upon yourself to try to break the curse."

"That's exactly what I plan to do," Evander said. "I'm going to kill the hag and set you free. When this is all over, we'll leave Alúine together."

"Saroise," Berengar interrupted. He'd given the lovers their moment. "Where is she?"

"She and Godfrey left to convince the brigands to join our cause, as you suggested," Evander answered. "They sent me to find you, if you lived. They plan to meet in the village, with or without the brigands."

"Then there's nothing left for us to do," Berengar said. Everything rested on the bard's ability to convert the outlaws to their cause.

When they reached Alúine, the soldiers were gone, returned to Blackthorn with their prize.

"There she is!"

The whole population of Alúine looked on as a crowd marched toward Rose, shouting *beast* and *monster*. The men Berengar had encountered outside the Green Flagon had formed a frenzied mob armed with crude weapons.

Evander drew an arrow from his quiver. "Run, Rose!"

"Get out of here—both of you," Berengar said. "Find horses in the stables and leave this place behind." He stared long and hard at Rose. "Don't come back." He strode to meet the approaching mob before she could reply.

When Berengar took out his axe, his strength threatened to rebel against him, and it took nearly all his will to maintain his hold. The sight of him standing in their path was enough to frighten the mob into remaining a safe distance away.

"Let us through," said their leader. "She's the monster!"

"And what are you lot?" Berengar's narrowing gaze

moved past the mob to settle on the other villagers watching outside their homes. "I thought you were keeping something from me. This whole time, it was Margolin abducting those girls, and you knew about it, didn't you? Maybe you even helped him, or at least kept quiet about it."

He looked over his shoulder and saw Rose and Evander flee the village on horseback. They were headed west, toward Móin Alúin. *They mean to slay the hag*, Berengar realized. *I must help them.* Succeeding might lift both their curses.

"You don't understand," said Iain, standing among the other villagers. "We've lived under the threat of the hag's curse for so long. Laird Margolin promised to free us from her torment if we helped him."

Berengar didn't bother disguising his disgust. It suddenly dawned on him that Phineas hadn't escaped by accident. Iain had set him free. "So you allowed your friends and daughters to be taken and sacrificed to an ancient evil. Was it worth it?"

He lowered his axe and turned his back. These people weren't worthy of his anger.

"Where are you going?" Iain called to him.

"To the bog," Berengar replied. "I'm going to kill the hag, and then I'm putting an end to this—for good."

H e ventured alone into Móin Alúin, not expecting to return. There was no sign of Rose or Evander, which didn't bode well for either. The sun faded behind him as he went deeper into the bog, until the light was no more than a distant echo. Crows watched from above as he staggered past the trees. Their eyes gleamed with malevolent intent in the torchlight.

Rain came down in torrents, but he could no longer feel it against his skin. His three days were nearly up. The hag's curse extended to his entire body, turning him to stone. Once it spread to his heart, the transformation would be complete. Even if it was too late for him, he could try to take the hag with him.

He pushed forward through sheer force of will. Each step was harder than the last. His muscles were so rigid he could hardly move, and the simple act of breathing required tremendous effort.

A vast darkness seemed to swell around him as he advanced. Berengar laid a hand on one of the trees to steady himself and felt a viscous, sticky liquid. Blood oozed from the tree. He withdrew his hand and surveyed the full extent of the hag's corruption under his torch's weak glow. The trees swayed and tilted toward him when he passed underneath, and the falling rains scorched the earth like acid. Monstrous shadows—hinting at nameless horrors better left unseen —lurked beyond the firelight.

Berengar held out the torch to ward away the dark. "Show yourself, witch."

A flash of lightning illuminated the hag's wretched form. Buzzing flies hovered over her and nested in her rotting flesh.

"Where are they?" Berengar demanded. "What have you done with them?"

The hag ignored the question. "You came alone." Her face twisted into something less than human, evidencing her displeasure, and her bulbous eyes simmered with malice. "A fool, even at the end. If the people of Alúine sent you here for me, they will pay dearly for their treachery."

"This is between us. Leave the villagers out of it." Berengar grappled with his sword, but his arm was nearly frozen stiff. "Since you're so fond of deals, I've got one for you. Lift Rose's curse and take me in her place."

She fixed a narrowing gaze upon him. "Your life is already mine, Berengar One-Eye, and you have nothing else worth taking."

The hag receded into the darkness before Berengar managed to wrench the sword loose.

"Find her," he said to Faolán. "We don't have long."

Faolán took up the hag's scent, and they stalked off in the swamp's direction. Whispers followed him along the path to the hag's lair. If he listened hard enough, he could almost hear words spoken in a black tongue. The hag was casting spells to keep him from reaching her before he succumbed to the curse.

"Boy," an inhuman voice called from the shadows, where a towering figure rose among the trees.

When the corpselike figure stepped into the torchlight, Berengar stopped dead in his tracks. His father loomed larger in death than he ever had in life.

"I killed you," Berengar said. "You're not real. This is a trick."

The figure's chest heaved with rasping laughter. Blood gushed from his throat where the dagger had opened it up. "You can't kill me, son. I'm a part of you. We're one and the same."

Berengar's face contorted in rage, and he rushed to meet the specter. They collided, and the torch slipped from his grasp. Berengar found himself alone, holding his sword in the dark. His father was gone.

He held onto Faolán and struggled to his feet, relying on the wolfhound to lead the way in the torch's absence. His limbs weighed him down like bricks, but he pressed on, dragging one leg behind the other.

"We're close," he said, as much for his benefit as Faolán's. "We just have to keep going."

A weak glow emanated ahead, visible through reeds along the swamp's edge. The light grew brighter as he approached. A woman's scream sounded in the dark, and the hair on his arms stood on end. Berengar followed the sound to its source and pushed back the tall reeds.

His wife lay on the birthing table, her sheets drenched in blood.

"You let us die," she moaned. "Why couldn't you save us?"

Berengar started toward her, but she vanished just before he could touch her. A hand from the swamp wrapped itself around his ankle. He managed to pull himself free as more corpses rose to the water's surface. Their decaying faces bore a strong resemblance to people he'd killed. The dead surrounded him, forcing him to the swamp's center.

"What are you waiting for?" Berengar shouted, his sword held at the ready.

"Murderer," their voices hissed. "Monster."

Berengar lashed out, but all the strength had drained from him. They closed in around him, ensnaring him in a rapidly tightening wall of bodies.

"I'll kill you," he muttered, hacking away with his sword. "I'll kill you all again."

The whispers stopped suddenly, and the dead were gone—all but one. The sword protruded from the chest of a small child.

Berengar uttered a tormented wail and released the sword, which disappeared into the swamp, along with the girl. He sank to his knees in mud and tried desperately to pull the black nail from his palm as the rains washed over him. It was no use.

Firelight beckoned him from a distance. The hag's lair was nearly within reach. He tried to find his footing, but it was too late. His legs had turned to stone. He grasped at the air, and the fingers of his left hand slowly stopped moving as Faolán barked and whimpered.

I'm sorry, Nora, he thought, *but they're right. I am a monster.*

He felt the curse creeping up his neck, slowly paralyzing him, and there was nothing he could do to fight it.

I wanted to be the man you saw in me, but I lost myself somewhere along the way. A long time ago he started down the road of vengeance and never turned from it. He chose to harden his heart—to love nothing—leaving no room for weakness or compassion. Now he was paying the price.

He felt his heart stop. No matter. The best parts of him died years before. In truth, he was a ghost already.

"You're wrong," a voice called to him. "You're not a monster."

A small figure stood in front of him, her features hidden by shadow. There was something strangely familiar about her, but he was too disoriented to remember how he knew her. With his head bowed, it was impossible to get a good look at her face. He wasn't sure if she was really there at all, or just in his head. She seemed a mirage, like the others but altogether different.

"You welcome death because you're afraid to live. You hide your pain behind your rage to hide from the world—and from yourself—but no matter how you try to deny it, your humanity is a part of you. Your heart is mangled, but it is not stone."

He could barely understand her words, but her presence radiated an overwhelming sense of warmth, even in the bitter cold of the swamp. Berengar longed to reach out to her, but he remained immobile.

The girl, who stood a hair's breadth away, bent down

beside him. "You saved the hobgoblins when you could have let them die."

The black nail quivered in his palm.

"You took time from your quest to help an innocent man."

The nail shook violently and loosened bit by bit.

"You spared the brigands when you could have killed them. Even now, at the end, you're willing to die so that others may live."

The nail fell away and vanished under the swamp's surface.

Berengar's heart restarted with a sudden kick, and air flooded into his lungs. His skin returned to its normal color as the curse lifted. His old strength returned, and energy surged through his veins.

With his mind cleared, his thoughts turned to the girl. He looked for her, but she was gone.

"Eileen?" he whispered.

There was no answer. He was alone. He wondered briefly if the girl was ever really there or simply conjured by his fevered mind. He pushed himself up, and his gaze fell on the hag's lair.

"Come on," he said after Faolán led him to his sword. "Let's end this."

Thorns and briars enveloped the hag's abode—a small, well-hidden hut in the deepest part of the swamp. Bone fragments and pagan symbols hung from crooked branches, and human skulls adorned spikes littered across the dark soil. Legions of crows looked on from their perches as the hag stirred an enormous copper cauldron, which bubbled and frothed with a particularly foul-smelling substance.

Berengar noticed Evander nearby, ensnared in thorns and unable to move. Rose was trying frantically to free him, even as the thorns bloodied her hands. When night fell, the blood moon would appear and cause Rose's transformation. The hag planned to make her kill her lover and feast on his corpse while in her werewolf form.

"I'm sorry, my love," Rose said. They reached out to each other through the hedge of thorns, and their fingers brushed.

Berengar took out his axe and stepped into the fire's sickly green light. "Turn and face me, witch."

The hag regarded the warden's sudden appearance with utter bewilderment. Her eyes swept his palm in search of the nail. "You should be dead. How did you break the curse?"

Berengar tossed Rose his sword to free Evander from the thorns. "Your days of terrorizing the people of Alúine are over."

"You dare challenge me—here, in my domain?" the hag hissed. "I am mistress of the black arts, and you are but mortal."

Berengar met her eyes with a steely gaze. "I'm going to take my time with you," he promised. "To make you suffer for everything you've done."

For the first time, he saw a sliver of fear in the hag's expression. She was right to be afraid. For the past three days, the curse had forced him to restrain his darkest impulses. Now he was at full strength and ready to unleash the full extent of his rage upon her.

She attacked first, calling the horde of crows down upon him. Berengar lowered his head and fought his way through the swarm. Faolán distracted the hag, causing her to lose her concentration long enough for Berengar to break through the crows. Vines and thorns shot out of the ground at her command, wrapping themselves around his axe, but

Berengar released his hold on the weapon and charged into her. He grabbed the hag's long, wispy hair, jerked back hard, and repeatedly jabbed his dagger into her rib cage. She fell backward and landed on the ground, knocking over the cauldron in the process. Berengar heard coarse, shallow breathing—a sign he'd punctured one of her lungs—as he stooped to retrieve his axe. When she spun around and contorted a webbed hand to cast a spell on him, he chopped the limb off with his axe. The hag tried to crawl toward her hut, but he pinned her to the ground with his boot.

"Any last words?"

Her eyes burned with hate, and she struggled to choke out the words. "One last curse. All the things you have lost —everything that has been taken from you—will be restored, only for you to lose them again."

The axe fell, and the hag's head rolled away. Berengar retrieved the head before making his way to Rose and Evander.

Rose returned his sword. "Why did you help us?"

"Because you deserved a chance," Berengar answered. "Because you're not a monster." He looked her over. "Did it work? Is the curse gone?"

"I don't feel any different," she replied. "We can't be sure until the moon appears."

Berengar turned to go. He'd done all he could.

"Wait," Evander called after him. "Where are you going?"

"The hag's dead, but the job's not done." Imogen was still out there.

"Then we're coming too," Rose said. "You'll need all the help you can get."

He nodded, and the trio started on the path from the bog. Villagers emerged from their homes and approached when they entered Alúine, where the brigands waited to begin the journey to Blackthorn.

Saroise approached with a replacement for his horse, but Berengar started past her. With the crowd looking on, he strode to the center of the village and left the hag's head on a spike.

CHAPTER SEVENTEEN

NIGHT ENSNARED the land like a tightening noose as Berengar approached Blackthorn under cover of darkness. Margolin's castle loomed in the distance, awash in an eerie, otherworldly glow. Flickering torchlight gave the appearance of life to neighboring thorn hedges, which cast grasping shadows along the castle walls.

Berengar kept to the trees, out of the sentries' line of sight, and searched for a weakness in the castle's defenses. The gates were barred, and guards patrolled the castle's outer perimeter. Margolin left nothing to chance. A series of ghostly wails rose above the pouring rains as the sluagh glided toward the castle and vanished into its walls. Berengar looked up at the sky, where storm clouds blotted out the moon. It wouldn't be long before the blood moon appeared.

He motioned for the others to follow him into the deluge, and they set about taking out the patrol one by one. There was no margin for error. Margolin's forces had an overwhelming advantage in numbers, and an early alarm would bring them running. Berengar was careful to avoid drawing attention, and the storm drowned out most of the sounds made by his victims.

As he inched closer to the castle, Berengar noticed Tuck among a patrol on its way back to the gate. He grabbed the guard and clamped a hand over his mouth to prevent him from crying out while the brigands peppered the remaining guards with arrows and dragged their bodies into the woods.

Once they were again hidden from sight, Berengar threw Tuck against a tree. Tuck tried to run, but the warden held the bloodstained axe inches from his face.

"Give me one good reason I shouldn't kill you where you stand." He held the blade against Tuck's neck. "Tell me how to get past the gate, or I'll carve you inside out."

Godfrey pushed Berengar's axe away with his wooden hand. "Wait."

Tuck averted his gaze, unable to meet the friar's eyes.

"I know what haunts you," Godfrey said. "I was there when Margolin's soldiers butchered my family."

"I'm sorry," Tuck mumbled. He again reeked of alcohol. "I'm sorry for everything."

Godfrey put a hand on the guard's shoulder. "I know, and I forgive you."

Tuck looked at him with complete surprise. "I don't understand."

"You let me go. Because of you I've been able to help countless others. You're not an evil man—just a lost one. It's not too late for you. The Lord offers redemption, but you have to ask for it."

"I want it," Tuck stammered. "What must I do?"

"If Laird Margolin's ritual succeeds, many more will suffer," Godfrey replied. "Open the gate and let us inside."

"What?" Berengar demanded. "You want me to let him go? He'll tell Margolin what he's seen the moment he's inside the gates."

Godfrey stared into Tuck's eyes for a brief moment. "No—he won't."

"He'll get you all killed," Berengar said.

"We must reach the castle without delay," Saroise reminded him. "It's the only choice we have."

Berengar backed away from Tuck. "If this goes south, I'll take your head before the night is through."

Tuck stumbled from cover and fled to the castle. After the sentries granted him entry, Berengar and the others began their approach. The companions relied on the storm and shadows to mask their movements and pressed themselves against the castle's lofty walls while waiting for Tuck to open the gate.

Minutes passed, and still the gate remained closed. Several of the brigands exchanged worried looks. Even with the patrol eliminated, the castle's sentries would spot them eventually, and they were running out of time.

What's he waiting for? Berengar thought, suspicious of treachery.

A bell tolled loudly above the thunder. Archers appeared on the wall, searching for them in the darkness. The gate opened without warning, and shouts rang out on the other side of the wall. Berengar tightened his hold on the axe and charged through the gate with Faolán at his side. Guards stormed the entrance to prevent them from making it farther inside the castle, and Berengar sprinted to meet them while Evander and the brigands exchanged fire with the archers.

He caved in the first soldier's breastplate with one swing of his axe. The man slipped in the mud, clutching his chest. The axe split the next man's helmet in two and cracked skull underneath. More soldiers rushed toward him, but the sudden attack had clearly caught them off balance, and with the sentries eliminated, the remaining numbers positioned near the gate were few. Following a brief skirmish, soldiers' bodies littered the area around the entrance, and the way forward was clear.

Berengar heard a whimper nearby and turned to see Tuck, with four arrows sticking out of his flank, slumped over the lever used to raise the gate. The guard's grip faltered, and he landed in a puddle.

"They have her in the courtyard," Tuck said. "Go." He reached out to Godfrey, who had stopped to administer last rites. "Do you think the Lord will forgive me?"

Godfrey nodded. "Aye. Be at peace, my friend."

At that, Tuck smiled and breathed his last.

"Follow me," Saroise said. "I know the way."

Apart from the storm raging above, Blackthorn lay quiet under night's embrace. Berengar and the others advanced deeper inside, where many of the castle's inhabitants hid in terror of the horrors unleashed by their master. He followed Saroise up a staircase to a wall that looked over the courtyard.

Imogen lay bound to a stone altar similar to the one on the hill at Alúine. Opposite the altar lay a well enveloped by a withered hawthorn tree. Even Margolin's soldiers appeared unnerved by the strange sounds emanating from the well. Thaddeus stood over the altar, reciting a sinister incantation with his arms stretched toward the heavens. At his side stood the Dullahan, so motionless he might have been mistaken for a statue. As Thaddeus spoke, the spirits of the dead slowly surrounded the altar.

Berengar turned his attention to the more than two

dozen soldiers between them and the altar. Behind them, Margolin observed the ritual with a stone face.

"Can you hit him from here?" he whispered to Evander. Margolin was at least seventy yards away.

Evander nodded, nocked an arrow, and quietly took aim. Before he could fire, the earth shook, causing the castle to groan. Margolin looked up and spotted them, and his soldiers followed their master's gaze.

Berengar and the rebels rushed into the courtyard, and the fighting began. The brigands struggled to hold their own against Margolin's elite soldiers' superior numbers. At Thaddeus' command, the souls of the dead departed the altar to prey upon the living as Imogen watched helplessly from the altar. Man after man fell beside him as Berengar fought against waves of attackers. Within minutes, Margolin's soldiers surrounded the remaining attackers.

Margolin raised a hand. "Stop."

The guards halted their approach.

"It is only fitting you should be here to witness Balor's rebirth, Warden Berengar. After all, it was you who made this possible."

"Go to hell," Berengar said, eyeing the Dullahan, who barred his path to the altar.

Margolin's iron crown seemed to glow in the torchlight. "I've already been there." He laughed, producing a grating, discordant sound that hinted at something monstrous within. "When the assassins opened my neck and left me for dead, I offered my soul to the dark powers in return for vengeance. That was when I heard it calling me—the voice of something other. Now the time has finally come to release Balor from his slumber to plunge this world into eternal darkness."

At the altar, Thaddeus stopped chanting and now held a black sword clutched in his hands.

"With this blade, we shall raise Balor to life anew." The sluagh dissolved into a shadowy blur that revolved around the altar before disappearing into the sword, which hummed with inner power. The spiritist held the black sword aloft and pointed it at the clouds as lightning struck the castle several times in rapid succession. "Souls of the departed, I sacrifice you to invoke the ancient magics. Rise, Balor, King of the Fomorians!"

The clouds parted to reveal the shape of the enormous blood moon stretching across the sky, as if a great red eye had opened above. When the red light fell over the well, the earth shook again, and a horrible presence emerged from the well and filled the courtyard.

Thaddeus passed the blade to Margolin, who approached the altar.

"With this sword, I spill the noble blood of my niece so you may again take form in this realm."

This is it, Berengar thought. He readied himself to make a last stand, but a bark from Faolán stopped him cold.

Rose's eyes glowed amber in the moonlight. Killing the hag hadn't broken her curse. Teeth and nails sharpened into fangs and claws, and by the time Margolin's soldiers realized what was happening, her body was already covered in fur. Arrows and spears from the guards found their marks, but none were made of silver, and the weapons served only to enrage her. She leapt at her attackers and savagely tore them to shreds, and renewed chaos broke loose in the courtyard.

"Rose, stop!"Evander rushed to aid her before Berengar could attempt to prevent him.

She turned to face him, her eyes bereft of any lingering humanity.

"This isn't you." Evander continued his approach and lowered his bow to show he posed no threat. "Fight it."

For a moment the werewolf's face betrayed a hint of recognition. Then an arrow from one of Margolin's archers struck her, and with an angry roar she leapt at Evander, who struggled in vain against her. Busy with the guards, Berengar was unable to intervene in time. Rose disemboweled Evander with her claws before scaling the walls and vanishing into the night.

Berengar sprinted toward the altar, and the remaining brigands followed suit. Margolin was forced to fall back to avoid incoming arrows. The tide of the battle turned, but Margolin's remaining forces held the rebels just short of the altar. Arrows flew wildly in every direction, and both sides suffered heavy losses.

"Kill the warden!" Thaddeus commanded the Dullahan.

The headless rider wielded a sword in one hand and the bony whip in the other. Berengar knew none of his weapons could kill the Dullahan, so he focused instead on holding his own. He parried each attack and drove his enemy from the altar, leaving Thaddeus and Margolin vulnerable. When the Dullahan's whip tore his axe from his grip, Berengar grabbed a fallen shield from the ground and used it to batter his foe until the shield splintered in his hands. A gold coin landed in his path, and the Dullahan froze just long enough for Berengar to recover his weapon. He nodded to Saroise, who cast a number of similar coins onto the ground, which caused the Dullahan to become confused.

"Stop him!" Thaddeus shrieked as Berengar reached the altar. The spiritist made his hand into a fist, drawing a shriek from the Dullahan. "You are bound to serve me. You have no will of your own."

Before Berengar could cut through Imogen's bonds, the Dullahan's hand shot out and gripped him from behind, pulling him away. The creature's whip wrapped around his blade, but the Dullahan stopped before delivering the killing blow.

Thaddeus looked down at an arrow lodged in his chest. Evander, who had taken up his bow with his dying breath, remained upright just long enough to watch the spiritist topple over. Then he too fell and succumbed to his wounds.

Hooves echoed through the courtyard as the headless rider's corpselike horse appeared. Berengar regarded the Dullahan warily, but the creature ignored him and reached for its head, which opened to hiss a single word.

"Margolin."

The Dullahan claimed lost souls, and Margolin had given his soul in exchange for power. Liberated from Thaddeus' control, the Dullahan was free to resume his task.

The bony lash wrapped around Margolin's boot before he could flee. His iron crown clattered to the ground as the Dullahan climbed atop his mount and dragged him screaming into the night.

With Margolin gone, it wasn't long before the rest of his men surrendered or deserted. As the fighting drew to a close, Berengar made his way to the altar and freed Imogen from her restraints.

"It's all right," he told her. "You're safe now."

Even as he said the words, the dark presence from the well swarmed around him. Suddenly, Imogen and the others were gone, replaced by a nightmarish scene of fire and shadow.

"You are too late," thundered a powerful voice. *"You may have thwarted the ritual, but I can still take possession of a mortal vessel."*

A giant loomed through a wreath of flame. Berengar felt the entity prying at his consciousness. Its terrible gaze left him spellbound and powerless to resist its will.

"Your rage and hate burn bright. You will make a powerful host. Soon this land will again tremble before me."

The giant's hand stopped short of him, and the hellish landscape vanished, replaced by the courtyard once more.

"In the name of the Lord of Hosts, I cast you out," Friar Godfrey shouted, forcing the evil presence back into the well, which Avery and Saroise promptly covered.

The red light faded as the clouds concealed the blood moon once more. A grim silence fell over the courtyard, and Berengar took a moment to regain his bearings.

One after another, the castle's inhabitants slowly emerged from hiding. All appeared relieved their former master was gone. As the others celebrated their hard-won victory, Berengar's gaze fell on Evander's lifeless form. He picked up his silver dagger and left the courtyard behind. The fighting was over, but his work wasn't finished. Not yet.

He found Rose on a hill within sight of the castle. With the moon again hidden by the clouds, she had returned to human form. Arrows and spear points covered her body, and blinded by the pain, she hardly noticed his approach. The image reminded him of the young woman he'd discovered in Skinner Kane's dungeon. He hadn't been able to save her either.

When she finally noticed him, she gave a start.

"It's all right," he said. "I'm here."

"I'm so cold." Rose's teeth chattered violently. "It hurts everywhere."

Berengar inspected her wounds. None were made with

silver. All would heal with time. He started to remove one of the arrows, but Rose grabbed at his arm.

"Evander. Is he—"

Berengar shook his head. "He didn't make it. I'm sorry."

"Did I—" She couldn't finish.

"No," he lied. "It wasn't you. Margolin's archers did him in. He died a hero." That last part was true.

"I can't do this without him." Rose trembled, and her whole body shuddered at once. "Help me. I don't want to hurt anyone else." Her meaning was plain.

Berengar held her gaze. "Are you sure this is what you want?"

She nodded through tears. "I want to die as myself, not some beast."

Berengar doubted Darragh would accede to such a request. Most of the other wardens would probably consider it murder.

He quietly grasped the silver dagger. "I promise it will be quick. You won't suffer."

When Rose reached out to him, he took her hand and held it.

"I want to see Evander again. Do you believe in heaven, Warden Berengar?"

"I don't know." If it existed, it wasn't a place he would ever see. "I used to think so."

"Do you think they'll let me in?" Rose asked. "After everything I've done?"

He squeezed her hand. "I do."

"You're a good man." Rose cupped his face, a tender gesture that surprised him. "It's not too late for you. You don't have to be alone. Having someone—it was worth the pain."

The clouds began to part. Berengar glanced at the castle, and when Rose followed his gaze, he slipped the dagger between her ribs.

He stayed with her, there under the light of the blood moon.

CHAPTER EIGHTEEN

THE TANKARD RATTLED when he brought it down on the table.

Empty. Berengar choked down the last mouthful of ale and beckoned to the bartender to refill the tankard. The bartender scurried forward to complete his task and withdrew to allow him to drink in peace, a routine well established over the course of Berengar's stay.

He'd taken up residence in a nondescript, out of the way tavern somewhere near the border with Munster. After renting a room, he'd immediately proceeded to make good on his pledge to drink himself into a stupor and try to forget about everything that had happened since he set foot in Alúine. The days soon settled into a familiar pattern, with one blurring into the next until he was no longer quite sure how long he'd been there. Three weeks or four—it didn't matter. He was in no hurry to leave. Although the tavern's proprietors seemed less than keen on his prolonged presence, they were either gravely in need of his coin or fearful of giving him offense.

Berengar raised the tankard to his lips and took

another sip. A warm, tingling sensation spread through his fingers, but on account of his size, it would be a while yet before the room was spinning around him. Faolán, who lay curled up at his feet, showed no signs of stirring. Enough time had passed for their injuries to heal. Usually, they would have returned to the road already. There was always something else that needed doing, but at the moment, he had a hard time making himself care.

He'd stopped the ritual and put an end to Laird Margolin's tyranny. That counted for something, didn't it? He sighed and took another drink. Regardless of how much he wanted to believe it, he couldn't quite convince himself.

Blackthorn had traded one despot for another. After her ascension to the throne, Imogen had reneged on her pledge to unite the land and set about exacting revenge upon her enemies. Many who previously demonstrated loyalty to her uncle were summarily executed without trial. She promptly proclaimed her intention to punish those who aided and abetted Margolin's schemes by imposing severe taxes and penalties on disloyal villages to establish order. Promising to return the land to the true faith, Imogen declared the practice of magic in all its forms prohibited under penalty of death and defied Friar Godfrey's advice, ordering the continued persecution of goblins and other nonhuman creatures in the area.

Berengar and Godfrey departed Blackthorn not long after burying Rose and Evander—finally joined together in death—within sight of the castle. Godfrey intended to return to Alúine and continue his work. Berengar, who had no desire to set foot in Alúine ever again, declined the friar's invitation to join him.

No one was innocent. The people of Alúine used their fear of the hag to rationalize their actions, but they were just as guilty as anyone else. The brigands claimed to fight for freedom but enforced Imogen's new edicts with enthusiasm, relishing in newfound power over their former oppressors.

No matter what he did, it never seemed to make a difference. He'd prevented Balor's return, but darkness would always find a way to spread. Everyone he'd tried to help, all the things he'd done—it was all for nothing. For a long time, the fight alone was enough. Now he wasn't so sure.

His constant anger had abated for the moment, leaving him feeling tired, empty, and defeated. Although he'd managed to survive the curse, he had not emerged unscathed. His heart wasn't completely stone, but that didn't change things he'd done or the man he was. Rose's last words weighed heavily on his mind. Despite everything she'd endured, she held out hope until her dying breath. He wanted to believe her. He wished he could see his way to finding that kind of hope, but he saw only darkness.

Then there was the hag's final curse. What did it mean, and what did it portend for the future? The tankard again rattled empty. At least the tavern was peaceful. He sat at a lonely table in the back of the room. Apart from the bartender and two patrons several tables away, the hall lay empty. A bead of sweat trickled down his brow. The days were growing warmer, and summer was on its way.

The door opened, and Faolán raised her head as Saroise entered the inn. She stopped to converse with one of the tavern's proprietors before making her way to his table. Berengar used his boot to push the chair opposite him out for her, and she sat on the other side of the table.

"I take it our meeting here isn't an accident," he muttered in a tone meant to imply he wished to be left alone.

"I've been looking for you. You departed Blackthorn in haste."

"My work there was finished. And you? I would have thought the Lady of Blackthorn had more use for you."

Saroise sighed. "It seems an iron crown is an ill fit for Imogen. She has little need of councilors now that she has an army. I left some time ago."

"And you came here," Berengar finished. "Let me guess. You want a song."

Saroise smiled, without a hint of the suspicion or dislike she'd felt toward him. It wasn't an expression others usually chose to grace him with. "You have me wrong, Warden Berengar. I came to apologize."

Perhaps he'd already had too much to drink after all. "Did I hear you correctly?"

"When you first came to Blackthorn, I only saw the man from the stories. Then I learned of your deeds in Alúine and all the people you helped. I was wrong about you, it seems. I was wrong about a great many things, I suspect."

Berengar leaned closer to her. "Why tell me this?"

"To the people of Fál, you're nothing but a killer without conscience." She looked at him intently, as if searching for the answer to a question she had yet to voice. "You made me pledge not to sing of your deeds. Why? Why not let people know the truth?"

Berengar regarded the empty tankard for a long moment. "Fál has enough heroes. Sometimes heroes aren't enough. The monsters out there need someone to fear, and if that means I'll never be beloved like Darragh or the others, I can live with that." He met her eyes with a cold gaze. "Besides—many of the stories are true. There's more than my share of blood on my hands."

If Saroise was troubled by his words, she gave no sign

of it. "You have nothing to fear from me, Warden Berengar. I gave you my word, and I will not break it." She hesitated. "I did not seek you for that reason alone. There is something else."

Berengar sensed something more was coming. Judging from her expression, he wasn't going to like it. "What?"

"Word of your actions at Kildare has spread through Leinster and beyond."

"I should have known Margolin would never keep his word. I gather there are already ballads on the subject?"

"Aye," Saroise replied, "but I'm afraid it's far more serious than that. Blackthorn received word from Dún Aulin."

"Dún Aulin?" A feeling of dread rose in the pit of his stomach.

"For the murder of Skinner Kane on the altar at St. Brigid's, you have been excommunicated from the church. There's a push to have you banished from Leinster under penalty of death."

Politics of church and state were so entwined in Leinster that excommunication from the church meant he was an enemy of the state. All servants of the Lord of Hosts would be encouraged to shun him or even do him bodily harm.

"Good," he muttered. "I hate the whole bloody kingdom. Gives me an excuse not to return."

Saroise didn't appear convinced. Both knew his actions had brought shame on the High Queen. Berengar didn't want to know how Nora would react to the news.

The door opened before either could address the matter further, and two messengers entered the tavern. Both wore white cloaks and carried blades sheathed at their sides. The pair engaged the tavern's proprietor in conversation with distinctly southern accents. After a brief discussion, the tavern's proprietor pointed the pair in Berengar's direction.

"Warden Esben Berengar?" one asked.

"Who's asking?" He inched his hand toward his sword.

One of the messengers handed him a rolled-up piece of parchment. When Berengar saw the sigil of the eagle on the message's seal, he knew immediately where it came from.

"What is it?" Saroise asked, noticing his grim expression.

Berengar broke the seal and unfurled the message before answering. "It's a summons—from King Mór of Munster."

"King Mór requests your presence at Cashel," the messenger said. "He asks that you come without delay."

Berengar's frown deepened. Why would Mór ask for him? There were other wardens more familiar with Munster. He hadn't had dealings with Mór since the war. The message was short on details, suggesting Mór feared its contents might fall into the wrong hands.

Whatever the king's reasons, Berengar owed Mór a debt. Besides, the summons gave him a reason to avoid returning to Tara to face the High Queen's ire.

He folded the message and tucked it into his cloak. "Very well. I'll go."

W hen they set out from the tavern the following morning, the proprietors looked more than a little relieved to see him go. Saroise too returned to the road, headed for parts unknown. They parted ways at a fork in the road, but not before she wished him well. Although it seemed unlikely that any bard with such a tale would decline to put it into song, for his part, Berengar actually believed her sincerity.

The messengers from Munster kept a quiet distance— which, considering his fierce hangover and accompanying ill temper, was probably wise. The throbbing in his temples eventually subsided, and before long his mood returned to its usual level of irritability. The companions traveled under bright sunlight, and the air grew warmer the farther south they rode.

They were almost to the border when Faolán sniffed the air and looked at him warily. Not long after, they encountered roughly a dozen corpses just off the road. Berengar slowed his pace, and the others followed suit. Flies swarmed around the bodies, which were scattered across the grass.

This was a slaughter, Berengar thought. He stared at the scene, unable to take his eyes away.

Alarmed, the messengers reached for their swords on the chance the responsible party remained nearby, ready to ambush them. Berengar didn't bother. Whoever committed the act was long gone. He dismounted and approached the bodies on foot.

"What are you doing?" one of the messengers called after him. "They're not human."

Berengar disregarded him and stooped to inspect one of the bodies, ignoring the smell. The corpses were the hobgoblins he'd saved from Margolin's men. Although Gnish was not among them, a trail of blood led into the woods, and Berengar suspected he knew what he would find if he followed it.

He guessed the bodies had been there for two days, maybe more. They'd been slain just north of the border, only a short distance from freedom. After a quick search, he concluded the thunder rune was gone, taken by whoever murdered the hobgoblins.

Berengar hung his head. *It really was all for nothing.*

A cry came from the pile of bodies. Faolán barked to get his attention, and Berengar made his way over to her side. Shielded by an arrow-ridden hobgoblin corpse lay one of the goblin younglings Gnish had taken under his care. Somehow it had survived.

Berengar took the goblin into his arms and trekked back to rejoin the others. He told the messengers to ride ahead to Cashel and let the king know he was on his way. He would answer Mór's summons, but not before finding the goblin a new home.

Maybe he couldn't make the world a better place, but he could at least do that.

THE BLOOD OF KINGS

Chapter One

It was never a good idea to keep a king waiting—even for a warden.

Berengar ignored the hunger that had been gnawing at him for the better part of two days. He'd ridden practically nonstop since crossing the border into Munster. Were it not for the subtext of urgency contained within the king's summons, he would have stopped for food or rest along the way. Further complicating matters, King Mór had not disclosed the reason for the summons.

Unlike the High Queen's other wardens, Berengar rarely ventured so far south—another reason the king's cryptic message was so surprising. Nevertheless, he had little trouble finding his way on the road. He followed the course of the River Suir where it originated on the slopes of the Devil's Bit, certain of his destination.

The summer air was warm and pleasant. Munster was the southernmost kingdom on the island of Fál, and its temperate climate accounted for fair weather throughout the year, in contrast to the harsh winters to the north. Berengar hadn't seen as much as a cloud in sight for miles.

He passed the first farm just after midday. More sprouted up along the road the farther he traveled. The castle was visible some distance away, looking over the land from atop a lush, green hill. The workers were already coming in from the fields as he approached the city, though sundown remained a healthy span away.

The Rock of Cashel—Munster's capital—was one of the most impressive cities in all Fál. Munster was the largest of the five kingdoms. In addition to the fair weather and an abundance of natural resources, the southern kingdom's easy access to the coasts ensured lucrative naval trade with Albion, Caledonia, and even Gaul. The sound of music coming from the city reminded the warden that Munster was also the cultural center of the realm, fueled by commerce and monasteries of higher learning.

The city teemed with life, a sign of its booming population. Berengar regarded the masses with a wary eye. The warden greatly preferred the open road to the walls of any city, despite Cashel's beauty. He was skilled in the art of killing, not conversation. Berengar suspected his manners were as dull as his axe was sharp. All the same, he was looking forward to sleeping in a bed for the first time in recent memory.

As closing approached, the marketplace was seized by a flurry of activity. Blacksmiths and armorers plied their trade near the sculptors and jewelers, just a few of the tradesmen assembled along the city square. Berengar spotted the pointed ears of several half or quarter fairies among the crowd, and even noticed a peaceful giant lumbering down the street. Historically, Munster was far more tolerant of magic and nonhuman creatures than the remainder of Fál. Berengar was of a similar disposition.

Men were just as likely to try to kill him as monsters, though that didn't make the latter any less dangerous.

Wherever he looked there were new sights, sounds, and smells to behold. Despite his hunger, Berengar forced himself to turn away the aroma of freshly baked bread. There was no sense in stopping now that he was so close to his destination. He might as well wait to enjoy King Mór's hospitality.

The warden deftly guided his stallion away from the marketplace. As the crowd's ranks thinned, various onlookers began to take note of him. Some stopped what they were doing and stood in silence, watching as he rode by. Others murmured amongst themselves, likely unsettled by his appearance. Berengar wasn't surprised. In fact, he was rather used to the reception by now.

It was the same wherever he went, and not without reason. His appearance wasn't exactly normal by any standard of the word. The right side of the warden's face was marred by three deep, uneven scars that ran in parallel from his forehead down to his lip. A leather eye patch covered the place where his right eye once sat, partially obscuring the scars where the band wrapped around his head. Berengar's hair was a blazing red, brighter than the color of an open flame. The sides were flecked with gray, like his beard, which had grown considerably during his time in the wild. He only trimmed the beard before he starting on a journey, and had not had time to do so before setting off for Munster.

He steered the stallion onto the cobblestone road that led to the castle. A monstrous-looking hound pursued him from the ground, a wolfhound mix Berengar had raised from a cub. Berengar appropriately named her Faolán, which meant *little wolf*—though there was nothing remotely little about her.

The castle lay in the heart of the city. The immense fortress was carved from the limestone rock jutting out from the earth beneath it. A wall surrounded the castle on all sides, barring entrance to the uninvited. Though originally constructed because of the site's defensive advantages, the castle had been improved over the centuries as Munster grew in wealth and power. There was nothing quite like it in all Fál.

"Halt!" a voice rang out as he neared the gate.

Berengar cast his gaze upon the place where two guards stood watch. Four more sentries looked on from the wall above. The warden's face took on an expression of annoyance but he brought his horse to a stop.

"You will go no farther," the guard said.

"I'm expected," Berengar replied tersely, his voice a low growl. He was hungry, tired, and not in the mood for games.

"Identify yourself," the guard said, his hand on his sheath. He was a young man, and Berengar doubted he had seen more than twenty summers.

When Berengar swung off his horse, the young man's companion grew pale. The warden was a great beast of a man, towering two heads over the tallest man among them. He wore leather armor and a flowing cloak made from the fur and skin of a bear. Both an axe and a bow were slung behind his back, and a short sword was sheathed at his side. Save for the overenthusiastic young man, the sight of the warden was enough to intimidate the guards.

"Stand back," the young guard said, but even he flinched when Faolán bared her fangs at the implied threat to her master.

Berengar lazily flashed his ring to the guard. The young man stared at it, puzzled. His defiant expression remained unchanged until the man beside him leaned closer and whispered something into his ear. The young man flushed a deep shade of red and bowed deeply. At the sight of deference, Faolán relaxed and let out a yawn.

"Apologies, Laird Berengar," the guard said. "We were not expecting you so soon."

"I'm not a lord," Berengar replied. "I'm a warden." His voice was deep and gravelly, like the stones from which the walls were built.

"Forgive me, Laird Warden," the young man answered.

Berengar sighed and shook his head in exasperation. "Take me to the king."

"Open the gate," the guard bellowed. "This way, sir."

Berengar led his horse by the reins and followed the guards beyond the wall.

"Warden Berengar has come to answer the king's summons," the older guard said to a messenger, who went sprinting uphill to carry the news.

The population inside the castle grounds was by no means modest, even in comparison to the city below. The group made their way across the busy courtyard, encountering nobles, priests, and soldiers engrossed in their own affairs. Their path again turned upward, where the castle waited, promising the end of one journey and the beginning of another. Golden banners waved proudly from a round tower, bearing the image of an eagle, the sigil of the king's house. Commanding statues of the great kings of old paid tribute to the realm's storied history.

The guards stopped just short of the castle entrance, and a young squire came running to greet them.

"Show the warden's horse to the stables," the older of the guards instructed as Berengar relinquished the reins to the boy. "And find a place for his hound in the kennels."

At the mention of the word kennel, Faolán's ears perked up, and she flashed the guard a toothy warning.

"Leave her here," Berengar said. "She won't attack unprovoked."

The guard looked hesitant but kept his doubts to himself.

Berengar held up the flat of his palm in front of the wolfhound. "Stay. Wait for my return."

Faolán snorted and trekked off the road, curling up under the shade of a birch tree.

A guard draped in a golden cloak and fine armor waited at the castle entrance, surrounded by a small number of subordinates. "I am Corrin, Captain of the Guard," he said by way of introduction. "Your weapons, please. None are to be admitted to his majesty's presence while armed."

Berengar glowered but did as requested, surrendering first his bow and then his short sword. "See that you handle these with care," he warned as he entrusted the battleaxe to the young guard who had challenged him initially. The warden said nothing of the dagger buried within the lining of his boot. Although he had not had dealings with Mór in years, they last parted on good terms, and Berengar did not expect treachery from him. Even so, experience dictated it was always better to be prepared.

Corrin nodded to the others, and the massive doors swung open, granting entrance to the castle. "This way, Laird Warden." He stepped under the detailed doorway arch and gestured for Berengar to follow.

"I'm not a…" Berengar trailed off. "Never mind."

They walked under a series of interior arcades, bathed in the sunlight that entered through magnificent stained-glass windows. Berengar's boots echoed over a well-swept floor. A tranquil quiet hung over the castle, where the thick walls provided a respite from the multitude of noises outside. The air was thick with the scent of lavender and chamomile. Rich tapestries and elegant silks adorned painted walls in the great hall, which currently lay abandoned.

The captain came to a stop outside what Berengar assumed was the entrance to the throne room. The door opened, and the captain ushered him across the threshold.

Let's get this over with, Berengar thought, grouchy from a long ride and empty stomach.

The throne room was larger and wider than the great hall—larger even than the High Queen's throne room at Tara. Aside from the throne itself, which lay at the opposite end, the chamber was largely empty. On the barrel-vaulted roof, there was a single rose window behind the throne. Berengar guessed the chamber was designed with the desired effect of making most supplicants feel small in the king's presence.

Mór sat regally on the throne, watching him quietly with the cautious, appraising expression Berengar remembered so well. He looked every inch a king in keeping with his notable ancestry. Mór's black curls were heavily streaked with gray, as was his well-trimmed beard. The king was dressed in gold and yellow, and a white cloak fell the length of his shoes.

A silver crown rested atop the king's head. Each of the five kings and queens of Fál wore crowns of silver. They were the *Rí Ruirech*—the overkings. Beneath them were the *Rí Tuaithe*, the underkings who wore iron crowns. Only the High Queen wore a crown of gold.

King Mór's crown was adorned with precious stones and other jewels that were without price, a way of setting Munster apart from the other kingdoms. In the days of old, the line of High Kings came from Munster. When the kingdoms broke apart, the throne at Tara sat empty for centuries, until Nora of Connacht again united Fál under one ruler.

The chamber was suddenly filled with the voice of the herald who stood between Berengar and the throne.

"Welcome, Warden Berengar," the herald announced. "You stand in the presence of Mór II of Munster, King from the Cliffs of Moher to the Celtic Sea, Lord of the Southern Islands, Master of the Golden Fleet, and servant of Nora, High Queen of Fál."

Berengar had other names too. Most were records of deeds, not titles of nobility. Many were not fit for polite company, and some others dared not mention in his presence. He was known throughout various parts of the realm as The Red Bear, Berengar One-Eye, The Queen's Favorite, Berengar Trollslayer, Berengar Goblin-Bane, and Berengar the Unbroken to name a small number. There were more than a few songs detailing his exploits.

Berengar did not kneel when the herald finished speaking, though he politely inclined his head in the king's direction. The gesture did not go unnoticed by Mór, who grimaced tersely in a sign of displeasure. It wasn't an unexpected response; most kings and queens were unused to anything other than complete and utter fealty. As a warden of Fál, Berengar stood apart. He was not subject to the king's laws and answered only to the High Queen. There were five wardens in all, tasked with keeping the peace across the land. Oftentimes this meant something as simple as settling disputes between local lords, or hunting a particularly dangerous monster. Judging from Mór's troubled expression, this was not one of those instances.

The two men stared at each other across the throne room for a long interval before at last King Mór's lips pulled back into a genuine smile. "It's been a long time," he said, rising from the throne.

"That it has, your grace," he said, respectfully addressing the king in the manner the royals of Munster were styled.

Mór approached, and the two men clasped hands. "It is good to see you again, my friend."

"And you, your grace."

Though they had fought side by side in the Shadow Wars, in truth, they had never been entirely close. Then again, when one was royalty, everyone—and no one—was your friend.

"You arrived sooner than we anticipated," Mór said, releasing his grasp.

"I came at once after I received your letter," Berengar replied.

"I thank you for your haste." Lines that were not there before appeared on the king's face. Despite his efforts at levity, something was clearly troubling him.

"What is this about?" Berengar asked. "Your letter was rather cryptic, your grace."

Mór let out a dark laugh that betrayed an undercurrent of tension. "Straight to business. You haven't changed much, I see." His expression brightened considerably. "Let us not yet talk of such things. The hour grows late. It will be dark before long. You must be hungry and tired from the long journey. You shall dine with my family and me, and then we will discuss the reason for my summons."

Having ridden with such urgency, Berengar felt a tinge of irritation at the prospect of having to wait even longer to discover the reason for his presence in Munster. Still, he was sure Mór would get to the point before too long, and he could live with waiting until after his belly was full before he received what was increasingly likely to be bad news.

Night descended over the land as the last vestiges of sunlight were replaced by muted candlelight and the somber glow of torches. Berengar dined alone with the Mór and his family at the king's table. Save for the servants and castle guards, the great hall lay empty. Music played softly from a band of court musicians gathered in their midst. The musicians of Munster were widely recognized as the best in the land, and their presence at court was a testament of their talent. As Berengar recalled, the king himself was a musician of some fame in his younger days, though Berengar had heard it said Mór rarely played since the Shadow Wars.

A servant girl approached carrying a *mias*—the wooden board on which food was served. "For you, sir." She laid the board before him and bowed low. Her eyes lingered perhaps a moment longer than necessary on his scars. He saw a familiar expression like fear flicker over her face, and the young girl promptly retreated to the kitchens.

Berengar turned his attention to the meal prepared for him. Anywhere else, the vast assortment of richly prepared dishes would have constituted a lavish banquet or feast. Given Munster's considerable wealth and commercial prominence, the king's table boasted foods found nowhere else in Fál. There was wild boar, rashers—strips of salted bacon, salted butter, *mulchán*—a delicious milky cheese, plums, blackberries and sloes, hazelnuts, and many others. In addition, the dishes at the king's table had been prepared with herbs and spices including garlic, chives, leeks, and peppers. Most impressive was salted beef. In other parts of Fál, the number cattle owned by a lord were a sign of social status. Only the exceedingly wealthy served beef, and rarely on an ordinary occasion.

The warden picked up the cutting knife with one hand and a loaf of wheat bread in the other. He ate hungrily, though he remained mindful enough of his present company to display a modicum of manners. As warm foods filled the space in his empty stomach, his spirits lifted considerably.

"How have you been these long years, my friend?" Mór asked. "There were rumors you had taken a wife."

"Just rumors, I'm afraid," Berengar said.

"But you were married once," Mor observed.

"That was a long time ago," Berengar said. "Before the Shadow Wars. At present, I've been rather busy about the High Queen's interests." The remark was a not-so subtle hint to steer the conversation in another direction. Some things were too sacred to discuss lightly with anyone, even a king. The death of his wife was one of them.

"And how are affairs at Tara?" Mór asked. "I trust the High Queen is in good health."

Mór spoke of the Hill of Tara, the capital of Fál where Nora ruled as High Queen. The Hill lay within the borders of the Kingdom of Meath, though the territory was considered separate. Tara was also home to the wardens, but Berengar spent so much time on the road in truth he no longer considered anywhere home.

The question was intended as small talk, to be sure. Berengar was certain the king's messengers kept him well informed of current events. He wouldn't have been surprised to learn the King of Munster had at least one spy among the High Queen's court.

"From what I hear, she's close to reaching a peace accord with Caledonia," the warden replied after swallowing a portion of bacon. "It's been some time since I was last at the Hill. I've only just come from an ogre hunting expedition in the Bog of Móin Alúin."

Mór's eyes danced in the candlelight. "Ogres? Fascinating."

"One ogre," Berengar said, holding up a single finger. "Though the bastard was almost the size of a troll." His gaze fell on the others seated at the table, and he quickly cleared his throat. "Pardons, your graces."

The king's wife and daughter sat beside Mór on the other side of the table. Queen Alannah's hair had not yet begun to gray, though it was not as luminous as Berengar remembered. She wore a silver crown to match her husband's, adorned by a single, prominent sapphire. The queen's reserved expression did not as much as flinch at the coarse language.

On the opposite side of the queen sat the princess. Ravenna was her name, and Berengar thought it suited her well. He had heard the Princess of Munster was a great beauty, and for once the stories held true. Her hair was black as the night sky, her complexion fair and milky smooth. She could hardly have been older than twenty, if that. Berengar saw little of her father in her appearance, except for the same appraising, calculated gaze. She said little, but he felt the weight of her attention on him throughout the meal.

When Berengar glanced in her direction, she held his gaze, which was unusual in its own right, regardless of sex or age. Her face was an expressionless mask, but there was something about her dark eyes that seemed older than the rest of her, almost weary. Ravenna wore a simple silver tiara with no stones, probably a statement of some kind, but he wasn't sure what, or whose message it was.

"How did you get involved in something like that?" the king prompted.

"I was hunting a group of mercenaries known as the Black Hand. There was...an incident in a church. The local lord agreed to keep the matter quiet if I rescued his niece, who'd been taken by the ogre. There was a vengeful witch involved, and a curse, but I managed to recover her."

Berengar lifted his drinking horn to his lips and gulped down a mouthful of sweet honeyed mead. There was more to the story, but Mór clearly wasn't interested in the details, whatever he said to the contrary. It was common practice for royals to deal in subtexts and hidden meanings with their words, a game Berengar had little patience for. Since he was dealing with a king, he would have to take part in the dance regardless, until which time Mór chose to reveal what was really on his mind.

A strong voice interrupted the lull in conversation. "What's she like?" the princess asked. "The High Queen, I mean. I've seen her thrice before, but never spoken to her. If she's anything like the tales say, I daresay she's quite formidable."

Mór slammed his drinking horn against the table a bit harder than necessary. Irritation was evident in his expression. "You must forgive my daughter, warden. She speaks her mind far too readily." His gaze fell upon his daughter. "You would do well to remember your place."

Ravenna shot her father a dark look but did not reply.

"She would have to be," Berengar said, "to bring an island of kings to heel. Not counting the Ice Queen, of course, who is formidable in her own right." Berengar casually raised the horn to his mouth. The mere hint of a smile on the princess' lips was reward enough to risk the king's displeasure.

"Will you be staying long, Warden Berengar?" Queen Alannah asked. Her hand fell gently on the king's shoulder, as if to diffuse the tension between her husband and daughter.

Berengar shrugged. "That depends entirely on your husband, your grace." He hesitated for a moment before addressing her again. "I was sorry to learn of the passing of your son."

Though the queen's expression did not change, it took a few moments for her to speak. "Thank you. You are very kind."

"I am young enough," Mór declared, as if the remark was addressed to him alone. "There is still time to produce another heir."

They ate the rest of their food in relative silence. The meal ended with a course of black pudding, made from blood, barley, and seasonings. Though served at breakfast in other parts of Fál, in the south the dish was considered a dessert. Once the table had been cleared, Mór waved a hand at the musicians, and the music promptly ceased. The others filed out of the chamber, until at last Berengar was left alone with the king and his guards.

"Leave us," the king commanded Corrin, and the guards left without a word. Mór pushed away from the table and stole closer to the hearth's warmth. Berengar followed suit, ready to hear what the king had to say. "I need your help, old friend."

"I guessed as much, though I'm curious why I received your summons when you could have sent for Darragh, or Niall," he said in reference to two wardens more closely associated with Munster. "You know I rarely travel south of the Silvermines, your grace."

Mór stared into the flames. "I would trust no one else with the task I set before you. It is true the others are all men of great renown, but you have no equal. "

A gruff chuckle escaped Berengar's throat. "Darragh might argue with that, but I'll accept the compliment." He saw that Mór's expression remained serious, so he added a hasty addendum. "I mean no offense, your grace, but I'm still not entirely sure why I'm here."

Mór appeared to weigh his next words carefully before turning away from the fire. "You will have to forgive my secrecy, for reasons I will explain presently. There are two matters with which I require your assistance. The first and most pressing concerns Morwen, my court magician. A fortnight ago I received word that superstitious farmers have laid siege to the monastery at Cill Airne where she currently resides. She's been trapped inside since then."

"You want me to deliver her to you," Berengar said.

"She is...precious to me," Mór replied with an expression that was almost pained. "That is why it must be you. Of all the wardens, soldiers, and means at my disposal, there is no one alive I trust more than you to return her safely to the castle."

This is what comes of earning a reputation steeped in blood, Berengar thought. "And the second matter?"

The king began pacing the floor. He peered past Berengar into the shadows, as if to ascertain they were still alone. "Now I must explain the reason my letter did not say more. A darkness has fallen over the kingdom, and I've begun to suspect powerful magic is involved."

Berengar kept his arms crossed. "Magic, your grace?"

The king came to a halt. Mór must have sensed his skepticism, for a flash of agitation came over the king's face, and he spoke through clenched teeth. "You think I don't know my own lands?" He lowered his voice, as if afraid of being overheard. "Famine has tainted our harvests. Our ships are sunk by strange storms that appear from nowhere. Bandits openly attack our merchants on the road."

"With respect, I fail to see what bandits have to do with magic, your grace."

Mór drew closer, until there was only a hair's breadth between them. Few dared such close proximity to the warden under most circumstances, but the king was blessed with that volatile mix of boldness and arrogance known only to those of royal stock. "Mark my words, there is a larger force at work here."

"Why not ask your advisers to root out the source of upheaval in your kingdom?"

"I am not sure whom I can trust. I sent Morwen to Cill Airne for this purpose. It was not an accident her location was betrayed. Perhaps she is close to the truth of the matter."

Mór led Berengar outside the room onto a balcony looking over the surrounding lands. He gestured to the city at their feet, which slept quietly under the cover of night. "I dare not speak openly of these matters. There is a peace between men and nonhumans, it is true, but it is tenuous at best. I fear voicing my suspicions will stir long-simmering resentment between the races, and I will not suffer a repeat of the massacres that marked my grandfather's reign."

The king's concern was genuine. Berengar knew Mór cared for the Kingdom of Munster above all else. The king was stern and fair, and he took his responsibility seriously. He was far from perfect; in addition to a quick temper, it was rumored the king had a string of mistresses. Berengar had a number of vices himself and was not one to invite judgment. Whatever his faults, Mór was by all accounts a good ruler.

"I see," Berengar said, though he remained unconvinced by the prospect of a magical conspiracy. However, Munster's Court Magician was in danger at the very least, and that was a matter he could do something about.

"Thus, these two tasks I lay at your feet: deliver Morwen here, and assist me in unraveling the threat to my kingdom. Do this, and I will consider any debt you owe me repaid."

The request seemed simple enough. Rescue the king's court magician from a group of peasant farmers and return her to the castle.

He reached out and clasped hands with the king. "I will see it done, your grace."

ACKNOWLEDGMENTS

Every time I try to write a novella, it turns into a novel.

I intended *The Wrath of Lords* to serve as a prequel novella that would explain events alluded to at the start of *The Blood of Kings*. Like my characters, my stories have a mind of their own, and *Wrath* quickly became something more—the true beginning of the *Warden of Fál* series. The Berengar we encounter in this story is even rougher around the edges (if possible) than the man we meet in *Blood*, which delves deeper into both the warden's past and the themes introduced in this book.

The idea for this series came from an interesting place. I'd dabbled in fantasy before—I have an as-yet unpublished fantasy series set in the same universe as *Warden of Fál*—but was busy with other projects when I read a mystery novel written by a friend. As someone who grew up devouring mysteries and thrillers, I wondered what it would look like if I attempted to write a mystery of my own. How would I do it differently?

That's when it hit me: I could write a series of mystery novels set against a fantasy backdrop. After that, all the other pieces quickly fell into place. Because so many fantasy series require readers to be familiar with all prior books, I've purposely tried to make each novel as stand-alone as possible (while remaining interconnected).

Having written in a number of other genres, including thriller, horror, science fiction, and western, I can honestly say fantasy is the most challenging and rewarding. There's something special about the combination of monsters, magic, and swords in a unique world with its own history and mythology.

The world of *Warden of Fál* was heavily influenced by Irish mythology. I was fortunate enough to take a trip to Northern Ireland, where it was as if the world imagined in my stories leapt off the page. Other fantasy stories that have influenced my writing or love of the genre include *The Lord of the Rings*, *The Chronicles of Narnia*, *The Kingkiller Chronicles*, *Bone* by Jeff Smith, *Game of Thrones*, and the *Skyrim* and *Witcher* video games. If you enjoy the genre, you owe it to yourself to check out these stories.

I'd like to say a huge thanks to Jeff Brown, my cover artist for the series. His work is tremendous. I would also like to thank Maxime Plasse, who did a superb job designing the map of Fál, and Matt Forsyth, who rendered a color illustration of Berengar. You each helped bring my world to life, and for that I am exceptionally grateful.

On the technical side, I'd like to thank my copyeditor, Katie King. I'd also like to thank my mom, Pam Romines, for helping to edit the book.

And finally, I'd like to thank you—the reader of this book. If you enjoyed *The Wrath of Lords*, I highly encourage you to read *The Blood of Kings*. Berengar's story is just getting started.

ABOUT THE AUTHOR

Kyle Alexander Romines is a teller of tales from the hills of Kentucky. He enjoys good reads, thunderstorms, and anything edible. His writing interests include fantasy, science fiction, horror, and western.

Kyle's debut horror novel, The Keeper of the Crows, appeared on the Preliminary Ballot of the 2015 Bram Stoker Awards in the category of Superior Achievement in a First Novel. He obtained his M.D. from the University of Louisville School of Medicine.

You can contact Kyle at thekylealexander@hotmail.-

com. You can also subscribe to his author newsletter to receive email updates and a FREE electronic copy of his science fiction novella, The Chrononaut, at http://eepurl.com/bsvhYP .

CPSIA information can be obtained
at www.ICGtesting.com
Printed in the USA
LVHW101100020622
720263LV00002B/172

9 781793 952448